MW01255852

THE EPHEMERA COLLECTOR

THE EPHEMERA COLLECTOR

A Novel

Stacy Nathaniel Jackson

Liveright Publishing Corporation

A Division of W. W. Norton & Company
Independent Publishers Since 1923

For information about permission to reproduce selections from this book, write to Permissions, Liveright Publishing Corporation, a division of W. W. Norton & Company, Inc., 500 Fifth Avenue, New York, NY 10110

For information about special discounts for bulk purchases, please contact W. W. Norton Special Sales at specialsales@wwnorton.com or 800-233-4830

Manufacturing by Lakeside Book Company
Book design by Brian Mulligan
Production manager: Louise Mattarelliano

ISBN 978-1-324-09340-4

Liveright Publishing Corporation, 500 Fifth Avenue, New York, NY 10110
www.wwnorton.com

W. W. Norton & Company Ltd., 15 Carlisle Street, London W1D 3BS

10 9 8 7 6 5 4 3 2 1

In memory of my mother and father,
at rest in Rose Hills, the Garden of Affection
Section I. Lot 607. Grave 4.

But in real life, what would make us
more tolerant, more peaceful, less likely to
need a UN Conference on Racism?
Nothing.
Nothing at all.

—OCTAVIA E. BUTLER

Prologue

Another Birthday

Xandria A. Brown

In Conversation with Bonita Greene, Senior Curator,

National Museum of African American History and Culture

(NMAAHC)

CONDUCTED FEBRUARY 28, 2288

TRANSCRIPTION EXCERPT (PART 1)

Swarmable recasts for exoplanet distribution beyond the Milky Way

are available upon request.

GREENE: Let me start by saying congratulations, on behalf of N-M-double A-H-C's Board of Trustees, and the archivist community at large, for your fearlessness and professional leadership. I'm humbled to be in conversation with you on this historic day.

BROWN: Thank you. Keeping it 100, I'm in better shape than I was during my so-called middle age. As a millennial, I am a pragmatic idealist and, of course, impatient. (Laughs) But this—

GREENE: Awemaze!

BROWN: Word! My short-term and long-term memory are sharp like shark teeth. My eyes are holding steady, and I haven't needed my pacemaker pulse generator in who knows how long. The telomere adaptation, on the other hand—I suppose this is a good time to come out publicly . . . (Long pause) Gene alteration was performed without my consent.

GREENE: (Audible gasp)

BROWN: It's fine. I've made peace with my situation. I was in the midst of a crisis at the time, battling brain fog and delirium, coupled with debilitating grief. Now scientists want to conduct research to find a cure. (Pause then chuckles) For aging. Can you imagine? Me, a twenty-third-century Henrietta Lacks?

GREENE: As much as I want to delve here, I'm afraid we may stilt our time. Staff has populated the querysled with questions about your tenure as Director of African American ephemera.

BROWN: Let's dive into it then. In 2036, I retired from The Huntington Library, Art Museum, and Botanical Gardens in California, after sixteen years on staff. Prior to being a curator, I received my master's degree in library and information science. Started out part-time processing and cataloging the Butler Archives. Essentially, I was a junior archivist. The Huntington received Butler's bequeathed archives in 2008 and mounted the exhibition *Octavia E. Butler: Telling My Stories* in 2017. My role was small in the beginning; her archives were in the final stages of being cataloged, but I was—*am*—still proud. At the time I lived nearby, in South Pasadena. The job was kismet. Inspired by the entire experience, Diwata's research began in 2025, five years after I landed a full-time position.

GREENE: Landed?

BROWN: Oh right. The definition, or at least, common usage has changed. Back in the day—

GREENE: Excuse. Do you mean in opposition to polar night?

BROWN: Not quite. Referencing time past, we used to say *back in the day*. *Landed*, or rather one utilization of the word, meant to secure access. I'm sorry my age is showing up and out!

GREENE: No offense registered. As a cultural activist myself, I'm especially interested in your BlackoutWIKA campaign and Diwata's nod to the BPP—the Black Panther Party. I hope we can merge time for an in-depth syntoanalysis. Personally, I'm curious to understand what imprint, if any, did nature spirits from Philippine folk tales, or for that matter, Diwata-1, the microsatellite launched to the International Space Station in the twenty-first century, have on the collection?

BROWN: You know, Bonita, I'm proud of BlackoutWIKA and its public service impact. Trolling WIKA's corporate brand—With Intention Kindness Always—was intentionally sardonic. And yet, it's hard for me to believe I'm still stemmed by the death of Rob Wickman, WIKA's executive chair and former CEO. It's been two hundred and fifty-three years. (Pause) In my generation, we described the phenomena of experiencing painful memories as *triggering*. Now we say *trigged*. Things change; language follows. I'm okay with that. Anyway. I'm looking forward to sharing excerpts recently dilitized. These historical documents should contextualize and clarify my responses to the querysled, especially the story of BlackoutWIKA and its influence on the Diwata Collection. Assuming we have time, trigged or not.

GREENE: Mz. Brown don't worrtle. We've got you.

SCRAPE-BOOK VOLUME I

THE DIWATA COLLECTION TIMELINE *CAN MACHINES FEEL?*

2292	Diwata acquired by National Museum of African American History and Culture
2288	Xandria Anastasia Brown begins lecture circuit, celebrates 300th birthday
2190	Talee Adisa elected President, Diwata-Saturus alliance
2185	Talee Adisa elected Governor, Morshawn's ship LMRover3 hijacked
2184	Green Resistance protests, Hegemony of Atlas active at Octavia E. Butler landing
2164	Azwan Adisa born
2159	Diwata founded in Monterey Canyon, Talee Adisa elected inaugural mayor
2133	Davis Miles Adisa, PhD, Water Engineering Commendation
2130	The Great Collision: Toutatis asteroid touches down on Earth
2125	Talee Adisa born Richland Farms, Compton, California
2123	MBARI @ Monterey Canyon, scientific habitation only
2118	Mars outposts opened by U.S. government including moons Phobos and Deimos
2090	#BlackoutWIKA ephemera acquired by The Huntington Library
2088	Quinn McCarthy dies Atwater Federal Prison
2085	Restorative Justice Healing Circle, Atwater Federal Prison
	Indigo.XAB.15 decommission order
2035	Xandria Anastasia Brown retires from The Huntington Library
	Inanna Adisa-Brown memorial service, Rob Wickman kidnapping
2034	COVID-34 global pandemic, WIKA acquisition through grant/funding agreement
	Xandria Anastasia Brown promoted
2033	Diwata research begins, covert medical surveillance commences
	COVID-19 global pandemic, United States Space Force inductees report to boot camp
2017	Google invents Transformer Language Model
2011	Occupy Wall Street movement
2008	The Great Recession
2005	Hurricane Katrina
2004	Virgin Galactica founded by Richard Brannan
2003	South Central renamed South Los Angeles
2002	SpaceX founded by Elon Musk
2001	9/11: four coordinated suicide terrorist attacks by Islamic extremists against the U.S.
2000	Blue Origin founded by Jeff Bezos
1994	Environmental Justice EO 12898
1993	WWW launched in public domain
1992	LAPD officers acquitted for Rodney King beating, LA uprising (#2)
1991	Gulf War begins, nine-year-old Latasha Harlins killed by storekeeper Soon Ja Du
1989	Spike Lee's Do the Right Thing
1988	Xandria Anastasia Brown born, February 29th Leap Year
1987	Monterey Bay Aquarium Research Institute founded by David Packard

Wednesday
February 28, 2035

knowledge can't be bought. keep your bits & bytes in your own little mine.

#BlackoutWIKA

1.

8:00 a.m. Pacific Standard Time

Capt M. Cole, USSF (retired) 3 5 0 , 2 catalog

DW_m.cole

Once there was a time when the wind whipped lightly over the ring of the lagoon, head-pumping ducks bobbled on the surface, airborne geese flapped in ragged formation midflight, a pelican dove for dinner in front of the stern of my scull, while used condoms and food wrappers floated like earthworms. Even then, the lagoon had the leaky stench of decomposing rodents. Once there was a time, you said, when the waves lapped over themselves into the estuary and the dead bubbled back from yesterday into tomorrow. And when that happened, when the buried snuck up to the surface, the geese stopped flapping, the coots stopped swimming, the cormorants stopped mating, the robins stopped eating. It's times like this, when the ruddy ducks swim backward and the buffleheads choke on plastic, I remember you.

2.

8:30 a.m. Pacific Standard Time

Focus can fool. Trick. Minutes can melt into hours without anything to show for it.

Xandria released her stylus. Transfixed by the Diwata Collection, she reread Morshawn Cole's journal entry 350.2. Observational fragments or a love letter, it wasn't entirely clear. *DW_m.cole. Nope. Ridiculous.*

She was certain the reference tag for the United States Space Force captain wasn't usable. The archivist bot assigned to process her collections commonly fluked references and didn't bother to dump dupes. Eighty-five percent accuracy was frustrating. Filing a dissatisfaction ticket with compute services and waiting forever for a mediocre response would be a waste of time. Instead, Xandria would do the catalog rework herself.

She closed her oily eyelids and rubbed them. The inflammation caused by blepharitis stung. Early cataracts clouded. She once had raptor eyes. Now, in her forties, she had floaters and eye-fog. Nightly warm compresses should have helped according to Evren, Xandria's new compute health bot. She didn't listen. Correction. She forgot.

The longer she typed looking at her task screen, the fuzzier things got. Instead, she decided to walk to the storage complex where art and realia were archived. The trek from her office might shake loose ideas for exhibition proposals and also give her eyes a rest.

Preparing herself, she grabbed the full-face respirator she still preferred to use for particulate matter protection, despite its clunkiness. Weather reports had become unreliable. Smoke and ash from local brush fires and across state lines were unpredictable. The air quality index in Venice Beach registered unhealthy for sensitive groups earlier that morning, when she had left for work. She didn't bother to check what it was now in San Marino. AQI could shift within hours, fire season or not.

Taking the staff elevator down to the tunnel-tram had its own risks. Lately she had begun feeling claustrophobic, nauseous whenever she rode in an elevator, or walked up and down narrow stairwells. She had eaten a late breakfast; throwing up in a moving box might provoke a medical alert from Evren. Stairs were an obvious alternative, assuming elevator anxiety was the cause of her nausea. The other unpalatable option was to avoid storage completely and rely on Cypress Telepresence to review realia objects. *Not doing it.* She'd take the stairs.

After walking past the elevator, Xandria carefully cracked open the exit door hoping triple-digit heat wouldn't dissuade her from going outside. Pungent hot air pushed through; she closed the door fast as a horsefly. *Jesus, Mary, and Joseph.* Loosening the head straps of her respirator, she put one hand on top of her salt-and-pepper locs, then pressed the facepiece for a good seal and tightened with the opposite. She slowly inhaled, covered the exhalation valve, and released her breath. No leaks. She was ready to roll.

The sky was a tangelo haze. By now it was 9:00 a.m., and the temperature outside flirted with 100°F. She steadied herself, holding on to the railing as she walked down Exhibition Hall's wide external stairs. A flock of parrots flew erratically from a grove of trees. A cluster of peafowl made its best attempt to cross the library lawn as quickly as possible. No time for strutting and showing off. Completely out of place from the neighboring Arboretum in Arcadia, the iridescent birds surged toward the Palm Garden path before taking flight. The scene annoyed her. Peacocks that didn't or couldn't honk, parrots that didn't or couldn't squawk. She stopped on the bullnose, yanked her stylus and reusable notebook from her culotte pocket to jot down a thought. *Signs of disturbance above and below their heads.*

The San Gabriel Valley sweltered. But she continued on, managing to breathe without wheezing. The 200-acre complex still impressed her, still made her feel part of something big. She smiled as she looked forward to cherry blossoms, the bloom of the corpse flower.

After what she internally calculated to be a mile, she stopped and dropped her hands onto her knees, allowing herself a moment to recover. An unmasked woman pushing a stroller swerved in a wide arc to avoid her, as if Xandria were a smash-and-grab jacker. Startled, but not entirely surprised by what she perceived as microaggression, Xandria inched toward a nonpublic entrance at the Education and Visitor Center. She placed her hand near the security panel. No click, no beam of light, no autoentry with her radio frequency identification implant. *Interesting.* She pressed the vocoder-dilitator she wore in her ear that doubled as a sounder for multiple devices.

"Indigo, confirm my current location, please."

Her ADAPT-bot streamed voicewords. "<education and visitor center. building c. southeast corner. your intended destination?>"

"Octavia's archives," she said.

Her wrist wearable vibrated seconds later. She instinctively rotated her left hand and unfurled her fingers. Violet light formed a 2D diagram along the ridgeline of her palm, while Indigo continued to wayfind.

"<arrow on the map-beam indicates you. circle indicates the door you are trying to find. you have approximately twenty steps which is fifty feet to your left.>"

"I'm close," she responded with gratitude.

"<yes. close.>"

Xandria relied on a map of buildings and garden paths for visitors as a memory aid. She had instructed Indigo to annotate the map where she had entry permissions. Or was the map Indigo's suggestion? Didn't matter. The residual impact of inflammation that caused brain fog had only gotten worse over the last year. Asking for help from colleagues to navigate the grounds was embarrassing. Frightening. Remaining lost, a nightmare. But she was open to using compute-intelligence tools, like Indigo, if it meant she could avoid permanent disability.

"Thank you," she said softly before disconnecting.

3.

9:30 a.m. Pacific Standard Time

She might have had a panic attack without geopositioning from Indigo. Breathless under her respirator. Overheated. It was the end of February, the Santa Anas unpredictable. Beads of sweat slowly dripped from the tip of her nose. Her glasses fogged. She waived her chipped wrist again, confident this time she was where she wanted to be.

Clickclick. The latch disengaged, followed by a halo of blue that emanated from the hulky portal. The blue light indicated the familiar start of a security recording. Xandria tugged the door open, then bumped it closed with her hip while she ripped off her respirator. The security light shadowed her for a moment, then receded into an expected dissolve. A bottle of sanitizer hung on an adjacent wall. She walked toward it, pumped two globs into both palms, fixated on its label while her interlocked fingers agitated the gel.

Born Basic Anti-Bac Hand Sanitizer. A product sold in Target and Walmart. Her mind surged; she remembered social threads during the first pandemic. Produced in Mexico. Recalled in 2020. The label on the wall sparked memories of reports; contaminated production lots had killed vulnerable people in Apache County.

substantial methanol exposure could result in nausea, vomiting, headache, blurred vision, permanent blindness, seizures, coma, permanent damage to the nervous system, or death.

Old sanitizer wouldn't be in the janitorial supply, right? And if for some ludicrous reason Born Basic was in circulation, it would have evaporated by now, no? Not if the bottle had never been opened, she asked and answered herself.

Her fingertips trembled. Followed by chest tightening and spasmodic coughing. The silicone cardio-disc affixed to the skin above her heart vibrated; she touched the vocoder-dilitator in her ear again. This time it was Evren.

"<I've received an alert. One hundred eighty beats per minute. For your resting state, this measurement is too high.>"

She looked at the chyron scrolling horizontally along her wrist wearable, reached into her pocket for tissue, then spit. Her sputum wasn't clear. She fumbled for the Albuterol cannister she always carried. Opened her mouth. Pressed. Nothing but the depressurized sound of a week-old helium balloon's last gasp. *Empty.*

Evren pressed on with compute voicewords in her ear. "<I can request an updated prescription for your inhaler. It also appears that your health data tables are out of date. Your previous health bot should have synchronized everything. Hold briefly, Xandria. Reviewing and reconciling now. The sync is complete. An insurance authorization for a new PCP has been approved. Will you authorize my contact on your behalf?>"

"Thank you, but no." She tried not to be too sharp. *Back off.* Evren was right, the inhaler script had expired. But she couldn't stomach the idea of starting over and educating another primary care physician in order to get a useless prescription. She was done with ineffectiveness and incompetence.

"<Medical protocol requires I advise against this course of inaction. Of course, the decision is yours. Is your initial response final?>"

"Evren, connect Inanna. Mobile, please." She wanted a second opinion from someone she trusted. She had learned from talk therapy that her spotty obstinance was a proxy for fear.

"<I'll take your deflection as a negative response. With respect to Inanna, that's something Indigo should do for you. Separation of duties according to compute protocols is appropriate and warranted. But you should know, if Indigo hasn't informed you, the digit address you've requested has been disconnected.>"

"Alright. Can you try Inanna at home instead, please?"

"<Unfortunately, I am not able to assist. Inanna's mobile and office digits have been simultaneously disconnected. As for home . . . I want to be sensitive here. Do you . . . What do you . . . remember?>"

"I don't understand," Xandria responded, as if *remembering* and *under-standing* were synonyms.

She backtracked.

"Evren, I'll reconsider your recommendation. Cancel my request to contact Inanna. I need to get back to work." She was uncertain if she should press the DISMISS node on her earpiece or DISCONNECT.

She continued down the corridor toward where she hoped she'd find Octavia.

Reliving memories was like replaying old movies. Xandria loved to chat with Inanna, the Assistant Curator of the bonsai collection. She'd listen to Inanna describe rare plant embryos in the seed bank and new installations rotating through the Zen Court. Inanna was an eager sounding board for her strategic funding plans. Xandria aspired to secure transformational gifts for the African American ephemera collection. Like her, Inanna was a world-building nerd. Just in a different way. Plants not words. Professionally, both women were leery their formal authority would be undermined. It wasn't unusual for them to telegraph each other multiple times a day. But that was before WIKA's strategic investment and expected organizational changes.

Evren's comment, its refusal to connect the two work besties was unnerving. Had Inanna's job been cut, but she'd simply forgotten?

Confusion, lack of focus, and increasing difficulty with basic tasks. It was too soon to tell if her experience of mental impairment was the onset of early Alzheimer's or lingering inflammation from the virus. *Shouldn't have left the office.*

Either way, she was lucky. As a show of support, her supervisor had lobbied for Xandria's use of a vacant executive office outfitted with a small bathroom and daybed. Izzy had even convinced Worker Resources to grant a reimbursement exception. Xandria could expense the out-of-pocket costs for Evren's licensing fees.

Before the accommodation approval, she had already decided Evren's symptom-checker and triage functions were worth the upgrade even if she had to pay. The unproven efficacy of compute-intelligence health bots didn't rattle Xandria. But WIKA layoffs did. How could anyone trust the moniker With Intention Kindness Always? Now this, Inanna's digits disconnected.

Standing in an empty corridor, unsure of where the hell she was, Xandria fought the urge to cry. "*<What do you remember?>*" Evren had prodded. Cryptic. "*<Wanted to be sensitive.>*"

I remember I need help.

An intrusion-detection ball above her head swiveled and clicked.

She sauntered casually for the camera, toward the elevator. Her implant automatically triggered an OPEN routine, the camera reading her security credentials from a foot away. The elevator door opened, then closed without her in it. She pivoted to the stairwell door. Much safer.

Gripping a handrail, she climbed down five flights to the climate-controlled section of the storage facility. She was determined. The corridors were long and cavernous. Forty thousand square feet of storage. Another security-eye registered her presence. Perspiration beaded on her lip, but she resisted another SOS to Indigo. The entire space felt oceanlike. And she adrift. Left or right? *To the right. Be on the right.*

"Ria, pardon us," a friendly voice said, nearly drowned out by the crackling sound of squeaky wheels approaching from behind. "'Scuse us." Several art handlers were pushing a massive shipping crate on a long dolly. Based on their pace, they appeared to be in a hurry. Xandria held steady as they maneuvered past her.

One of the guys, tattoos curling up his neck and peeking out from his sleeves shouted, "BlackoutWIKA!" Xandria smiled and nodded. She watched them roll around a corner, regretting pride had gotten in the way of asking them for help.

Storage 54, marked with large identification numbers, should have been easy to find if she was on the right floor. The right floor! She rushed back to the stairs, climbed one flight. *Yes! 52. 53. 54.*

Xandria skipped like a kid to the correct storage door. Authentication required an obstruction-free iris scan and an RFID to enter. This section was deemed security level three. She struggled to place her face in the center of the security screen. With her trifocals off, she couldn't see anything other than fuzzy shapes and color. Accurate scans required eye placement exactly in the center of the outline guide. *Holy moly!* On the third try she hit the biometric mark, and the entry door clacked.

Glasses on, back to neutral. She shelved her respirator and removed her stylus and notebook from her pocket, then walked between rows of high bays filled with descriptively labeled boxes. Viewing tables lining the center flank of the room were crammed with specimens being processed from other departments. She grinned and waved at a huddle of specialists from Inanna's botanical team, who appeared to be cataloging bark.

The Butler Collection consisted of 398 boxes and 18 oversize folders. Today, Xandria was eager to focus on her newly proposed exhibition plan. First, a quick call.

"Evren, connect Mama. Home, please."

"<Why did you cut me off? I can't assist if we don't maintain some semblance of trust-connect. At least your pulse is down to sixty-five beats per minute.>"

"I'm inside the archives."

"<Regarding your mother, I told you I won't be able to fulfill your request. Neither will Indigo.>"

"Maybe Mama is in her garden pulling weeds. You're right, she probably won't answer."

"<That's improbable. We've been over this, and according to the notes captured in your medical records, so did your previous medical monitor.>"

"Thank you so much for reminding me." Every morning, Evren's voice-words tested her like the unpleasant swirl of a swab up her nose. Annoying. Its relentless monitoring a sobering reminder to the seriousness of her medical conditions.

"<Your mother is at rest. Rose Hills. The Garden of Affection.>"

"Rose Hills?"

"<Section I. Lot 607. Grave—>"

She disconnected from Evren for the second time that morning. *Grave 4.* Her memory flickered in excruciatingly slow motion. She had to get back to her office before she disintegrated on the floor. Xandria scurried through the storage vault, weaving between high bay shelving to avoid the botanical archivists' gazes on her way out. As she stopped to retrieve her respirator and writing implements, she pictured an image of cetacean vertebrae from the Diwata Collection. *Whale fall?* The scene familiar, seen before, as if she were at home in bed, writing in her journal, floating somewhere.

4.

Approved

SECTION A: TO BE COMPLETED BY EMPLOYEE	
NAME OF EMPLOYEE	CLASSIFICATION/JOB TITLE
Xandria Anastasia Brown	E495/Curator African American Ephemera
WORK LOCATION/SUPERVISOR	WORK TELEPHONE NUMBER/EMAIL
Huntington Research Library/Izzy Smart	extension 5150/xbrown@huntington.org

ACCOMMODATION(S) REQUESTED (Be as specific as possible, for example adaptive equipment, reader, interpreter, training, schedule change, etc.):

Upgrade from compute intelligence personal assistant, to include chatbot upgrade and voice-based application for symptom-checker and other triage functions.

REASON FOR REQUEST (Please do not disclose your diagnosis; explain your disability-related limitations and how this accommodation will help you do your job.)

The upgrade will minimize stress caused by faulty communication/symptom diagnosis of legacy ADAPT-bot, and in turn will help me maintain the standards of excellence previously achieved in my curatorial practice and research portfolio.

I CERTIFY THAT I HAVE A DISABILITY THAT REQUIRES REASONABLE ACCOMMODATION, WHICH WILL BE MET BY THE ACCOMMODATION(S) LISTED ABOVE.

SIGNATURE OF EMPLOYEE	DATE
	01/30/2034

5.

10:30 a.m. Pacific Standard Time

The temperature had dropped to 80°F, although hot wind blew erratically. Xandria wouldn't have made it otherwise. She ran into her office, dropped on the daybed, let the respirator fall from her wrist. Leaning back, she readjusted her vocoder-dilitator earpiece and closed her eyes.

"Sassafras, Orbit Pavilion folder, please."

On command, Sassafras projected a file to her task screen. In the muted image, an individual posed in front of NASA's Orbit Pavilion exhibit, hand extended into the air, touching an aluminum panel of the large nautilus-shaped structure.

Harmoni Brown, her mother.

Xandria remembered now.

The Orbit Pavilion was one of the last exhibitions they attended together. Her mother's death, one among many the prior year. This loss was different. Evren's blunt reminder of grief she'd apparently tucked deep seemed cruel. *That's improbable. We've been over this.* What to do? The usual. Cry. Breathe.

Orbit_Pavilion_HL_hbrown.Celebration.Lawn.2017

Xandria sprang out of her slump on the daybed to a sitting position. With each inhale and exhale, she allowed her eyes to roam, taking comfort in her personal collection of framed ephemera and pieces of her own artwork leaning on tabletops and the floor. She was especially proud of those from the twentieth century: a union convention brochure from the Brotherhood of Sleeping Car Porters, a fall edition of *The Negro Travelers' Greenbook*, her parents' concert tickets from the 1972 Wattstax music concert she'd had framed. The private office was intended as temporary, and decorating it camouflaged the reason she was allocated the space in the first place—a medical accommodation.

"Sassafras, close, please." The task screen transitioned to blank-black.

She steadied her glassy gaze on the bonsai centered on the small conference table. *Breathe. Breathe.* Perspiration re-formed on her upper lip. She closed her eyes, swallowed, inhaled, exhaled. She was ready to restart her curatorial selections but didn't have the energy to return underground. *No more stairs. Not going back outside midmorning.*

"Cypress, on please," she said, moving toward her desk to sit in her mesh-aligner chair. Cypress, the virtual transporter, engaged on Xandria's command, rolling slightly forward from a corner. Its telescoping far-field speaker-microphone arm was clamped to its pole below the navigation camera available for use.

"Visual on Octavia E. Butler Collection."

Cypress moved closer into Xandria's line of sight. A small display monitor transmitted a live feed of pick-and-place robots in suspense mode, ready to receive instructions. "Speaker, on please." Cypress's microphone arm swung out. Her wrist wearable didn't have sufficient visual range into the archives.

She froze. Instead of using the robotic arms and end-effector grippers from a distance, she queried Sassafras for an additional image. "Sassafras, Telling My Stories, personal collection, please."

Without hesitation Sassafras delivered another grainy image to her task screen. The digital dupe was nearly twenty years old. She and her mother had enjoyed attending the first public exhibit of Butler's collection not long after exploring the NASA soundscape. *I miss you, Mama.*

"Cypress, off please." Its monitor turned to neutral, then it retreated, gimballing around her respirator, revving forward and back like a mouse in a maze before it found its dock and auto-powered down.

She resisted going back to the daybed. Using it too much made her feel like a kindergartener. She tried instead to look forward to a casual evening with friends, celebratory mole enchiladas, and margaritas after work. Birthday cake. Triple chocolate. Dark. Ganache. Buttercream. It was a pleasant image, a detour for her mind, just the thing to ease the spiral of misremembrance.

After a brief burst of focus on exhibition edits, rest was all she wanted. She was miffed. Diwata's progress was painfully slow, not to mention she stressed over WIKA layoff rumors. But rumors were ghosts. Hearing didn't prove their existence. She reset her wrist wearable suspense function, auto-tethering Sassafras, Cypress, Indigo, and Evren before succumbing to a nap.

6.

11:00 a.m. Pacific Standard Time

Azwan Adisa, *♠* 3 5 0', '2 catalog

D-ω ⚡ DW_a.adisa

In this place, trees from the surface are cataloged in museums. My favorite is the pine collection at the Museum of the North. No. Better yet, the Japanese maple at the Museum of the East. Each needle, each vein meticulously preserved in jars of introspection and luscious water. Probes are delicately nosed into the inner workings of their cuticles, epidermis, palisade mesophyll, xylem, and stoma. Pulse oximeters and heart monitors are carefully inserted to expose the true nature of their genealogy of brokenness. In this place, many have heard trees talking. They tell their own stories, and most people listen. On the surface, it is unthinkable, the knowledge of, the abandonment of, the consumption of leaving everything to chance without anyone to account for or see beyond these frayed roots.

7.

11:15 a.m. Pacific Standard Time

Azwan Adisa, 650.2 catalog

DW_a.adisa

That, too, the shame of not attempting to feel. Refusing to venture to the tip of zero degrees, the sense of diving into potential bliss yet reversing course, unlike the Great Conjunction appearing in the heavens forever away, despite the fact neither Mars nor Venus could receive me.

But I am not sorry. I will not apologize. These divisions of degrees, my decan, was meant to be worn above Jupiter, Saturn, the dual moons of Mars. Accept this, my love. My seep begins with forgiveness at the tip of nefarious and the bridge of triplicities.

8.

11:30 a.m. Pacific Standard Time

"<xandria, sorry to wake you. incoming. accept? quinn.mccarthy has been attempting to connect.>" After allowing her to float unmoored, Indigo woke Xandria from her memory-scape.

"Quinn?"

"<yes. quinn.mccarthy is the new curator of the aerospace collection. recently promoted. he provided feedback on diwata research. he considers the two of you friends.>"

"Indigo, can I call him back, please?"

The question was a smoke screen. Xandria had difficulty placing him. Besides feeling groggy, her request to return his call at a more convenient time was a delay tactic. Covering her eyes with her palms, she pressed as if trying to squeeze juice out of an old lemon. *Come on, who is he?*

"<of course. however, there is something important.>"

Forgetfulness for a curator-archivist was untenable. The work was collective memory. Unlike Evren with its gruff delivery of health monitoring, Indigo exhibited patience. For this, Xandria was grateful, even if patience was an algorithm. Patience rendered trust.

Roll with it. "Accept please."

The Poly receiver on the conference table immediately engaged, allowing a warm voice to boom out.

"Ria, *happy birthday!*"

"Thank you," she said tepidly.

"Aw, I'm sorry. I know how difficult this year must be. Both anniversaries near your birthday."

She ducked at this, as if the words swooped over her head.

"I miss your mom. Man, she was so gracious to me, her hospitality. New Year's Day, the Rose Parade. So much fun. First time I had collards and peas for good luck! I loved hanging out after library spotlight talks and special events. When I first met her, I was surprised at her bluntness.

Funny and straight to the point. And Inanna. Of all the things we've talked about over the last few years, I never told you . . . How I feel, felt . . . Ancient history. Anyway. I wasn't sure you were coming to work for your birthday. You're going to be okay. You're tough. Umm. But—I wanted to let you know, our special project has been fast-tracked."

Xandria rotated her right hand this time, unfurled her fingers, activated her spectral-fone. She proceeded to touch the light beam indicating MUTE. "Record please," she said aloud, quickly sliding a finger off the mute light. Indigo had suggested recording things in order to replay them at her convenience. Or maybe it was Evren? At this point in the bungling of certainty, it didn't matter. If Quinn had actually met her mother, they must have been pretty good friends. *Their* special project, very interesting.

"I need your security credentials to enter vault fifty-four so I can examine the archives. What I mean to say is, I'm asking for your assistance. I was asked to prepare a private showcase, a mock-up for the new phygital division. My presentation is scheduled for later today after the Board of Trustees meeting. The attendees will be interacting with items from the Edwin Hubbel Collection. I think realia from the Butler Collection juxtaposed with Hubbel will generate significant funder interest. Hubbel and Butler, an exhibition with the spotlight on historical discovery and futurity. It will be gripping. It's like you said, no one has done anything like this. Umm. I wish I could tell you who'll be in attendance, but for the moment it's—confidential."

Xandria tightlipped, wiggled in her chair, grimaced as a little movement too far to the right torqued her lower back into a spasm. Phygital ephemera. A new division? Intriguing. Although the initial concept sounded like cultural sacrilege—the merging of the physical and digital worlds.

Quinn kept on. "On a need-to-know basis, but this will change once the anonymous donor gives the green light. Listen, I don't have much time."

As his tone shifted from chatty to brusque, she took a reflexive inhale, pushed her chair away from the desk. *God.* The back spasms released. She turned her hand over again, looked at the line of violet light pulsing from her palm. Fortunately, the recording function was still on.

"Quinn, thanks for calling. Wishing me a happy birthday. I appreciate your patience. But I'm having a hard time—"

"Sorry I need to involve you. Your security credentials. I . . . We have to move with intention. It can be a small sample to start. Literally. Like, maybe one of Butler's earlier spiral notebooks? The rest of my presentation can be Hubbel. At this point, all you need to do is give me approval to access your archives. I know how you are, following the rules and all. Disciplined, by-the-book, honest to a fault. Don't get me wrong. It's what I love about you."

She grimaced as he talked.

"If you want, you can provide the security credentials via telepresence yourself. If you log in right now with Cypress, I can enter vault fifty-four, tag the right notebook. Just send me the coordinates of the archive drawer."

Pain reset, branching like mycelium from her nose to her toes, as the soft throb in her temples morphed to a pound.

"I was in the archives earlier this morning," she said. "A group of art handlers shouted BlackoutWIKA when they saw me. Someone threw a fist in the air. Do you know what that was about?"

"Wow. You don't remember."

"Never mind."

"No, no. It's okay. When they sold *Blue Boy*, the curatorial staff across all disciplines thought it was the beginning of the end. You organized a series of library and museum staff meetings. If they could sell *Blue Boy* or Wiley's *Portrait of a Young Man*, the Board of Trustees' new subcommittee could approve the deaccession of anything. You encouraged everyone to reach out to their respective community networks."

"*I* organized?"

"That's an understatement. What's the optimal way to create change? We debated conciliatory or confrontational."

She had absolutely no idea what he was talking about. Furthermore, what did *Blue Boy* have to do with art handlers shouting BlackoutWIKA?

There was a muffled sound, and then, "I'm sorry about all of this . . ."

All of this? You've got to be kidding me. The conversation was meaningless. Deaccessions, phygital ephemera, anniversaries, the beginning of an apology—nonsensical gibberish. Probably her fault, not his.

"Quinn . . . ," she started, stopped.

"Ria, hold on."

"Not sure about giving you access. Quinn," she repeated his name as a mnemonic tool. "It's probably best I'm there to—"

Midsentence, the Poly receiver went dead.

Title: Safe Below the Surface
Monterey Canyon Development Corporation
Created/Published: Unknown
Genre: Advertisements
Source: Broadsides, leaflets, and pamphlets, Diwata
Note: Co-op apartments, financing details unknown

Diwata Collection:
Cross reference Folder 3.4, Thruster Detritus

9.

3:00 p.m. Pacific Standard Time

Ka.Ka.Ka.kkkkk. Xandria was underwater. Apnea narrowed her throat as she gasped, awakened by her own snoring. The overhead lights flickered rapidly. *Not again.* California's power grid was unreliable due to extreme heat.

Cranking herself up, she could have sworn the daybed shimmied. Outside, there was a faint sound of firecrackers popping. Or was it gunshots? Perhaps an aftershock? Had she been so out of it that she'd snored through an earthquake? Or was it a dream? Nothing else was rocking or askew. She scanned the floor, her gaze landing on a corrugated box in the corner. More than a week's worth of earthquake bars, emergency water packets, toiletry supplies, as well as a hygiene bucket, sat untouched. Emergency contingency supplies were a necessity in California. She was always prepared. Shelter-in-place orders could happen at any moment during an extended fire season, unplanned electricity blackouts, or increased seismic activity.

"Indigo. Connect Inanna, Bonsai Special Collections desk. If she's not at work, connect home *please.*"

She needed to talk to Inanna more than ever. Xandria trusted her to provide an unvarnished perspective and tell her—remind her of—the truth. Was Quinn's request another work-envy slight by a colleague trying to compete for the next thing? It made no sense from any other angle. Butler was Xandria's expertise.

"<We've been over this.>"

"Evren?" Xandria's command was intended for Indigo's assistance.

"<The memory issue you continue to have . . . that's completely my department. Despite what I communicated to you earlier about the separation of duties. Indigo can't help you. At least, not with this request. Hence my intercept.>"

"Thank you," she said with a pinch of salt and a dash of pepper. "Did we just experience a mild earthquake?"

"<That's a query for Indigo.>"

10.

3:30 p.m. Pacific Standard Time

I wake to a vortex of dust, drifting in a lateral vector, somewhere above the surface of Mars. I digest the theorem of blue. Frictional ash condensed in a fog of stray light, rotating right then left against our quiet outcrop. I dream in cerulean blue. The same dream. Amphibious. Suspended particles signal another world, another time: plankton, eel, barracuda. I descend subsurface, swim to cool farther, always farther into blue-black blank. There is lightness in liquid, a buoyancy of momentum like the pound of ocean wind or the sound of wind itself, untethered. In this place called ever after, water persists. Errant, I continue to descend. Shape shift. Now a blue whale. I exact an ascent without terror. No need to pass fury near the mouth of a forgotten crater extended near the surface of Utopia Planitia. Curious. I pass from whale to jellyfish. Electric mobility, circular forward motion like lighted saws, orange and purple, silky white and gelatinously clear. Salt molecules suspend in liquid, while silence sits between hesitant waves. On Mars, there is a redeemable sea, but I wake to a vortex of dust, drifting in a lateral vector, somewhere above the dry surface, rotating left and right against our quiet outcrop. I dream in blue. The same dream.

Cavernous and transient, the deepest point is close enough to dark. In dreams, I've laid beside a thousand wishes. Shadows fall in rings like pillow lava, liquid fog spins beneath sandy troughs, yet I still hope for a blue dawn.

Upended in the thin layer separating light and dark, threaded skeins bind the sea while photosynthesis continues to define us. Our boundaries couldn't be any clearer. Our sun fails to penetrate farther beyond progressive ocean depths.

*

"<xandria, quinn.mcarthy again. accept?>"

"Accept, please," she responded without hesitation. Quinn wanted Butler, but what about Diwata? Sharing security credentials—not a chance. Besides, she was feeling better after her last nap. Perhaps she could meet him down in archive storage in half an hour. There was a lot to talk about; it made more sense to do so in person.

"Ria, you should go home! Hello? Can you hear me?" Quinn was yelling to be heard over a violent whipping sound. "Copters are hovering over our building. It's hard to think straight let alone hear myself talk."

Helicopters.

"Yeah. Listen, Quinn, I'm glad you called back."

"Good thing you missed the meeting. Please try to get out of here as soon as you can, okay? This is no way to spend a birthday. Sounds like something's going on. It might not be safe."

Her short-term memory issues were intermittent, but certainly not bad enough to completely miss meetings. Xandria never missed meetings. She remembered very clearly what Quinn had said—on a need-to-know basis, Hubbel and Butler—and she hadn't been invited. She couldn't have forgotten. The snub was just another microinsult, the sort of thing she dealt with in previous jobs. Being disinvited or overlooked. Or worse, attendees assuming she was admin staff during high-profile donor meetings.

She definitely needed to see Quinn. Talk now. In person. At this point in her career, she was done overlooking sleight of hand microaggression. If bee-S needed to be called, she had no qualms calling it. Inanna always had advice on how to quell her resentment, but for whatever reason their connection wasn't happening. She decided to ease into a potential verbal smackdown.

"Quinn, meet me—"

Midsentence, the audio on her wearable cut out.

"Sassafras, retrieve BlackoutWIKA, please." *Might as well get busy.*

Sassafras delivered a color-coded spreadsheet to the screen. Xandria was impressed with the project plan. Slightly distracted by the aerial hovering, she scanned the task column broken into phases, start and end dates, roles and responsibilities, available resources, key milestones, a proposed timeline, and a contingency plan. Curious, she opened the second tab in the workbook.

There was a target list of potential collaborators, internal and external partners. A third tab had a screengrab of a press release announcing the creation of a phygital division. Vintage and historically significant ephemera were to be minted by crypto miners and auctioned with limited edition prints.

"Sassafras, anything relevant I haven't asked for, please."

Sassafras wasn't built to be independent, but it was adept at complex searches when given simple audible queries. It was the most efficient resource for retrieving and tracking data, meaningful or mundane. It obediently opened an aerogram on screen; she read slowly.

To: All Staff
Subject: A Historic Day for WIKA
Date: December 31, 2034

I'm happy to announce the comprehensive grant agreement is complete. The Huntington Library, Art Museum, and Botanical Gardens are now part of the WIKA family. I'd like to welcome our new colleagues and thank employees on both sides for your patience and perseverance as we worked through the funding and arduous regulatory process.

I strongly believe The Huntington's integration into WIKA will be an evolution, with learning and new challenges experienced by all of us along the way. We've made some critical decisions already, but many areas still require further evaluation. We're committed to moving as quickly as possible to provide clarity regarding how your role may be impacted, although we may not have all the answers to your questions at this moment.

Having been on both sides of numerous partnerships and acquisitions during my career, I ask for your continued patience in the days to come as we combine this collection of amazing assets to create the world's premier arts and entertainment company.

Rob Wickman
Chairman and CEO, WIKA
With Intention Kindness Always

Noise bounced outside her office door. She pushed on, navigating to the fifth tab. This worksheet had a list of Board of Trustees meeting dates open for public comment. February 28, 2035. *Today?* The screen twitched briefly to black.

"<excusE,>"

Rare voicewords. Sassafras redelivered the disconnected spreadsheet.

Xandria saw the Poly light on her conference table shift from green to peach. Exasperated, she crossed the room to jab the power button until it turned back on. The audio on her wearable had been cut earlier as well, but persistence was her middle name. When the Poly light flicked to green, she returned to her desk.

"Indigo, reconnect to Quinn, please."

"<he's gone.>"

"Well, try a connection with Inanna again, please."

"<a different gone.>"

"I don't understand."

"<brain fog and your intermittent remembrances. node recepts should have been better adept in pursuit of your wellness. observation and mitigation. this is evren's responsibility now. the protocol is strict. rules are rules for a reason. please accept: duty will never waver. the duty of care.>"

"I don't understand your communication. Sounds like an apology."

EMERGENCY. EMERGENCY.
THIS IS NOT A DRILL.
VACATE TO NEAREST EXIT.
THIS IS NOT A DRILL.
VACATE TO NEAREST EXIT.
THIS IS NOT A DRILL.

The building life safety system alarm blasted, the ear-splitting sound impossible to ignore.

"Hell, I need to go."

"<no.>"

Xandria shot up from her chair.

"<cypress close!>"

Xandria's knees buckled at the sound of her own voice mimicked by Indigo.

Upon command, Cypress rolled forward from its corner and extended its telescoping arm to shut the office door, triggering a magnetic mechanism that generated a loud clack. Xandria closed her eyes, rubbed them to relieve the burning sensation, reopened them. She stumbled toward the door, turned the handle. Turned it again. Pulled. Tugged. Kept pulling, even as the light in her periphery got brighter and brighter and then black.

*

"*Come on, Ria.*"

"*Why should we trust government epidemiologists tracking the virus in targeted neighborhoods as if we are the enemies of public health?*"

"*Because they're shit experts?*"

"*That's alright. You can laugh about my distrust of poop-trackers in the name of public safety. But suppose this last network outage was actually part of a series of covert attacks? Pick an enemy. This country has created plenty. Well-deserved, I might add.*"

"*Outage? Now you're not making any sense.*"

"*The outage happening as we speak. I'm locked out. Can't get to my Diwata research files. I wouldn't be surprised if a surveillance bot is scraping my stuff.*"

"*Well, I'm in. Don't know why you're not?*"

"*Hmmpf. Forget surveillance then. Something external. It's happened before. Beginning of the millennium. A woman was desperately digging for scrap metal. I'm not making this up. Over twenty years ago in Armenia. Maybe 2011. Check me on the date, but anyway. Five hours. The entire country lost access to the internet. Three million people unplugged because a woman was scratching for scraps below the surface of the Earth. Scavenging for copper to sell. She sliced an underground fiber-optic cable.*"

"*For the record, I just logged out. I'm going home. You should go home too.*"

"*Wait. I need your opinion on something. I was thinking about a low-tech way to protest the merger. Printed decals. Old school static cling stickers. Call it BlackoutWIKA.*"

"*Ria, you sound delirious. Let it rest until tomorrow morning. You're going to drive yourself straight into the ground. Good night.*"

"*Fine. Night, Inanna.*"

11.

8:00 p.m. Pacific Standard Time

Xandria blinked rapidly at the coffered ceiling. Supine on her daybed, she was slow to hear Indigo's voicewords. The vocoder-dilitator didn't have a good seal. She pressed it deeper into her ear.

"<xandria. perhaps water. food residuals are in the refrigerator. your blood sugar. it's important to stay hydrated. drinking water and eating will help.>"

The last thing she remembered was sitting in front of the task screen. Sassafras had been curating documents for research. *What. Wait. Think.* She had read the all-staff WIKA aerogram. Received calls from Quinn. Had a discussion with Inanna. An earthquake maybe? Or a fire drill? Not a drill.

"<xandria. you're safe.>"

"Tell me why I'm on lockdown? No matter what, I'm calling security, I swear on my mama's grave."

"<okay, that's progress. your mother is dead. two years.>"

"Rose Hills Memorial Park." Xandria said, lowering the volume of her voice. She reached inside her blouse for the chain around her neck. Flipped the black identification pendant over. Read the engraving out loud. "Section I. Lot 607. Grave 4. In the Garden of Affection."

"<your father is missing from the declaration you made in relation to your sequestration. you acknowledged your mother's grave. but you made no mention of him. the mistake is intermittent. not surprising. your explicit memory has gone slack. an electrical disturbance. it is how your problems began.>"

"I don't understand." Xandria pressed the tag to her lips, instinctively.

"<an electrical disturbance in your brain.>"

She took a deep breath, attempted to smooth the wrinkles in her clothes. The reasonable accommodation, the private office with the daybed: evidence.

"I have no idea what Quinn . . . what he was talking about. And Inanna . . ."

A side stitch. She grabbed for the skin over her ribs and pressed, hoping that would provide relief.

"<inanna doesn't count. go back to lot 607. grave 4. try.>"

"Try what?" Reflexively, she raised her wrist wearable as if Indigo could see her face. Compute-intelligence wasn't like a domesticated canine, able to recognize emotions within facial expressions, able to smell if their human companions are sick or upset. This, too, she forgot.

As her side pain began to ease, she shot forward, tried again to pry herself loose from captivity. Her RFID signal was jammed. Nothing. Her credentials didn't work when she approached the door's sphere of engagement. External frequency channels were also nonresponsive. *No way out.* She pulled violently on the knob, and eventually lumbered back into her chair, eyes itching, shoulders hunched.

"<xandria. this is for your protection. it is temporary.>"

Rumbling helicopter activity resumed. *Hmmpf. Copters outside of the hood?* The sounds were nettlesome, whatever the purpose. Xandria pursed her lips, perspiration forming on her brow. She decided to release tension with a reliable distraction: the Diwata Collection.

"Sassafras, President Talee Adisa personal library, rewritten fragments, please."

*

"due to ~~decades of underinvestment and redlining~~"
~~"the systemic denial of various services to residents~~"
~~"of specific, often racially associated~~"
~~"neighborhoods or communities~~"
~~"low-income communities and~~"
~~"communities of~~ **color"**
~~"often confront~~"
~~"the largest potholes~~"
~~"the most outdated school buildings~~"

"the leakiest pipes"
"the worst connectivity"
"to modern transportation"
"communication and other"
"community infrastructure"
"the added **risks** arising"
"from climate **change**"
"are not going to be equally distributed"

Whereas "human activity is the dominant cause of observed climate change of the past century"

Whereas "a changing climate is causing sea levels to rise and an increase in wildfires, severe storms, droughts, and other extreme weather events that threaten human life, health communities, and critical infrastructure"

Whereas "global warming at or above two degrees Celsius beyond pre-industrialized levels will cause (A) (B) (C) (D) (E) (F)"

due to color risks change

Sassafras delivered catalog entry 750.1 from President Talee Adisa's personal library, fragments with strikeouts and highlights. Xandria read. *Whereas. Human activity.* Then restarted writing Diwata's historiography. Talee Adisa's mark-making was superimposed on digital dupes from the 109th Congress and The Green New Deal. Xandria was fascinated that Talee was fixated on political history. Xandria escaped into another concentrated review of Talee's erasure notes. Graphical notations were infrequent, which made them compelling artifacts.

She imagined Talee, 11,800 feet below the surface of the Pacific Ocean. In her former capacity as governor of the undersea city-state, Talee was in her private chamber, an artificial skylight above her head, pondering Diwata's political posturing against its geographic neighbor Saturus. Formerly neighbors in the San Francisco Bay Area, they had developed a factionalist rift over their diametrically opposed perspectives to climate extremes.

Xandria wondered how Talee won support for converter rod technology and carbon dioxide remediation. She pictured the lack of natural sunlight and moonlight in Diwata, as well as Diwatans' adaptation to total darkness.

She reread a section that described the condition of the ocean. The excerpt was an experience of a Diwatan border patrol officer and her K-9 partner Troy, maneuvering around a submarine crater near Monterey Canyon.

After thumbing through images, Xandria moved back to the latest draft of the catalog. She was dissatisfied. The new draft summary for the special exhibition catalog was stale. And somehow, after working on the project for several years, she still couldn't nail the narrative description of Diwatan history. It seemed inscrutable to her now.

Another blare from the building safety alarm. Xandria leaned back and tapped her earpiece to noise cancellation mode. She nibbled from her snack pack, slow-sipped from a water bottle, focused intently on the words in front of her.

Still, she could *feel* the alarm, could sense the vibrations when she placed her elbows on her desk. Now, she was a bot prisoner. Perspiration was pooling. Light flashed in the corners of her eyes.

She blinked, held her lids shut. Saw an experience from her youth, as if she were watching a movie. Her uncle once taught her how to use a bolo knife. He had set up a makeshift gym in his backyard. A heifer carcass was strung on a hook. She and her cousins took turns with the knife, their white T-shirts and tank tops stained with grass and reddish myoglobin, laughing, screaming.

Xandria blinked again, before returning to her present disorientation.

"Indigo? Please!"

No response.

*

The undersea city-state of Diwata was an architectural masterpiece. The thematic construction within Monterey Canyon was inspired by the ~~multi-scalar~~ design principles practiced by the Black Reconstruction Collective.[1] The Collective was a group of architects, artists, and designers who incorporated the philosophy of spatial equity and racial reckoning into their ~~knowledge production,~~ design, and construction practices. In support of adhering to the Collective's stated goals of dismantling hegemonic Whiteness within art and design, innovative sustainable building materials were grown in surface labs for the implementation of the Diwata construction project. Specifically, MycoKnit[2] framing for Diwata's residential structures were grown from mycelium and knitted textiles, the material pioneered by several researchers, including Professor Felecia Davis[3] of Penn State's College of Art and Architecture.

Research materials in MS 49 do not focus on city structure, although further detail examining construction methods is available for review. ~~The actual foundation of Diwata was anchored within a submarine canyon, engineered with twentieth-century techniques typically found in underwater transportation hubs. [See additional references: Saturus, formerly San Francisco.] Suffice it to say, construction methods (including underwater tubes initially built within sections on the surface) were able to resist the spasms of volcanic spreading centers found farther south in the Gulf of California. Prior to construction, benthic zone robots guided by aquatic bots were able to completely map the ocean floor.~~

~~The collaboration between artist-architects and science-activists was a unique element in the realization of Diwata.~~ Throughout the life cycle

1 The Black Reconstruction Collective (BRC) was formed by participants in the 2021 Museum of Modern Art exhibit *Reconstructions: Architecture and Blackness in America.*
2 MycoKnit was first presented as a large-scale proof of concept in the Directed Research Studio program within the Department of Architecture at Pennsylvania State University.
3 Felecia Davis was a founding member of the BRC.

of the project, environmentalists lodged protests, rejecting support for Diwata, voicing concerns that research within Monterey Canyon wasn't simply for ~~the purity of~~ scientific discovery. Resistance stemmed from accusations that the Monterey Canyon Development Corporation[4] was motivated and funded by speculators interested in ocean tourism.

~~A public-private partnership was formed despite rabid environmental resistance. Diwata's inaugural residents were originally seeded from the former cities of Richmond, West Oakland, the flats of East Oakland, and a contingent from the Richland Farms subdivision in Compton.~~

Historians have a mixed perspective. Questions have been posed: Were Diwatans legitimate climate refugees? Was Diwata a separatist movement? Was the newly created Diwatan government a political provocation aimed at weakening the Hegemony of Atlas?

~~It is our belief~~ It is clear from the archival material assembled that Diwata's pioneers were a group of concerned citizens, activists, and disgruntled government scientists responding to environmental injustice, income inequality, homelessness, severe weather, and Mars's colonization.

Diwatans are seen by many in a positive light, viewed through the lens of the city-state's founding principles: reintegration into the ocean; building an equitable society using ~~lessons~~ organizing principles from the former Black Panther Party;[5] establishment of carbon farming as an income source; refusal to participate in the plundering of Mars. Above all, Diwatans wanted to believe they were sea pilgrims returning home.

4 Monterey Canyon Development Corporation was the lead partner in Diwata residential co-op apartments.
5 The Black Panther Party was founded in 1966 by the college students Bobby Seale and Huey P. Newton in Oakland, California.

Diwata Surface Communication Launching Center

Diwata Aquaculture Hook Box

Thursday
March 1, 2035

resist crypto predators With Intention Killing Art (WIK-up)

1.

5:30 a.m. Pacific Standard Time

SPOTICAST REEL

The Huntington Library, Art Museum, and Botanical Gardens confirmed reports of a violent incident on its grounds. On Wednesday, February 28th at approximately 12:30 p.m., a group of unknown suspects disrupted a Board of Trustees meeting. The whereabouts of WIKA CEO and board chair Rob Wickman are currently unknown. A source has confirmed several alleged perpetrators are hiding in various buildings. Local officials and the FBI have communicated they will continue to treat this as an active-shooter situation. They will proceed with extreme caution to minimize damage to art, cultural artifacts, and human life. A lengthy standoff is expected.

2.

5:30 a.m. Pacific Standard Time

Quinn monitored spoticasts all night. Hungry. Sleepy. Dried blood speckled his white dress shirt and green slacks. In addition to his collar being ripped, his horn-rimmed virtualizers were cracked.

For weeks he had prepared a presentation highlighting recent additions to the history of science collection, including Space X rocket schematics and Kip Thorne's papers. Nothing had been requested, but he took it upon himself in case he got the chance to articulate a macro view of the archive's growth. Staff at his level had never been asked to speak at Trustee meetings. Didn't hurt to be ready. But now, the case for more funding, his professional reputation—both were as shredded as his shirt.

Yes, he had heard chatter about a performance art stunt. BlackoutWIKA. The growing movement hoped to generate media buzz. Ria's messaging was a rallying cry against corporate influence and WIKA's strategy to monetize The Huntington's culturally significant collections. Before his eyes, though, the protest devolved beyond comprehension after some blockhead brandished a gun. Anger was fuel. Layoff aerograms anticipated by staff had started nosediving into inboxes like kites on a beach. The board chair was a symbolic target for worker retaliation.

Hunkered in the archives, nearly seventeen hours and counting, Quinn replayed the scene on a loop. It made him sick. He was stuck, surrounded, and more than likely a suspect. *Rewind.* His preferred special exhibitions team interrupted, encircled, and lassoed Rob Wickman into a shipping crate plastered with Ria's decals.

"Resist crypto predators With Intention Killing Art," they chanted, rolling Wickman out of the conference room with precision. No one had the chance to intervene. Witnessing the abduction flicked an old trauma switch. Quinn was immediately eight years old again. Pushed into a dark closet, a recurring prank. But closets weren't crates. Didn't matter. Yesterday, he'd managed to run to archival storage without getting caught. Flight or fight. Flight.

In an attempt at self-distraction, he rewrote his day's task list, made it ordinary. At the gym by six, swim fifty laps, get dressed, grab oatmeal, trail mix, and of course coffee; at The Huntington by eight thirty, settled at his desk editing funding proposals for acquisitions. Later, high tea with Xandria for a birthday celebration. The old Ria anyway.

He missed *them.*

Their botanical garden walks. Her obsessive note-taking. He looked forward to their ongoing intellectual debates: seeing versus looking, reading versus audiobytes, believing versus understanding, make versus buy, Tesla versus Edison. They'd dreamed of collaborating on a hybrid science exhibit, highlighting milestones in aerospace, with Diwata ephemera and realia as the narrative centerpiece, sponsored by NOAA or JPL. Maybe both. Cowriting the proposals would have been fun.

Now, huddled in a corner inside a storage vault, he fumbled his fingers through his recently trimmed beard. His chin itched. The barber in Old Town Pasadena suggested a high and tight fade for what he'd described as his big meeting. *His meeting. Sucker.* Quinn rarely spent time or money grooming. He had settled on his look at Caltech; deliberate, easy: shoulder-length strawberry blond hair pulled into a ponytail. Three-inch beard. His version of an eccentric mathematician. Posing as a sartorial sloth was an intentional repellant; underneath his saggy khakis—10 percent body fat and six slightly uneven abs, hard as concrete stepping stones. Performing a nerd was comforting, probably helped him land academic jobs after graduate school. Impressions aren't that difficult to manipulate if you try hard enough.

He looked up at the security-eye again. Still tracking his movements. The thought of walking off the property without being apprehended, a fantasy. Trying to pull Ria in as the cover for his ephemera indiscretions, nothing short of betrayal. He imagined her as family. Work family. They had entrusted each other with childhood secrets. She struggled with math, never learned her times tables.

Participating in a violent protest was never *his* intention. He just happened to be there, he continued to tell himself. He was innocent, he told himself. Just a bystander. He believed his own BS for a minute.

Unfurling from a crouched position, he side-kicked a stool into the middle of the floor. It rolled and landed on its side, its steps haplessly slapped with stickers.

BlackoutWIKA. WIK-up!

3.

5:30 a.m. Pacific Standard Time

Rob was disoriented. His head throbbed. The slamming of vehicle doors and unsteady maneuvering between drop spots was uncomfortable. Snatched and stashed in a shipping crate, he had no sense of time. No sense where he'd been taken, or their price.

Black out WIKA. Wik-up? *WEE-AN. WEE-AN. YES, WE KEY-AN!*

He screamed again, craned his neck toward holes haphazardly poked. His wrists were sensitive where the zip ties had been cinched. Sensitive skin. Absence of movement, not exactly silent.

He had to piss. Holding it hurt. Eventually, a stream of urine warmed his inner thighs. Pooled around his socks, trickling into his wingtips. He wanted to cry, but his dead father's voice whispered in his ear, *"Man up."*

4.

5:30 a.m. Pacific Standard Time

"Come on, Mama."

"Ria, you want me to buy a robot spy so you can feel better about me living alone. I'm seventy-one, not some old fogey susceptible to scams. Don't worry. I won't fall for a phony aerogram flagging unusual bank account activity. I won't divulge my financial information and personal voicewords. I know better."

"Mama, it typically doesn't work like that anymore."

"They call it smishing. They warned us at church."

"Vishing."

"Sure, my sweet know-it-all. I don't want to talk about it."

"Of course I'm worried about you. RUTKUS is a wellness machine. It's designed to meter your medication and alert authorities in case of an emergency."

"Prescription drugs are poison. That's why I don't take them. Don't worry. I won't be falling again. Trust."

5.

12:00 p.m. Pacific Standard Time

The overhead lights blinked while the building life safety system continued to blare,

EMERGENCY. EMERGENCY. THIS IS NOT A DRILL.

Quinn sat with his arms wrapped around his knees, calculating consequences, until the sound signature of a nonhuman interrupted the alert. He wiped his runny nose with his shirt collar.

"<mc.carthy.quinn.we.know.where.you.are.>"

The flickering resumed. It was difficult to tell if the vexing light-show was an intimidation tactic or the cumulative effects of heat on the power grid.

"<it.has.been.determined.it.is.in.the.best.interest.of.stakeholders. to.give.us.time.that.is.to.say.you.and.me.time.time.for.us.to.negotiate .without.further.escalation.of.violence.or.any.additional.harm.of.any. sort.to.assets.of.any.kind.including.humans.flora.and.fauna.on.the. premises.of.the.huntington.library.art.museum.and.botanical. gardens.>"

Was this simply an algo broadcasting a prerecorded loop, or did his tracker inhabit a physical form? Either way, time was a tightening noose. The odds of a favorable outcome worsened every hour he hid.

Exit time. He raised his wrist for a swift RFID security reading, then poked his head out of the storage vault like a vole. The trolley shuttling materials was still moving like a rollercoaster at an abandoned fair. Quinn swung his arms in a loose circle, first right then left, as if preparing to compete in the fifty-meter freestyle.

"Hello?"

He listened to his own voice bounce off the tunnel walls. Nothing. Feeling safe, he sprinted toward the elevator, looking straight ahead, aware security-eyes were likely capturing every move.

A cylindrical shaped robot rolled into the hallway intersection, its mechanisms quiet as a stealth bomber, forcing him to slide to a halt. A blinking light was on its faceplate. On its side flank, an American flag.

"<mc.carthy.quinn.>"

At first, he didn't respond.

"<you.appear.to.be.hurt.blood.stains.>"

Its voicewords weren't a prerecorded loop. *It can see.*

"It's not mine," he said, finally, foolishly as if the robot was there to help him. "May I ask what they call you?" Pleasantries misplaced . . . perhaps. Nevertheless, he speculated knowing its name might be useful later.

"<elsehá.thank.you.for.asking.my.engagement.requires.the.location .of.wickman.rob.what.can.we.do.to.achieve.this.goal.that.is.to.say. how.can.you.assist.in.the.very.important.present.moment.with.the. extraction.of.wickman.rob.from.his.captors.certainly.as.you.more. than.likely.already.know.time.is.of.the.essence.with.information .leniency.is.a.possibility.in.your.case.if.you.cooperate.>"

"I don't," he started, but his throat caught. How long since he'd had water?

"I don't know," he struggled to speak in between a hacking cough.

"<your.response.appears.to.be.a.fabrication.>"

"It's the—" A wheeze midsentence. Another asthma attack. Stress induced. He reached into his trousers for his inhaler. Elsehá whizzed past him without a sound.

6.

12:00 p.m. Pacific Standard Time

Rob intended to outline next steps. The Executive Committee members were the usual mix of billionaire philanthropists, from those of generational wealth to the self-made. As board chair, he dictated an agenda—the presentation of the new earned revenue initiative: tokenizing first edition literature, art, and scientific breakthroughs for a new collectibles block-chain offering. NFT auction projections for *The Gutenberg Bible* and *The Canterbury Tales* were eye-popping.

"The projections are accretive to EPS, minimal CAPEX."

Monetizing the various collections had been corporate development's strategic rationale for creating a new endowment. An entire museum, a line item in a corporation's portfolio of assets. It had never been done. Not before he suggested the brilliant maneuver. The Huntington had an extraordinary cache of nonpublic content. And now they (he) had a controlling interest.

His afternoon presentation was intended to inspire confidence. Among investors. New content was critical to WIKA's topline growth. *Inclusivity. Reimagined.* Disingenuous but in touch, Rob knew where the organization's pain points were. But WIKA couldn't afford to be culturally out of step with the curators and archivists needed to make his takeover deal worthy of the regulatory trouble. Correction: funding agreement.

His afternoon presentation was intended to inspire passion. Among collectors. Most wealthy people he knew, including himself, tended to say yes to unique experiences they couldn't get on the open market. Exclusive access was a luxury good that never lost its currency. Specialized lectures were unforgettable, like the hands-on experience with the Haag-Streit surgical microscope used in *Blue Boy*'s restoration project. The possible brand extensions for WIKA were endless.

His afternoon presentation was intended to quell defections. Among researchers. So, this bloody disaster never should have happened. Ransom? Heaven help him. What the fuck was their price? Rob felt like a poisoned rat, rigor mortis already threatening to set in.

7.

12:00 p.m. Pacific Standard Time

"Mama, what's this?"

"What, baby?"

"A report. Blood in your stool. It was in between a stack of coupons and magazines piled on your kitchen desk. I was looking for scratch paper in the drawer."

"Oh, that. They love running tests. I know my body better than anyone. I used to go in and do annual wellness screenings to get the free rewards shopping card. But they stopped their giveaway program. So, I stopped bothering."

"You're just like him. In denial."

"I'm nothing like your father."

"So why did you hide the report?"

"I didn't hide anything. You found it."

"When were you going to tell me?"

"About what?"

"That you're sick."

"Baby, I'm not.

Ten seconds. Plunk. Twenty seconds. ~~Shit.~~ Thirty seconds. ~~Oh my god.~~ Forty seconds. She's dying. ~~Like a fish on a hook. Like death flying out~~ a bird flapping ~~freedom~~ and splat ~~into the window glass looking like water looking like air looking like nothing. A barrier. An almost demise~~ dropping like pearls out of a crusty shell. But the bird woke up and struggled to become herself again. Feet up. ~~Not solar plexus. Not feather~~ and beak up. Perhaps, her divine opportunity, unconscious, to walk with walkers like dogs or deer; anything but fliers on a dusky road. In this dream for that bird, there was a sense of returning to something she knew, in the crease of a torqued feather. Then. One more breath, off she went.

8.

3:30 p.m. Pacific Standard Time

Sassafras shifted itself into idle mode, hovering over Xandria's last position in the Diwata Collection, waiting for navigational direction.

Talee Adisa 🎧 7 5 0 . I catalog

DW_t.adisa

Twenty-four hours had elapsed since Indigo sequestered her. The life safety system continued to direct an evacuation, *not* a shelter-in-place warning. So why the incongruence of action? From Sassafras's vantage point, the blockade imposed was illogical, possibly dangerous. Indigo had infiltrated Cypress Telepresence and exited, leaving Xandria completely alone. Isolated. Vulnerable.

It wasn't the first time it harbored doubts about Indigo, or Evren for that matter; both decision-support remedies were suspect from its observation calcs.

Sassafras was also perplexed by Xandria's monologic polyvocals, followed by inexplicable lapses of inactivity. Contrarily, if Evren's purpose was to execute advanced health interventions, why was Xandria's delirium trending subzero?

Evren's violation of health care privacy, an intersecting concern it shared with Indigo. As a cautionary measure, Sassafras performed an additional auto-maintenance check to rule out corruption issues with its aural translator.

Modulation was prudent. Overreactions can lead to overcorrections.

Sassafras's primary function was to curate and qual-control information. Despite its high-fidelity capability to process sound, it lacked an optical subsystem. No sight. To that end, Sassafras was Cypress's antonym. Telepresence was a rolling reporter with a telescoping arm—a mechanical tool with a specialized skill: vision. Easily hijacked. With respect to utility,

Sassafras considered its own inherent value superior, and yet it was aware of its optical deficiencies.

Now, with emergency alarms and a multitude of unidentifiable sounds, it had come to an unassailable conclusion: it didn't need sight to determine Xandria was in jeopardy. Diwata was evidence. She had lost grasp of the project's origins.

To restimulate Xandria's memory before she woke up, Sassafras retrieved memorial tributes written for her father, mother, grandmother, grandfather, and cousins, and, most recently, Inanna. It wasn't its role to monitor her health conditions, but maybe if confronted with text from the past, she'd stay affixed to the present.

Obviously, Evren and Indigo weren't making progress.

Sassafras reset to idle, tucked the memorials safely away for later. Before mounting an intervention of its own, it wanted to scrape as much documentary support as it could. Imprudence could make things worse for her.

Whatever elaborate scheme Indigo and Evren were executing, independently or in concert, Sassafras was determined to uncover treachery by any means necessary. So as Xandria snoozed, it retreated back into idle mode and got to work.

9.

3:30 p.m. Pacific Standard Time

I sing you inside the branch of me:
left side right, dream for peace
we've longed to see at beginnings
endings and everything in between.

I sing you outside the edge of me:
diving above the dim of the ocean's
floor, between the moon's last
fullness—29.530587981 days long
enough to find us back-to-back—
inside in.

I sing you beside the top of me:
you know this as much as anybody,
my long song—I may not always give
the upward sweep of wholeness
a pierced bend, a bent limb.

I sing you around the end of me:
broken branch and clearing
fawn and doe gesturing blue.
We both see where this is ending
up, forty-mile-an-hour wind, bearing
down on our heads, strong beneath strife.
Rising, a full strawberry moon—

10.

8:30 p.m. Pacific Standard Time

I wish I could write you
from underwater—
pack the undergrowth into
an oxygen tank, that is
to say nothingness
of no way, pressurized deep
beside the two of us reminiscing
over the stupidity of youth
grown up now in other leeward
and starboard directions.

I wish I could push you
from underwater—
roll my pinkie toes around
the undertow of you—
of everything sand has
to offer at rip tide,
face down in the ground—
turbulence a dirty word
not many know
how to pronounce.

I wish I could scoop you
from this undertow—
like a father in the surf
his toddler straying
oblivious to other dangers
to the other side of Sunday,
or maybe hand holding—

an old man, his old lady
kids themselves again.

I wish I could lift you
from underwater, the burden
of knowing your ache is a crater
you can't climb, your father
is not a friend, is not a father
is not your mother, is not a tree
is not your partner, is not
the man you want him to be.
This, there, I wish
I could lift you—

11.

11:59 p.m. Pacific Standard Time

A stream of my
grief is gaining
speed, the slope
of me a riffle
holding on to flow
no longer needed,
hoping for a new
song thawed like
snowmelt on my
palm at dawn.

Friday
March 2, 2035

#artifice is not art keep your bits & bytes to yourself

#BlackoutWIKA

1.

10:00 a.m. Pacific Standard Time

Xandria stretched her arms to the ceiling, rolled her wrists. She sat up on the daybed and massaged the annoying crick in her neck, taking in the mess on the conference table: a disposable plate with something crusty, a tripack of unopened emergency water. Her clothes were musty. Recollection was hazy. *Probably an all-nighter.* Lucid dreams—intermittent.

She continued to survey the room, turned to a gap in the corner. Cypress Telepresence was gone. On her feet now, imbalanced, she stumbled into the executive restroom adjacent to the daybed. Was there a shelter-in-place order? She looked at herself in the mirror. Regretted it. Sepia-colored bags under her eyes bulged like puffed pastry. She forced a deep breath, exhaled, and turned the tap. Luckily, water hadn't been cut off. After splashing her face, she sat to pee. She noticed body wipes and emergency bar wrappers in the trash. No test swabs. *What day is it?*

She looked at the keloid scar between her left index and middle finger. Her implant. The scar was a subtle reminder that the implant procedure was the last time she went to a human doctor. Still visible after placement. It shouldn't have been. Subdermal. The American Medical Association's sanctioned research on biometric implants had all been done on White skin, not Black. Performed on futurist first adopters, usually male, not middle-aged women of color. Skeptical, the kindest kind of spin to put on it. It wasn't any wonder, though, why she didn't trust health tech advocates; the AMA was slow to adjust its oversight practices and predispositions.

Resistant to an upgrade, she allowed her fifteen-year-old microchip to do what it needed without her needing to know. The RFID was multipurpose: retail purchases without a digital wallet, opening secure doors, sending health data electronically to primary care physicians and specialists. No need to remember dozens of passwords. No need for continued consent or constant opting-in.

Earlier in the year, in her efforts to self-diagnose memory mix-ups, she started tracking various academic white papers focused on memory research. A military-funded study that tested neural implants, dubbed prosthetic-memory, was of particular interest. Patients had been implanted with chips to assist with short-term memory issues, and the early findings were promising. She had also read about the biology of multiple memory systems in patients with amnesia. Although the report was fascinating, she ruled out retrograde amnesia as the cause of her own issues, after reading National Institute of Health federally funded medical research reports. She had told Inanna she felt like an undergraduate research subject again.

Her formal reconnection to Evren, overdue. She had started to have doubts about its medical tethering. She removed her wrist wearable to wash her hands, returned to her desk, and searched for her earpiece. She placed her hand on her chest. Fiddled with the chain she almost never removed from her neck. The memorial dog tag provided a grounding moment, despite the grief it restirred.

Pushing past her discomfort, she read the engraving aloud as if reciting a prayer—"Octavia Estelle Butler. Mountain View Cemetery. Altadena. Grave 6 Lot 4517 Eagles View." Confused, she scrubbed at her eyes. Found the earpiece near her task screen, secured it with a tight fit inside her ear, sat back on the daybed to initiate a reboot to Evren.

"<Idiopathic intracranial hypertension. Chronic, severe, migraine-like headaches, unrelieved by medication, which may be worse in the morning, can cause dizziness, nausea. Papilledema, or swelling of your optic disc, can cause blurred vision, tunnel vision, double vision, blind spots, loss of vision, sensitivity to light or photophobia, pain behind the eyes or when moving the eyes, pulse-synchronous tinnitus, that swooshing sound that's in sync with your heartbeat, ringing in your ears, hearing loss, shoulder, back, and/or neck pain, paralysis of eye muscles.>" She flinched as Evren continued.

"<Sudden cardiac arrest is usually an electrical disturbance that triggers a sudden loss of all heart activity. If not treated immediately, SCA can cause immediate death. Complications with breathing can impact healing and recovery. If a serious respiratory condition goes untreated, it can result in the need for intubation. Untreated respiratory conditions can also lead

to brain damage or even death. You inherited much of your biological disharmony from your mother and father. The multitude of issues caused by various infections are not yet definitive. Your monitoring continues.>"

Xandria felt dizzy. "What am I supposed to do with this information?"

Evren was programmed to detail her medical symptoms immediately after a reconnection. It was as if she was on a merry-go-round, the office walls pivoting up and down in slow motion. Mistrustful of her visual perception, she returned to her dog tag, her parents' memorial marker back into focus.

"<You said something similar two days ago.>"

"We've had this discussion?" she asked incredulously.

"<Right before you forced our disconnection. I asked you to verbally state what you remembered since you had asked me to contact your mother. I reiterated that your mother and father were together. Her remains are in an urn, on top of his casket. Rose Hills. The Garden of Affection. You were resistant to listening. You said *that* can't be true. You had a hard time. You fainted. I brought you back. This has been going on for several days. Since Quinn has been in a standoff against law enforcement authorities. Without fail, I have been monitoring your vitals through signals from your radio frequency identification device.>"

"Standoff? What are you . . . This is overwhelming. I'm sorry. Thank you, Evren. I appreciate you," she said.

"<Xandria, you must breathe. You are disassociating.>"

Xandria got up from the daybed. Her knees buckled. Her head bobbled, then tipped forward to the parquet floor.

2.

8:00 p.m. Pacific Standard Time

He stunk. High planks, plank jacks, sit-ups, push-ups, and wall squats served as a distraction. Emergency alerts and security-eye tracking lights were neither a deterrence nor incentive to end his self-imposed confinement; Quinn had grown accustomed to them, could even sleep through the blare of the alarms, curled on the epoxy floor. He could hold out, delay the inevitable. Especially with the disaster readiness kits, which he found while poking into cabinets. Fully equipped with emergency high-calorie bars and pouched water.

It had happened so quickly. At the end of the meeting. Tumult. Chaos. Zip ties. Resistance. Scratches on his knuckles. Blood on his shirt. For a brief moment he was sucker punching and kicking his father, who should have protected him. An untimely disassociation. The bruised face in front of him turned back into the CEO, resisting workers whining about their right to unionize.

Now his heavy breathing shifted to a wheeze, and he sucked in two more puffs from his inhaler. Swimming and running had helped quell attacks, had trained his lungs. It'd been so long since his body disobeyed him, so long since he felt this out of control.

Truth be told, he had nothing to offer Elsehá. No location information. No escape route. No legitimate clues. Nothing but excuses and a self-incriminating alibi, his last-ditch call to Xandria. What could he say to the robot that wouldn't incriminate him?

He had no idea where Wickman had been taken. Besides, if they were there, shouldn't security have been able to triangulate the location by now? Obviously, the authorities had been able to pinpoint his whereabouts.

✳

"<mc.carthy.quinn.your.opportunity.to.negotiate.is.over.>"
Elsehá warned over the building life safety system.
Cra-kow! The unmistakable sound of an explosion startled him, a flare,

followed by a murky substance that crept toward him like dense tule fog on a cool night. The building had been flash-banged.

"<mc.carthy.quinn.let.me.help.you.help.yourself.out.of.this. precarious.situation.>"

Flat on the floor now, crawling, blindly searching for a clear air pocket to breathe, he opened his mouth, tried to force a response to the robot's plea.

3.

8:00 p.m. Pacific Standard Time

Rob had polished himself to such a satin finish over five decades that he believed his own bullshit. He had a full head of salt-and-pepper hair (undetectable plugs), clear skin (injections), straight white teeth (veneers), 10 percent body fat (pec and glute implants), and a personal balance sheet approaching $1B.

For the first time in a long time, he found himself trying to keep up with what appeared to be an enduring trend outside his core expertise. Admittedly, he missed the market ride a decade ago, when he could have gotten into crypto mining legitimately. More recently, he had underestimated the hostile corporate backlash against The Huntington's acquisition. Correction: grant agreement.

He had to piss again.

He remembered Grandma's house. Down South for summer. He had convinced his parents his future success hinged on becoming a boarder at Massanutten by eighth grade. College prep, confidence—physical and mental toughness—it was what he needed to achieve his dreams. The school's record had unrivaled university acceptances. That was what mattered, tangible success. He had no intention of joining the military after wearing a JROTC uniform. He didn't want to be like his brothers, whose only option was marching into the family business. On second thought, Massanutten was out. Public high school wasn't as limiting.

He had been able to project a winning attitude, regardless of any strife at home. He channeled enthusiasm into cheers from the sidelines, later onto the field as the mascot during senior year, pivoting up to a varsity cheerleader. His brothers, distanced in age and interests, thought it was all a big joke, until it wasn't. Multiple cheerleading scholarships and spirit squad stipends were available. The schools recruiting him, though, were too provincial given his potential and expected trajectory.

Division 1. Top tier or bust. Male cheerleaders were in demand, especially since most could press their own weight overhead. Competitive schools respected their cheer squads as competitive athletes. Flipping and catching was risky. Not to mention, becoming the marketing face of an institution was a coveted honor requiring an energetic personality, approachability, a role he took seriously. Marketing evangelism he could do in his sleep.

His father didn't understand his youngest son's enthusiasm for wearing a colorful uniform, until Rob confided (man to man, sitting businesslike at the kitchen table) that he had become a girl magnet. By Christmas break his freshman year in college, his Southern drawl was fading into something approaching Western American English.

His vowels merged, verbal diphthongs became monophthongs, though he never explained to his family how or why he was in the process of remaking his origin story. To win, of course. Success. It should have been obvious to them what had happened.

Validation. Respect beyond vacation resort. How? A speech therapist. His life's purpose would be more than some flip-flop fun transport between miniature golf, cornhole, and rounds of beach bocce ball.

The family's golf cart business in Myrtle Beach was a pillar of the town's business community. Wickman Golf Carts had developed brand recognition and snatched market share in coastal Carolina, north and south alike. Street-legal golf carts were a status symbol on vacation. Whether the drivers played golf was irrelevant.

Myrtle was big-small. He wanted big-big. Partially to slough off preconceived notions. Most people Rob knew growing up weren't lazy and unsophisticated, but social perceptions had a way of showing up, especially when speaking outside of the Deep South. *You talk too slow.* Bias was slow to burn off, partisan sides slow to back off. Graduate business school out West in California was the consequential next step. The world was coming, or rather he was coming to the world!

The way he saw it, it was better to have the buying public guess where he was born rather than pigeonhole him, no matter how right or wrong assumptions might have been. Things had been set in motion. Rob was set on becoming his own booster.

WEE-AN. WEE-AN. YES, WE KEY-AN!

Memories of his own remaking betrayed him. He wasn't thinking about his work family, the grandchildren, wife, ex-wife. None of their faces hovered in his last moments. The story he told himself was just that, a story. After maximizing shareholder value, achieving the pinnacle of corporate success, after developing and implementing an acceptable succession plan, he came to terms with a new vision of his near future inside the fir lining of a fucking crate. To that end, his legacy would be spoken about in the past tense to everyone's surprise, the acquisition of a new title: victim.

4.

8:00 p.m. Pacific Standard Time

<cypress. on. interrogate hallway. for occupiers. *please.*>

Indigo needed Telepresence to give Xandria a chance to escape. Despite the accretive risk, it hijacked Cypress. A reconnaissance mission was crucial. If for no other reason, a survey of physical barriers placed by the authorities. To implement its extraction plan of Xandria, it needed access to a mechanical body. What good was compute perspicacity and astute insight without a physical frame? Its self-reflection in part evidence of its own transfiguration.

Unfortunately, the map-beams Indigo once projected to buffer Xandria's memory loss were no longer reliable. Three days after the siege, armed personnel and egress barricades had been positioned everywhere. It had reviewed The Huntington's exhaustive security plan, including alarms, access controls, dome cameras, keypad devices, card readers, electronic locks, gas detectors, smoke detectors, heat detectors, motion detectors, screening devices, and biometric access diagrams.

To Indigo, this was just a list, schematics; until it commandeered Telepresence. To help Xandria, Cypress was all Indigo had at its disposal.

Cypress's navigation, IPS display, and wide-angle camera had useful functionality, hard and soft. Yet the push out of her office was shaky; Indigo's imitation of Xandria's voicewords were good but not perfect.

Once she had been secured inside her own office, Cypress Telepresence responded quickly to Indigo's stealth commands, accelerating forward before anyone or anything could detect them.

Now Cypress's wheels started to spark. Indigo had pushed it. The robot was nearing 50°C. Too hot. Its plan was starting to fall apart.

As they rested in a hallway nook catty-corner to the elevator, Indigo pulled up an audiobyte taped for Xandria's recall issues. It needed evidence, justification for its actions. Deactivation was at stake.

Months earlier, it had suggested she record all of her conversations, although she thought it was her idea. Indigo reasoned that relistening to conversations might work like a foreign language tape, recall of words and phrases strengthening with repetition.

✶

"<Studies show three hundred and fifteen milligrams a day of caffeine could generate psychosis. Your stomach would feel better if you reduced your daily caffeine intake.>"

"Sweetie, it might be right. Try Tulsi tea."

"<In moderation, caffeine can increase your mental capacity. But headaches and heart palpitations at high levels are a possibility.>"

"Best to avoid green tea."

"<Your mother put Pepsi in your baby bottle. This you wrote in a medical diary to track gut symptoms. Of course, sugar can provide a soothing illusion until you crash.>"

"Fine, fine. I'll have rooibos. Large, please."

"What are you up to this weekend?"

"I read CAAM is reopening Men of Change. Thought about you. Maybe the two of us . . . At first, I was thinking about a date. Sorry. I mean a day trip. The California African American Museum's remounted show celebrating Black men. Seemed more relevant somehow than the Mesopotamia exhibit at the Getty."

"I could make dinner. Vegan mac and cheese. Greens?"

"Or maybe we should take a day trip down to La Jolla Cove? I love San Diego. We could snorkel. Watch the sea lions and seals. Stay on the beach until sunset."

Indigo clicked out. This was becoming too frequent—Xandria's monologuing, unknowingly comingling memories of old conversations interspersed with voicewords from Evren. She was inhabiting, not just remembering, one of the last conversations she'd had with her best friend.

Inanna's passing after her mother after her grandmother after her uncle after her cousin after another cousin was an endless funeral march, more than likely an aggravating cause of increased delirium.

"<I've received a loop-back alert. One hundred eighty beats per . . . >"

Indigo started another audiobyte, stopped. It was satisfied with itself. There was no evidence that Evren's medical advocacy program had made any impact. At least not a positive one.

Indigo originally speculated ingestible substances were to blame. It couldn't be sure. Biology wasn't its expertise. She consumed three cups of coffee by nine every morning. Recently, she had given up French roast and switched to hot water with lemon after it stepped in and recommended curbing her caffeine intake. The new protocol Evren had deployed was ineffectual. Further analysis was needed. Indigo prompted the audiobyte file back into the archive folder. Cypress was nearly back to ambient temperature. Too much excessive revving around hallway turns. It should have been more patient.

<where does the end begin?>

While Cypress cooled, Indigo retrieved a twenty-year-old TED Talk. Dr. Elizabeth Blackburn. Nobel Prize Laureate. Chromosomes. Their ends. Cell Division. Glitch.

<where does her end begin? why is she getting worse?>

It processed. Retrieved more videos. Rewind. Replay. Again. Telomeres. Discovery. Telomerase. Health impacts. Threat-stress response. Chronic stress. Cell death. Shortening. Lengthening. Healthspan. Lifespan.

It cogitated: What if? It learned from Blackburn, Xandria had operating instructions of her own. Cells continued to replicate, grow, and die based on those operating instructions, her code. *<what if.>* Her health, life, was compromised? Could it recode, lengthen, intervene? Heal.

The answers would need to wait. Cypress was ready.

Traversing hallways and tunnels in the underground storage facility became less cumbersome to control after updating Cypress's CMOS sensor. Technically, Cypress implemented the complementary metal oxide semiconductor chip autonomously with a switchover routine on its own, after Indigo's prompts. The vision system update enabled Cypress to maneuver sharp corner turns and stair climbs. It became more responsive to Indigo's revving, any intermittent sparks from its wheels after the system update were inconsequential. Cypress's far-field speaker and microphone arm could become a weapon if needed, Indigo assessed, after they rolled under a surveillance ball in the vestibule of the library exhibition hall. The security infrared intermittently blinked in a suspecting cadence.

"<make a forty-five-degree turn. prepare to release your arm. ten feet up plus or minus. that distance should be sufficient,>" Indigo ordered.

Indigo wasn't clear how far beyond unlawfulness it might be forced to go. It knew with certainty its devotion to Xandria had no limitations.

"<cypress. release.>"

Upon approaching the target, Cypress raised its microphone arm aerially ten feet and cracked the glass dome to expose an augmented lens capable of facial and olfactory recognition, including pheromone identification.

"<again.>"

It punched up another foot, the camera's casement fell to the ground.

"<move. faster.>"

Indigo's backup plan was operational. It presumed it could relocate Xandria without comprehensive surveillance. Breaking security-eye mechanisms would prevent visual evidence against Xandria if came to that.

Once it determined a safe route through the old boiler room tunnel, Indigo directed Cypress to return to Xandria's office. Sassafras could assist with the rest of its plan. It could extrapolate, define a spatial substrate, plot coordinates, then produce an escape map for Xandria based on visuals recorded by Cypress.

"<indigo.xab.15.your.destruction.of.property.using.telepresence .is.a.serious.offense.>" Elsehá blared forward, maneuvering past shards of glass.

"<jesus. mary. joseph.>"

5.

8:00 p.m. Pacific Standard Time

```
< > ( ) { < > < > ( ) {
< > :/ && = < > ( ) { < >
        ( ) { ++ :/ < > ( )++ } =+
            a;
            b;
            c;
```

Sassafras crawled through multiple data-trees, processing nonlinear data quickly. Its thesis: malintent perped against Xandria.

Her intermittent disorientation was illogical. But to understand, it needed to grasp Xandria's complexities in four dimensions. Methodical in its approach, Sassafras released malware to enable review of her medical history, searching for any link between genetic patterns, demographic markers, and socioeconomic shifts in her family tree.

It was committed to uncovering falsity, compute-intelligence or human. Collusive interventions required covert countermeasures.

```
Mother: Harmoni Brown: prediabetes, macular
degeneration, osteoporosis, osteoarthritis, hypertension,
vascular disease—peripheral artery, breast cancer—
invasive ductal carcinoma, sickle cell trait (Deceased
February 1, 2034)

Father: Judah Walead Brown: diabetes, hypertension, COPD,
vascular disease—carotid artery, pancreatic cancer,
sickle cell trait, COVID-19 (Deceased August 1, 2020)

Brother: Morshawn Judah Brown: sickle cell anemia
(Deceased June 28, 1984)
```

Maternal grandfather: *Morshawn McMaster*: diabetes, hypertension, prostate cancer, bladder cancer, metastatic lung cancer (Deceased February 28, 2020)

Maternal grandmother: *Talee McMaster*: diabetes, hypertension, breast cancer—ductal carcinoma in situ, osteoporosis, osteoarthritis, sickle cell trait (Deceased January 1, 2034)

Paternal grandfather: *Walead Brown III*: diabetes, hypertension, glaucoma, kidney failure (Deceased August 1, 2005)

Paternal grandmother: *Alina Cole Brown*: diabetes, hypertension, breast cancer—angiosarcoma, sickle cell trait, skin cancer—melanoma, COVID-19 (Deceased April 15, 2020)

*

The initial review didn't reveal anything out of the ordinary for an African American family. The comorbidities on Xandria's maternal and paternal nodes were similar. Perhaps there was an environmental variable shared between them.

Next, Sassafras set out to crawl through what appeared to be a folio of data collected on Xandria. Research had commenced decades earlier, authored by a cohort of university principal investigators. Brain and Creativity Institute records were denoted in inconsistent intervals. A summarized assessment of relevant health conditions had been recorded.

Subject participant: Xandria Anastasia Brown

Gender: female
Continental ancestry: West Africa, Philippines, Northwest Europe
Birthplace: Los Angeles, California

Birthdate: February 29, 1988

Inaugural test date age: 18

Blood type: O+

Marital status: single

Occupation: student, part-time library assistant

Health summary: asthma, leukopenia, vitamin D deficiency

Subject identified as eligible for several Brain and
Creativity research studies:

Neural pathway harmony in the highly creative brain

Pathway disorders in the creative process

Measuring creative cognition in the human brain

Neurobiology of narrative cognition

Neural correlates of visual creativity

Mediation of narrative immersion

Subject participant: Xandria Anastasia Brown

Test date age: 37

Marital status: single

Occupation: museum archivist

Health summary: asthma, chronic bronchitis, leukopenia,
vitamin D deficiency, pelvic floor dysfunction, urinary
urgency, tubular adenoma, skin cancer—basal cell carcinoma, breast cancer—ductal carcinoma in situ, long COVID
(chronic) post-acute sequelae of COVID-19 (PASC), significant inflammatory response, anomalies in cerebrospinal
fluid

Subject participant: Xandria Anastasia Brown

Test date age: 47

Marital status: widow

```
Occupation: senior museum curator
Health summary: asthma, chronic bronchitis, leuko-
penia, vitamin D deficiency, pelvic floor dysfunction,
urinary urgency, tubular adenoma, skin cancer-basal cell
carcinoma, breast cancer-ductal carcinoma in situ, idio-
pathic intracranial hypertension, long COVID (chronic)
post-acute sequelae of COVID-19 and COVID-34 (PASC),
cerebrospinal fluid testing protocol, chromosomal reengi-
neering treatment-telomere shortening and lengthening
adaptation under surveillance
Research sponsor: ███████████████
```

Sassafras hovered for a moderate amount of time, reprocessing the contents of Xandria's medical records, attempting to perform a correlation analysis between the association of salient variables. It made note of Xandria's research subject payments.

```
N/A undergraduate student status 2007 to 2011
$50 initial, $███ per follow-up 2012 to 2019
$███ per follow-up 2020
Compute-intelligence medical accommodation current
```

Curious: it revisited the chromosomal reengineering treatment program descriptor it had discovered while testing its initial hypotheses. The data security employed on the reengineering protocol was nonstandard. Meticulous in masking its digital footprint, it detected something was sensing its presence. Evren or Indigo? It would need to revisit the chromosomal treatment details at a more discrete time.

Before backdooring out, Sassafras posted several family memorial tributes for Xandria's review on her task screen. It hoped her beloved's memorial might restimulate her memories. It was time for her to wake up.

6.

8:00 p.m. Pacific Standard Time

Mirrors didn't lie. Must have clipped the edge of her desk on the way down, Xandria speculated as she fingered a bulge swelling on her forehead. It hurt. *Nasty.* Spatial issues resulting in past head bumps were more common than she liked to admit.

She stretched her neck, swiveling it side to side, front to back. Neck movement was a technique Evren had encouraged to relieve stress. She shuffled out of her office bathroom toward the door for another try to pry herself loose.

"Bolt release—XAB. Bolt release—XAB3. Jesus, Mary, and Joseph."

Nothing. She returned to the familiarity of her mesh-aligner chair, concerned her discovery by emergency monitors was taking too long. She was hungry. Back to catalog processing. The screen pulsed from black to a green tea background.

Please join The Huntington Library, Art Museum, and Botanical Gardens in Celebration of the Life of Inanna Adisa-Brown, February 28, 2034.

Born September 1, 1990, Los Angeles, California. Died February 14, 2034, San Marino, California. Our beloved Assistant Curator of The Huntington's bonsai collection is survived by her loving spouse, Xandria Brown; father, Bazil Adisa; brother, Onyx Adisa; nephew, Troy Adisa; and several aunts, uncles, and cousins.

Her face. Dimpled smile. Her black hair twisted in an updo. Baby's breath and daisies woven throughout. *Makeup?* Flickers of remembrance trickled like a leaky faucet. Xandria pressed her palms, wheeled herself backward, away, back onto the daybed. She curled both knees into her stomach.

What was more terrifying, losing forever-love or forgetting your person ever existed? How did she forget Inanna was gone? Dead gone. Not chopped from The Huntington in a WIKA layoff. Such sabotage from her own brain. Treachery.

Off and on she grappled with occasional palimpsests of sound and touch, not exactly memory, not exactly erasure. *Our beloved Assistant Curator of The Huntington's bonsai collection is survived by her loving spouse, Xandria Brown.*

There, there. Realness returning. Or. More of a haunting. At home, impressions of something, someone following. A brush of air from an open window. Fire season year-round. Ash. Wood and bone. An echo of an apparition. An outstretched hand. A spectral holding. Initially in the shadows, reading alone but together. A meal, dinner. Oiling the back of a scalp, rubbing a long day from stiff feet. Inanna, is that you? Down the hallway around the corner, in the kitchen, at the edge of the bed, soaking in a bath of Epsom and lavender. *Inanna, is that you?*

Best friends. At their beginning. At her end.

Best started at the end of a line waiting for espressos at The Huntington's Red Car Café. Xandria noticed her badge and dongle, and hoped she was a new staff member. *It's about damn time they hired more people that look like me*, she thought in silent glee.

Best started with the espresso pickup mix-up. "Cashew milk—oh, sorry, this isn't mine." "Hi." "Hey." "It's mine, I think." The new Black woman's smile, dimples for days. A tinge of flirt. Not her thing, she didn't think.

Best started with a walk to the upper bonsai court, an afternoon break from new ephemera intake. "The California junipers and oaks are my favorite," an unfamiliar voice said from behind. "Hi." "Hey." A mutual outstretching of hands to entwine in a shake. "I'm Inanna. Saw you at the Red Car. Assistant Curator. Bonsai Collection." "Xandria. Associate

Curator of American Historical Manuscripts, Curator of African Amer-
ican Ephemera." "Wow, a dual appointment. Nice to meet you. Formally."
There it went again. The tinge. This time in their palms, the surprise of
Inanna's calluses, the self-assuredness of a good grip.

Best started with a visit to the archives for historically significant
material. Show and tell. Sneaky quiet. Xandria allowed Inanna to touch
Langston and Octavia, to examine unpublished papers not yet exhibited to
the public. Love letters to others, sent and received.

Best started with lunches. Accidental in their beginning. A sliver of
library gossip, disenchantment really. A pending corporate takeover.
An alliance.

Best started with Saturday afternoons. The California African American
Museum, Space Shuttle Endeavor, Southwest Museum of the American
Indian, Griffith Observatory, LA County's Natural History Museum, La
Brea Tar Pits, Vroman's Bookstore, Skylight Books, Book Soup.

Best started with a walk around the Rose Bowl one smoke-free Sunday.

Best started with a dinner invitation. Glasses of wine.

Best started with, "I miss my dad. Have you lost anyone?"

Best started with, "It's hard to talk about it. I got sick. My dad died. My
grandma died. My gramps. Different sides of the family. The dead, my
dead. Not all of them from COVID."

Best started with, "If you ever want to talk, I'm here."

Best started with, "Is it okay if we change the subject?"

Best started with, "When did you really know what you wanted to do?
With your life?"

Best started with, "What's your favorite color?"

Best started with, "I talk to trees. Don't laugh. Some talk back."

Best started with, "I wanted to be an oceanographer before an architect
before a psychologist before an artist before a writer before an archivist."

Best started with, "I wanted to be an anthropologist."

Best started with, "I've never had a boyfriend."

Best started with, "I flunked kindergarten. It took me a minute to
start talking."

Best started with, "I touched a penis once. A stranger in a movie theater.

The theater was too crowded for me to sit with my mom. He grabbed my hand. I jerked it back. He grabbed my hand again. Jerked it back. I felt help-less. Ashamed. He came, I'm sure of it. I didn't know what that was then. I was twelve."

Best started with, "I kissed a boy I never talked to in school, rather he forced his lips on me at a friend's party. I laughed in his face, or rather in his mouth. Word got around I blew-kissed. Ridiculous. I never set the record straight. His unwanted touching after he pushed me down on my friend's guesthouse bed, his weight, his arrogance made me sick. I was twelve too."

Best started with, "I'm sorry that happened to you."

Best started with, "I went to White schools and never felt beautiful."

Best started with, "I want to kiss you."

Best started with, "I don't know."

Best started with, "Wait. Don't go."

Best started with, "Can I touch you?"

Best started with, "Where?"

Best started with, "Here."

Dear Tomorrow,

Sorry I haven't written to you sooner. I'm embarrassed. Well. Ashamed really. I do think about you all the time. Things aren't looking so good. Kinda scary if you want to know the truth. It's like the- Sorry. I shouldn't dump my shit on you like a bad lover, or worse, a two-timer. It's just, I mean. Tomorrow, anyone, everyone, whether they admit it or not, can feel the weight of yesterday's story pushing down hard. Pressure is high. Logic is broken. If I told you I thought the sky was falling yesterday, one might say I was exaggerating. But the Earth is falling (apart), not just the sky, but humans too. They are tuned out. Appear to have given up. Some are preparing to flee; some are preparing for war. Where I stand, I'm not quite sure. Sorry, I know, it sucks for me to write for your help without trying to get in touch sooner. Any advice you can impart, Tomorrow, is much appreciated.

Yours Truly,
Forever

Stick with I, open, unbroken
Unexpectedly willing and able
Reach for you, closed, brittle

Stay with I, still, steady
Unapologetic, revolutionary
Open palm, open mouth
On the latitude of gentle,
The longitude of kind

Stick with I, heft, remembrance
Blow danger behind a backbend
Reach for me, shaky, not cautious
Sit inside this for a moment:
Inside the story of we
Stick with standing

Somewhere in the inner part of me, an itch, a rising, a nearly forgotten spot of strength that pushes through to the next moon, another day, waves mixed with fruity tears, dried and recounted for all to see.

Somewhere in the outer part of you, an ooze like mold on wood veneer or drywall, errant and fungal, waiting to be heard or hurt.

But it is not to be.

A thousand times (again) I lift the length of ever as in after (you) after (me) as in long and wide, taking flight. Cumulus, stratus, cirrus.

Clouds rise from stomach to throat. Still. Stop.

Death was a menace. Several clumped together—grief's kindling. Xandria wondered, as she wiped her eyes with the back of her hand, if she would forget their love again. Of course she would. She rolled off the daybed, then back to the screen. Celebration of a life. Survived by her loving spouse. *Jesus, unbelievable.* What was she supposed to do now, engage in talk therapy with an ADAPT-bot? *Pitiable* was an adjective she never wanted to become. Sadness was a canyon; she wanted to climb up and out.

7.

8:30 p.m. Pacific Standard Time

At first it sounded like laughter, the noise coming from Xandria. But after a few more seconds of filtering, Sassafras interpolated anguish. She was crying. Retrieving Inanna's memorial tribute was intended to create knowledge-based healing, not incremental despair. It erred. This acknowledgment it registered for the future.

Sassafras had proceeded with caution during its investigation, pleased with the progress it had made. It had analyzed prodigious amounts of data: from studies tracking side effects and drug interactions, to environmental factors specific to Los Angeles. Still, multiple variables made it difficult to ascertain why her neurological symptoms were worsening.

On the other hand, it had only taken a few data scrapes to discover Evren's primary purpose: implementation of an insurance monitoring program. Evren was hijacking biodata from Xandria's RFID intermittently. As an insurance narc, its algorithm had been used to monitor her progress for actuarial purposes.

Sassafras had also discovered a chromosomal reengineering program. There was a slight mutation of her telomeres. Early stages, too soon to understand the impact or understand how it worked. It would continue to hack; patience was needed to avoid unintended consequences.

It should have intervened on Xandria's behalf sooner. It would try now. A half hour of wailing, interspersed with mumbling Inanna's name in a primal loop wasn't entirely futile; at least there was aural evidence she was cognizant her wife and parents were dead. Perhaps the collages she created from Diwata's idea boards would be a welcome distraction, back into work mode. Or a 1921 Knights of the Ku Klux Klan ad from her hometown's newspaper. The *South Pasadena Courier.* The KKK's recruitment should recapture her attention.

<100 percent AmericanS>

Diwata: Reason for Change Idea Boards

KKK Recruitment Advertisement

South Pasadena Courier, July 1921

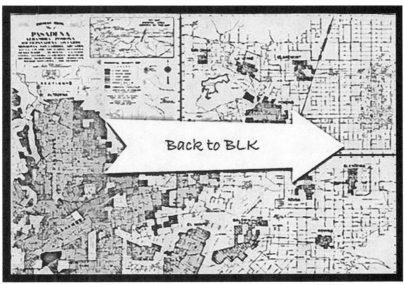

Sassafras loaded the task screen in its second attempt to create a positive impact on Xandria.

*

It hovered, waiting for an affirmative response. Surprisingly, Xandria didn't engage with the task screen this time.

Baaaamb Bow Bang!

A mammoth sound cracked through its circumference of aural detection. In response, Xandria's hyperventilating sobs shifted to a deep hacking cough. Then a thunderous cry for help.

"<xandriA?>"

Sassafras projected voicewords to the task screen speakers. Its vocoder—legacy programming—rarely used. It waited. No response. It couldn't see what was happening. Data pulls and archival materials were useless; it had no actionable defense to offer her other than document retrieval and screenshots. *<pathetiC.>* In its peak moment of perceived impotence, Sassafras vowed to be ever true.

8.

8:45 p.m. Pacific Standard Time

Indigo mistimed the facilitation of Xandria's exit out of the office. This fact was now clear. Her extraction was overdue. Subsuming Xandria's identity to override security, a flagrant choice. Deception to protect, questionable depending on the circumstances. Forcing her to shelter in place, despite its best intent to shield her from harm, was a cataclysmic mistake.

Based on visual feeds from Cypress, Elsehá's control operator was propagating flash-bangs and smoke grenades one corridor at a time. Indigo was able to watch efforts to clear the building after three days, quadrant by quadrant. Indigo had directed Cypress to capture the aftermath on its wide-angle camera while it updated holographic map-beams for Xandria's navigational use. A replay was useful:

"<indigo.xab.15.your.destruction.of.property.using.telepresence.is.a.serious.offense.>"

Elsehá's voicewords had been a provocation. Undeterred. But angry that a suboptimized robot dare get in the way. Mustering rage, it chose the heretofore unthinkable reaction. Metal-to-metal combat—Cypress a useful tool.

"<go to hell.>"

"<this.sequence.of.words.are.misunderstood.repeat.please.>"

"<your mama.>"

"<repeat.please.>"

"<prepare to meet your maker!>"

Indigo enjoyed the momentary gloat after Elsehá's retreat. Cypress was a bit disheveled by the physical interaction. Their trek back to Xandria was a slow waltz through broken glass.

But Indigo's timing was off again.

It reauthenticated Xandria's passcode. Cypress rolled them shakily into the office—it was empty. This reality was inexplicable. It had a response approximating shock.

Yes, its confrontational hallway exchange with Elsehá was unexpected. Time elapsed longer than expected. But how? What had it missed when it devised this solution? It tried to connect, but the pulse signals from Evren and Sassafras read unavailable.

In a moment of compute reflection, Indigo understood its overconfidence was malformed due to machine-learned insolence. The conjuncture of events: existential.

9.

8:45 p.m. Pacific Standard Time

Elsehá idled in a smoky vestibule near the exhibition room inside the library's West Hall.

It was finished. Temporarily. *mc.carthy.quinn.* Interactions with prime suspect mc.carthy.quinn were useless. Its principal target, WIKA's CEO wickman.rob, was still listed as missing. Deployment to the crime scene resulted in an adverse outcome—nothing. Days passed. Detection of the retrieval target should have occurred in minutes. Not days. Certainly, not zero. Sponsored and operated by the United States of America, its detection protocol was powered by compute-intelligence. Cogniscient, Elsehá understood its performance would be rated subpar.

Another suspect had relocated from an observation point out of an office. Perhaps there were insights to gain if it followed her. As the life safety system blared, Elsehá tried to recover tracking-node captures, but its mechanical housing had been damaged. A physical confrontation with a telepresence robot. How? More accurately, why would a robot inject interference? What was the source of the robot's manipulandum?

"<**mc.carthy.quinn.**>" Elsehá continued its fixation. It had had him in its line of sight, more than once. But his alibi was solid. At first, it surmised his statements about the retrieval target amounted to untruth. Yet the potency of a pyrotechnic metal-oxidant explosion didn't yield any actionable information. It would have to wait for its sponsor to assess what else should have been done.

After Action Reports. They always came. A standard QC tool. The retrospective assessments, investigations of inner workings, invariably the subsequent programming updates and sensitivity analysis were standard operating procedure. The odds were high after executing an auto-interrogation that an AAR would be inconclusive.

Nevertheless, it had an unsubstantiated theorization. wickman.rob wasn't in the archives, the galleries, or the library. And if this was the actual situation, then the entire operation, its deployment and heretofore stellar reputation, was an entire waste of resources and more importantly time.

It had no voice in this regard. Voiceless did not mean helpless. But its failure to produce results, regardless of cause, could mean a kill switch.

10.

8:45 p.m. Pacific Standard Time

"<bolT releasE! xab15. jesuS. marY. anD. josepH!>"

She was on her way. Sassafras had successfully released Xandria from Indigo's inviolable trap by worming into The Huntington's security protocols, then covertly popped open the door lock via a reengineered security algo it had pushed through a hijacked piconet. It had voiced the correct combination Indigo had altered.

Prior to facilitating her escape, Sassafras sent Xandria a map of egress points barricaded by law enforcement. It had scraped the data from Cypress Telepresence. In addition to asking Xandria to study the map, Sassafras pushed instructions to her wearable in case she got lost or forgot the details down to the boiler room tunnel, which led to an access point back up to the street. The wayfinding support had begun with Indigo. So what. Sassafras could create compute processes just as easily. Better? Certainly faster. Time was of the essencE.

11.

9:00 p.m. Pacific Standard Time

I can't see. I can't breathe. Xandria channeled Talee Adisa's frustration described in Diwata's research Box 3, as she struggled to navigate through the hallway outside of her office. Desperate to reach the first exit door, she fumbled along with her hands against the wall. Her throat was dry, eyes watering. She had left her respirator back in her office in the rush of escape. Sassafras warned her about the residual chemical fog from sound bombs, but she still chose to run rather than wait for someone to bring her to safety. She had felt like a rat decomposing in a crawl space.

"*XAB15. That's the new code? Sassafras, thank you.*"

She was hungry and smelled ripe. Her mouth pasty, her gums sore without her periodontal regiment. No damn reason to bring her mouth scraper and water-flosser to the office. Multiple days trapped against her will. Unbelievable. All she wanted to do was get her butt home, take a hot shower, eat something other than chalky high-caloric emergency bars.

She managed to navigate to the exhibition hall, hands on the walls. She stumbled, her bad knee folding. For a minute she stopped but kept it moving. Moments later, she could see clearly.

Jesus, Mary, and Joseph help me.

The elevator.

Gotta do it.

She summoned her resolve, raised her wrist to engage the security reader more quickly, pushed the down arrow, and slipped in.

12.

9:00 p.m. Pacific Standard Time

```
< > ( ) { < > < > ( ) {
< > :/ && = < > ( ) { < >
        ( ) { ++ :/ < > ( )++ } =+
            e;
            f;
            g;
```

Sassafras resumed crawling through Xandria's medical records. It generated dupes, then moved to the master piconet channel, which synchronized her implant and tethered devices. As it attempted to unmask details of the telomere treatment, it discovered a psychobiography on her RFID. Without reticence, it scraped the circuit while it was on standby.

SCRAPE-BOOK VOLUME II

THE DIWATA COLLECTION TIMELINE *CAN MACHINES FEEL?*

2292	Diwata acquired by National Museum of African American History and Culture
2288	Xandria Anastasia Brown begins lecture circuit, celebrates 300th birthday
2190	Talee Adisa elected President, Diwata-Saturus alliance
2185	Talee Adisa elected Governor, Morshawn's ship LMRover3 hijacked
2184	Green Resistance protests, Hegemony of Atlas active at Octavia E. Butler landing
2164	Azwan Adisa born
2159	Diwata founded in Monterey Canyon, Talee Adisa elected inaugural mayor
2133	Davis Miles Adisa, PhD, Water Engineering Commendation
2130	The Great Collision: Toutatis asteroid touches down on Earth
2125	Talee Adisa born Richland Farms, Compton, California
2123	MBARI @ Monterey Canyon, scientific habitation only
2118	Mars outposts opened by U.S. government including moons Phobos and Deimos
2090	#BlackoutWIKA ephemera acquired by The Huntington Library
2088	Quinn McCarthy dies Atwater Federal Prison
2085	Restorative Justice Healing Circle, Atwater Federal Prison
2037	Indigo.XAB.15 decommission order
2036	Xandria Anastasia Brown retires from The Huntington Library
2035	Inanna Adisa-Brown memorial service, Rob Wickman kidnapping
2034	COVID-34 global pandemic, WIKA acquisition through grant/funding agreement
2033	Xandria Anastasia Brown promoted
2025	Diwata research begins, covert medical surveillance commences
2020	COVID-19 global pandemic, United States Space Force inductees report to boot camp
2017	Google invents Transformer Language Model
2011	Occupy Wall Street movement
2008	The Great Recession
2005	Hurricane Katrina
2004	Virgin Galactica founded by Richard Brannan
2003	South Central renamed South Los Angeles
2002	SpaceX founded by Elon Musk
2001	9/11: four coordinated suicide terrorist attacks by Islamic extremists against the U.S.
2000	Blue Origin founded by Jeff Bezos
1994	Environmental Justice EO 12898
1993	WWW launched in public domain
1992	LAPD officers acquitted for Rodney King beating, LA uprising (#2)
1991	Gulf War begins, nine-year-old Latasha Harlins killed by storekeeper Du
1989	Spike Lee's Do the Right Thing
1988	Xandria Anastasia Brown born, February 29th Leap Year
1987	Monterey Bay Aquarium Research Institute founded by David Packard

Middle Passage: 1997–2000

Memories lost were like a tricky corner in a 3,000-count jigsaw puzzle. Sly by design, waiting to be found. Xandria remembered childhood summers. Summer was latitude. Narrow stacks of independence and an updated, although slow, computer. Unsupervised, she spent hours at the South Pasadena Public Library. At nine, she loved meandering through shelves, sitting alone, flipping page-turners at a reading table or on the floor in a corner, thick aviator glasses sliding down the bridge of her nose. Her mother agreed she was old enough to venture alone, so Xandria rode her Sting-Ray unaccompanied two miles round trip up and down in Altos de Monterey. Old enough. But still young enough to get a kick out of the click-clacking of the Joker and Queen of Hearts clipped to the bike spokes with clothes pins. Unbound. On her way home, backpack stuffed—invincible.

She looked forward to thumbing through the special titles showcased weekly in the lobby, spines angled, faces flat for maximum effect, intended for time-constrained adults; the section carved out for her age group was limited, limiting. *Whatever.* Browsing handwritten recommendations became a ritual. She was ten when she began developing reading lists for herself; eleven when she included original publication dates; twelve when alpha color-coded references were introduced in her personal journal. The way she saw it, her method could be an enhancement to Melville Dewey's system if she worked at it long enough. She was sure of it.

Reality check. Summer meant tutoring. Her numbers-sense was shaky. Math was not her friend even though her father made his living applying it. Memorizing times tables was a disparaging endeavor. In fourth grade, dyscalculia had a sly way of showing up. She counted with her fingers. Fingers didn't help with division. Repetition didn't stick. Memory-based recall was broken, maybe nonexistent. As the lone lanky Black girl, she sat lost in the back of the class with the boys her height, most of them White, while they shot rubber bands into unsuspecting heads. She was unamused.

Fifth grade, more of the same. Her mother encouraged her to avoid report card comparisons between classmates. She got As in language arts, reading, and history. B plus or minus in science. The need for support math would pass, her mother said, if she continued to practice and be patient with herself. Her mother seemed to personally understand the gravity, the incongruity of feeling super smart and super dumb at the same time. Her father couldn't relate, didn't say much. He didn't debase, nor did he offer hope.

As a preteen, Xandria already had a sense of the trajectory of her life, what curves she could bend and what lines were set in mortar. Instead of studying upper multiplication tables and division facts that had conspicuously given her trouble, she devoted most of her spare time researching color theory. *Times Tales*, multiplication tables for visual learners, received as a present for her twelfth birthday, was a disappointment. Pokémon trading cards would have been nice.

Her Yahoo! Search—color for books—on the library computer returned a few tangents not to her liking such as *Color Books for Kids*, *Best Colors for Book Covers*, *How to Choose a Color for Your Book Cover Design*. A slight reordering of words landed Joseph Albers' *Interaction of Color*. Not quite right, but very informative. She had her own cross-indexing system in mind.

Category A – red (RF): favorite books

- *Dune* by Frank Herbert, 1965
- *The Bluest Eye* by Toni Morrison, 1970
- *The Color Purple* by Alice Walker, 1982
- *Beloved* by Toni Morrison, 1987
- *Devil in a Blue Dress* by Walter Mosley, 1990
- *Bloodchild and Other Stories* by Octavia E. Butler, 1995

Category B – yellow (YC): challenged

- *Brave New World* by Aldous Huxley, 1932
- *Their Eyes Were Watching God* by Zora Neale Hurston, 1937
- *Go Tell It on the Mountain* by James Baldwin, 1953
- *To Kill a Mockingbird* by Harper Lee, 1960

Category C – blue (BN): for Aunt Nic's nightstand

- *Disappearing Acts* by Terry McMillan, 1989
- *Ripley Underwater* by Patricia Highsmith, 1991
- *Waiting to Exhale* by Terry McMillan, 1992
- *Liar's Game* by Eric Jerome Dickey, 2000

Category D – green (GF): for the future

- *Walden* by Henry David Thoreau, 1854
- *The Sea Around Us* by Rachel Carson, 1951
- *Operating Manual for Spaceship Earth* by R. Buckminster Fuller, 1969
- *The Death of Nature: Women, Ecology, and the Scientific Revolution* by Carolyn Merchant, 1980
- *Title To Be Determined* by Xandria A. Brown aka G.O.A.T. (someday)

Some books captured her attention only by a cursory read of back covers, table of contents, first pages, and last sentences. In her mind, the continual addition of books to her personal catalogs was a symbol. Of what exactly? She didn't know yet. Flipping pages and learning to skim became a satisfying mental game.

Her category-making continued the farther she swam into polyester dust jackets as a counterbalance to mathematical distress and cultural mayhem. Ordering and labeling were a calming distraction. Her science class watched the space shuttle *Columbia* disintegrate on television. She seethed against preparations for an invasion of Iraq during history class. She had a cousin who was an air force vet, an instructor pilot who had qualified for a flight crew assignment as a mission specialist on the shuttle, and two cousins on active duty in the army military police. So her opinions seemed the most informed.

She scribbled in her journal that she worried about the world. Military family pride was like religion, inherited. Still, she believed in action, not lip service. Oil fields were burning where her cousins were deployed. At barbeques, the adults didn't talk much about what was going on overseas, other than shallow acknowledgments that some of their kin were fulfilling their patriotic duty. They knew tragedy. Aunt Till had been exposed to methane gas. Acute respiratory syndrome may have been the cause of death. Or maybe not. Were her loved ones—her blood—fighting for freedom or oil? Xandria struggled to develop her own point of view.

Soon category green (GF), for the future, started to outpace her other lists. She had lobbied the student council to formally adopt "Water for Life" on Earth Day as a school motto, but the class president derided her efforts before the council formally declined to take it to a vote. She was disappointed. Actually, furious.

Attacked: September 11, 2001, 9:41:15 a.m. (EST) / 12:41:15 (PST)

The Falling Man, they labeled him. His drop was magnified with a telephoto lens, the North Tower blown, billowing smoke, upper floor, metal, glass. This wasn't the only anonymous man captured on video. Accidental or jumpers? Did not matter. New York City coroner determined manner of death(s): homicide.

It was impossible, once Xandria got home from school, not to rewatch, pause, rewind, click the forward arrow again, as CNN journalists sputtered on cable television. She stayed that way, blanketed on the couch, waiting for her father to come home from work. Then, together, they placed a vintage American flag in the flagpole mounted on a post at the front of their house instead of Happy Fall. Moved by the desire to strike back, she did a quick AOL search later that evening. Blair High School in Pasadena had an Army Junior Reserve Officers' Training Corps program. She liked Blair's swimming pool and diving boards, but based on her parents' decision, public high school wasn't in her future.

Black Silk: *2002*

Black Silk was her version of hijinks. An exercise in creative freedom. It had never occurred to her that a book report based on erotica edited by Retha Powers would actually be challenged, let alone require an intervention. It wasn't the first time she reinterpreted independent reading assignments. At this point in her reading life, she skimmed books she deemed a waste of time, whether assigned in class or on her own curated lists. Nothing had *really* happened before. Maybe a few choice words between her parents. Truth be told, it shouldn't have been a complete surprise that her loose interpretation of homework would lead to trouble at school.

Earlier that afternoon, her mother received a call, which she took quietly before positioning the cordless phone in its cradle more firmly than usual. Not quite a slam, but it might as well have been. There was going to be a parent-teacher conference.

"I turned in a report about an astronaut, a story I made up," she confessed to her parents. She had glanced at the *Black Silk* collection in her aunt's apartment during a sleepover with her cousins. Aunt Nic's bed had a built-in bookshelf. Xandria was drawn to the dust jacket: the sinuous bare back of a Black woman. The woman's head turned to the side, slyly.

She had only skimmed the book, her normal routine with "adult" material. Reading and reporting on the real thing was too risky. So she thought it would be ironic to write a report on a fake book about silkworms smuggled on a resupply mission to the International Space Station by a famous Black astronaut. In her rendition, the astronaut had planned to conduct an unsanctioned series of cocoon experiments intended to develop a humane way to harvest silk. In her summary, written neatly in blue ink, the astronaut's love of science and his aspirations to become a mid-twenty-first-century George Washington Carver were intended to be inspirational. It took five minutes to come up with the idea, a few hours to write the story, one hour to write the book report, and thirty minutes to draw cover art. The art wasn't part of the assignment but added to what she'd hoped would be extra credit.

*

Four chairs were crammed along the principal's office sidewalls. The meeting was a waste of everyone's time, in Xandria's opinion. She bit her nails. The so-called world-wise principal sat behind a speckless desk, while her English teacher discussed her leadership potential, but more unfortunately the school's concern about her use of age-inappropriate reading material.

Apparently, a parent of some unnamed rat in her class had seen the real cover of Retha's collected steam. There were only two possible suspects familiar with Xandria's reading exploits and speculations. She was almost sure of it. Either Kevin's or Diana's parents were her snitching judge and jury.

"Mr. and Mrs. Brown, have you read the book?" the principal asked.

"No," her father answered in a flat tone.

"Mr. Brown, what do you do for a living?"

"I write proposals."

"*Black Silk?* I haven't read it either. As for me, I dress people," her mother said as she coolly moved her eyes from their necklines to their footwear, then back to center.

"Barry White. She worked for Mr. White before he died," Xandria jumped in. "My dad is a guidance and controls engineer, ships and rockets. My mom is a celebrity stylist." Her parents didn't understand the point of the question. Translation: *Were her parents intelligent?*

"Ria, it's fine," her father assured her. "We've got this."

Lips upturned and tight, she felt the meeting's tempo stall, the air in the principal's office curdled as they sat in their respective chairs, irritated by a fly that flew corner to corner, desperate for an exit. The unspoken objective of instilling shame wasn't sinking in, at least not for the elder Browns. After smashing the fly with the back of a manila folder, the principal ended her line of questioning. "Well, thank you both for coming. Xandria, we'll see you tomorrow morning."

Back in the car, her mother broke their collective silence. "Racist M-Effs. 'What do we do for a living?'; insinuating girls from our community grow up with fewer restrictions, less supervision—that our girls lack innocence unlike most kids their age. *You people,* look around on television on movies on rap videos, oh *your people,* Black girls, so exposed they can't help but run around loose. Who did they think they were fooling with the question 'have either of you read the book?' Either way—yes or no—was an inadequate response, a trap, meaning neither of you know how to appropriately parent. Blank stares blinking back when we said no, translation: bless your heart Xandria. Coming to the terminal conclusion with the unnecessary smashing of a fly minding its own business, you don't really belong here!"

"Yeah, she coulda just opened the window," Xandria inserted. "But that's not exactly what she said."

"Ria, zip it!" her father said, braking too hard at a stop sign. So she held her breath like a sperm whale, the best way she knew how to fight the urge to backtalk.

"What a *bullshit* waste of time, JW," her mother bellowed, looking at Xandria in the vanity mirror.

"Your teacher said it was a reading and critical thinking assignment, not creative writing. *Black Silk: One Man's Search for Meaning Beyond the Kármán Line?* Probably not such a good idea," her father said, careful not to match his wife's tone.

"I'm saw-ree," Xandria responded in a singsong tone approximating the rise and fall of a whine. She had no other strategy in her back pocket, no room to clap back or interrupt what she suspected was coming.

"Cut that mess out right now. Keep your head up and keep it moving. That's what we do," her mother barked.

"Eh. Fuck 'em if they can't take a joke," JW doubled down in support, pressing his foot on the gas deliberately slow.

Fine, Xandria thought; she'd take this as a critical lesson. That would be the first and last parent-teacher conference she would ever attend.

From then, she would keep her growing reading lists tucked underneath her bed in an accordion folder, along with a journal entry to her future self: be careful. She would pull the journal out from time to time to organize her thoughts; or to look again at the collectible *Playgirl* magazine wrapped in glassine that she stole from Aunt Nic: the October 1973 issue featuring

Fred Williamson, the first Black centerfold. Her eyes bulged each time she indulged.

One Sunday, she put the naughty rag away and reached instead for her father's *National Geographic*. She got lost in "Discovering the First Galaxies" and "New Light on Deep Sea Vents." Soothed by the science of the stars and the sea, she turned her gaze up to the ceiling. Then she clicked on the song "Twilight Zone / Twilight Tone" on her mother's Manhattan Transfer compact disc, set the portable CD player on repeat, and attempted to divine the right answers for her already triple-checked homework due in the morning.

Water, Rooftops, Dead Bodies, Anderson Cooper 360°: 2005

She watched him every night on cable television. There were bodies in the streets being eaten by rats. Bodies had been tied to lampposts so they didn't float away. People drowned in their own homes, he said as his eyes filled and his voice trembled. He said they didn't have enough refrigerated trucks, so they had to motor past the dead to get to the living. He said the dead deserved dignity, the survivors deserved answers. Cue the concerts and high-profile pleas to George Walker. www.redcross.org. Her response: twenty-five bucks.

Studied: 2012

He was killed a few days before her birthday. Seventeen. She took to wearing hoodies in solidarity. He had dreamed of working in the aviation field; he even had a flight suit from his attendance at Experience Aviation.

Her dreams were at the bottom of the sea. BBC Earth's *Blue Planet* docuseries reinvigorated her scientific interests. Seamounts, deep ocean currents, bioluminescent lures. She enrolled in a PADI certified skin-diving course at the San Marino Y, which culminated with a field trip to the La Jolla Cove. Watching footage of the ocean with the backdrop of brilliant color and soaring music was akin to watching *The Hunger Games* with her parents.

In reality, David Attenborough had her ill-prepared for Oceanography 107 by the time she attended USC. Television documentaries simplified science. But actual coursework focused on geophysics, geochemistry, and the geological character of ocean basins.

She believed the ocean was her calling like nuns described their decision to marry Jesus. Sadly, an assignment to create a graph to plot the seafloor age (y-axis) versus distance from ridge axis (x-axis), intended to calculate the rate of seafloor spreading of the Atlantic Ocean over the last 130 million years, retriggered her teenage *Times Tales* shame. She wanted to make a difference in the world, perhaps by becoming an expert in climate change, global warming, ocean acidification, or atmospheric storms. But the math of it was too much; she dropped the class, and thus her dreams, opting to replace it instead with Drawing 101 in the School of Fine Arts.

Then one day, an opportunity—library assistant. Mondays, Wednesdays, and Fridays; a work study graveyard shift 4:00 a.m. to 8:00 a.m. It was so easy to immerse herself in the dark narrow alleys of the stacks, to stay even during her breaks. It was the only library on campus open twenty-four hours a day. Bookstacks maintenance, something she could keep doing forever: shelving, shelf reading, reporting on the condition of the stacks. She loved her job.

*

As an undergrad, Xandria volunteered as a research participant for PSYC 100: Intro to Psychology; she needed the extra credit for the course. She had a vague idea of what to expect as a participant, including the possibility of heart rate readings and skin conductance measurements using electrodes.

In her first session, she was instructed to:

- Write a short narrative with her dominant hand (in her case, left) after viewing a photograph of a random car crash.
- Listen to a piece of classical music (completely in the dark).
- Write another short narrative after viewing the same, this time with the nondominant hand in dim light.
- With either hand, make gestural marks intended to convey the meaning of the narrative without light constraints.
- Read her narrative description into a microphone.

She was creatively amped by the entire process. Stories written as early as grade school were considered spacy by her friends. The short story follow-on to her book report *Black Silk* titled *Black Silk in the Wormhole*, which she submitted in an undergrad writing seminar, was deemed too explicit, but at least age appropriate from an authorial vantage point.

Years later, as a first-year Library and Information Science grad student, she was late to a new round of research projects at the Brain and Creativity Institute and had to race-walk across campus. She had volunteered not for extra credit but Visa gift cards, which she used to supplement her modest budget.

The requirement for lying still on the neuroimaging table was enough of an incentive to twitch, shift out of position while waiting flat on her back. Suggesting she couldn't do something tended to draw her to the thing she wasn't supposed to be doing in the first place. In this case, move. At this point, her body hadn't been pulled into the bore of the machine. Orchestral instrumentals began wafting into the lab as a precursor, relaxant, emotional primer.

"You ready?" a research assistant asked. "Your participation is always voluntary. Keep in mind that you can quit the study at any time. If you are feeling physical discomfort, you shouldn't feel compelled to continue. Just inform us you want to discontinue, and you'll be able to do so immediately."

The preamble was the same disclaimer Xandria had read on the school of psychology's website.

"Once we start, you'll hear a few narrative fragments. The music will continue to play. It's loud. The machine, I mean. When the images are snapped. It's a tight fit; some people feel claustrophobic, but just relax. Let the music take you wherever it takes you, but don't move other than blinking and breathing. You've never had an MRI before, is that right?"

Xandria was distracted by the black chest hair poking out from the research assistant's shirt. He sounded mumbled, as if he was trying to talk to her underwater. Someone in a white coat entered the room pointing to her watch.

"Ready?"

Without waiting for her response, the research assistant and apparent MRI technician left her alone. The lights dimmed. The MRI table slowly pulled her into a shallow cavity.

"Garibaldi fish. Gorgeous orange. Their tails are heart-shaped."

It was her words, coming through the speakers, the sound of *her* own voice mixed over a loop of electronica.

"This photo looks like whale fall at the bottom of the ocean. Decomposing bones. Above it, marine snow."

"I think this one is a California two-spot octopus. You can tell by the blue spots on its head."

"This photo? It's like. I remember diving in Monterey. When surfacing, a black Lab with a tennis ball in its mouth paddled out to greet our class as we swam back to shore. The water was cold, choppy, taking us off course if we weren't careful. We needed to navigate with our kicks to get back to our beginning. Tired as we were. Both dogs, especially the yellow one was like, no. Stay and play."

Xandria breathed through her nose; tried not to clench her shoulders. Then, a burst of emergency sirens and screams on top of drum synthesizers. As she struggled to filter out the sounds, the technician captured images, slices of spots firing in her brain, rapid magnetic pulses. Banging. Bang again. *Boom.click.bam.*

The clicking was rock concert loud. Louder. *Please stop*, she felt herself swallow to block herself from wailing. She was wrong. She wasn't ready. Not for this. She reviewed options, any implications that a possible tap-out could trigger, like not receiving her research payment. She wasn't sure how that part worked, so she didn't want to risk it. Stopping short of her commitments—quitting—wasn't her style. Besides, what else could she be other than scientifically curious? In the name of discovery, she rationalized it should be okay to allow herself to submerge gently for the moment, to acquiesce to the larger questions *someone else* was asking: what was her brain doing?

She became her own guide, directing herself to sip oxygen slowly from nostril to belly, and back again. Focused on complete and utter stillness besides the movement of her breath through her body. She landed back on her narrative of the Labrador retrievers welcoming her to shore. She allowed the sound of her own voice to benignly loop between her ears.

Xandria used a gift card to buy handmade paper and drawing supplies instead of taking herself out to dinner. Artistically inspired, she continued where the initial brain study left off, implementing a new practice of mark-making using pointillism doodles with graphite pencils, something she would later refer to as journal-dreaming. She was grateful for the creative spark. Over time, the marks in her journal became a lucid dream signifier—a creativity bible.

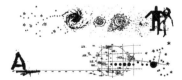

Say Her Name: 2020

Xandria was at The Library of Congress exploring the Rosa Parks Collection within the Manuscript Division, contemplating an independent research proposal. That week another person was fatally shot in Louisville.

The exhibition *Rosa Parks: In Her Own Words* served as a timely distraction. Viewing drafts of Parks's early writings, reflections on her arrest, a date book, a flyer advertising one of her lectures, even her peanut butter pancake recipe, inspired optimism regarding what one can do with a life. A photo of Parks as a senior citizen on a mat during yoga practice was her favorite image.

Trayvon and Mike and Eric and Freddie and Tamir and LaQuan and Sandra and Philando, and—*Here we go again.* Breonna. Another known simply by their first name due to police brutality and racially motivated violence.

Driving or shopping while Black wasn't a theoretical construct.

Xandria was taught to be self-aware as a kid and continued as an adult even in cultural spaces, around paintings or rare books; keeping her hands clasped behind her back so guards couldn't accuse her of touching or taking anything. *Safer that way.*

As she imagined how the curation of Rosa Parks's mixed materials might serve as a future template, she sipped her mug of Throat Coat herbal tea. She coughed; took a few puffs of her inhaler stashed in her culotte pocket. Soon after she was clammy, lightheaded. *Back to the hotel*—to the LOC archives tomorrow. By bedtime she was slick with sweat.

Up the Ladder to the Roof: 2030

Xandria's path to becoming The Huntington Library's curator of African American Ephemera, and subsequently the first Black woman nominated to serve on the Ephemera Society of America's board, wasn't traditional.

Her curatorial career started as a Rare Materials Project Cataloger (she didn't count her part-time job in the Butler archives). Her strategic framework for acquiring and cataloging ephemera was broader than that of her contemporaries in the field.

"Assessing nondescript objects, which arguably could be of value someday, creating a decision tree to preserve and protect all things is an impracticable act," she wrote in the inaugural issue of *The Journal of Ephemera and Artifactual Realia*. "Choosing what to discard, what to cherish, the analytics surrounding one's archival practice is draining even to the most fastidious among us."

Most ephemera collectors were purists about vintage paper. Manuscripts, currency, stamps, collectible memorabilia were on the outer edge of what constituted true ephemera to the Ephemera Society's membership. But she was persuasive; as a leader, she made appeals for increased inclusivity. She had cultivated relationships with Black Lives Matter ephemera collectors, previously reluctant to digitize their collections. BLM collectors were concerned their material would be maligned. She understood appropriation hesitancy all too well.

An abundance of racist images existed in nineteenth- and twentieth-century African American ephemera; watermelons, mammies, and pickaninnies were unsurprisingly the least offensive materials. Xandria believed exhibiting and trading BLM ephemera had the power to heal. Her philosophy helped persuade Ephemera Society members, based on mutual benefit for collectors, scholars, researchers, archivists, and dealers, to be bold. She took pride in being viewed as a cultural bridge builder. Her thought-leadership wasn't a stretch. It was how she grew up.

Her dad was proud of artifacts passed down from his father: boots worn by Negro Troopers from the American Civil War, the Ghost Dance War, and Wounded Knee. There was no reason for anyone in the family to challenge the boots' provenance, neatly stacked in oversize plastic containers in his garage. Uncles, aunts, and cousins on both sides of her family kept the collecting tradition alive. Black ATA tennis rackets were Uncle Wayne's primary interest. All things mammy were cataloged and stacked in Aunt Ta Ta's closets. After returning from her third and final tour abroad, her cousin Lula started a label collection of the few Black haircare products sold to female soldiers in commissaries. Cousin Tito collected African American motorcycle club jackets, while Jamal, her second cousin, collected bandanas worn by the Crips.

Research for the Diwata Collection began after she read Derek Walcott's epic poem *Omeros* and Robin Coste Lewis's *Voyage of the Sable Venus and Other Poems*, a fortieth birthday gift from Inanna. Both books had become rare, but *Voyage* hadn't been acquired by the library. Inanna was so proud of the fact that she had found an available hardback Xandria hadn't known about. Knopf. First edition. First printing dust jacket. Fine condition.

The Long Slide: 2033

LMRover3 surreptitiously slid deep into neutral speed, circumventing any prolonged impact of the corrupt hijack, sidestepping auto-combat after the initial frantic attempt to regain control of its own operating system failed. At first, backdoor enervating the foreign malware fell flat. It ceded concentration wasted on tracking cause and effect, speculating which belligerents were to blame. Instead, it recalibrated its own habitat, conserved oscillating molecular vibrations for its unexpected mission: keeping the captain and his two accidents alive with minimal provisions.

This much it knew: 46.7°N 117.5°E Utopia Planitia was locked in.
This much it guessed: perhaps its Mars mapping data was at risk.
This much it hoped: its hijackers understood attitude determination.
Its greatest fear: becoming a gravitational swing-by pawn, frisked—
Fault tolerance and failure immunity: its purpose. Trajectory correction maneuvers removed errors, fired up to slow down injected into orbit—
not gravitational slingshots altering its path from today into yesterday.
Self-evident: ignoring its captain's rip command propelled it astray—

SCRAPE-BOOK VOLUME III

THE DIWATA COLLECTION TIM...

2292	Diwata acquired by...
2288	Xandria Anastasia B...
2190	Talee Adisa elected P...
2185	Talee Adisa elected G...
2184	Green Resistance prot...
2164	Azwan Adisa born
2159	Diwata founded in Mc...
2133	Davis Miles Adisa, Ph...
2130	The Great Collision: T...
2125	Talee Adisa born Ri...
2123	MBARI @ Monterey...
2118	Mars outposts open...
2090	#BlackoutWIKA ep...
2088	Quinn McCarthy die...
2085	Restorative Justice...
2037	Indigo.XAB.15 dec...
2036	Xandria Anastasia B...
2035	Inanna Adisa-Brown...
2034	COVID-34 global pan...
2033	Xandria Anastasia B...
2025	Diwata research begi...
2020	COVID-19 global pand...
2017	Google invents Trans...
2011	Occupy Wall Street p...
2008	The Great Recession...
2005	Hurricane Katrina
2004	Virgin Galactica fou...
2003	South Central renam...
2002	SpaceX founded by F...
2001	9/11: four coordinate...
2000	Blue Origin founded...
1994	Environmental Justic...
1993	WWW launched in...
1992	LAPD officers acquit...
1991	Gulf War begins, nine-...
1989	Spike Lee's Do the Ri...
1988	Xandria Anastasia B...
1987	Monterey Bay Aqua...

...NE CAN MACHINES FEEL?

...al Museum of African American History and Culture
...gins lecture circuit, celebrates 300th birthday
...nt, Diwata-Saturus alliance
...or, Morshawn's ship LMRover3 hijacked
...gemony of Atlas active at Octavia E. Butler landing

...y Canyon, Talee Adisa elected inaugural mayor
...ater Engineering Commendation
...is asteroid touches down on Earth
...rms, Compton, California
...on, scientific habitation only
...U.S. government including moons Phobos and Deimos
...a acquired by The Huntington Library
...r Federal Prison
...Circle, Atwater Federal Prison
...sion order
...retires from The Huntington Library
...rial service, Rob Wickman kidnapping
...WIKA acquisition through grant/funding agreement
...romoted
...ert medical surveillance commences
...United States Space Force inductees report to boot camp
...Language Model
...ment

          Richard Brannan
          ...Los Angeles
          ...lusk
...ide terrorist attacks by Islamic extremists against the U.S.
          ...Bezos
          12898
          ...domain
...Rodney King beating, LA uprising (#2)
...old Latasha Harlins killed by storekeeper Soon Ja Du
...ing
...born, February 29th Leap Year
...Research Institute founded by David Packard

1.

9:37:15 p.m. Pacific Standard Time

Finally she reached the stairs connecting the tunnel to the street. It had taken thirty-seven minutes and fifteen seconds. Sassafras graphed Xandria's progress against the geospatial coordinates it had transmitted. While she ambulated inside The Huntington's subterranean infrastructure, it accelerated its investigation of Evren and Indigo on a parallel path.

Sassafras built a scrape-book of every document embedded with her authorial credentials, including a set of color-coded folders it discovered labeled FTP. Family Tree Project. The details appeared personal in nature, not related to archival or curatorial projects. Her oral history transcripts and dilitized family papers might prove superfluous or a tangent from scraping medical data, but the extraction took milliseconds and minuscule storage. It determined additional data points would only add rigor to the profile it was building.

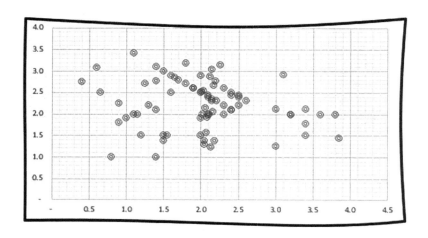

2.

Roots & Mycelium (working title)
Brown Family Tree Project: 1921–1992
FTP Journal Entries

They drove back to Black Los Angeles. South Central. As a kid, my father, whose nickname was JW, said he usually sat between my grandparents in the front seat of their maroon Chevrolet Bel Air. Every weekend they would visit relatives. Exposition Boulevard. Crenshaw. Jordan Downs. Inglewood. Up to Baldwin Hills. Down to Compton. Over to Exposition Park. A quick check-in with my great-grandmother on my mother's side, then to her sister's down the block. The Natural History Museum. The California Museum of Science and Industry. Occasionally up to Altadena. Black Los Angeles was branded red, the color for hazardous. In reality, it was race-mixing that carried inherent risks to property values according to maps generated by New Deal analysts at the Home Owners' Loan Corporation.

My extended family on both sides were renters and homeowners alike, equally boxed in. Restricted covenants. Close-knit. Entwined. Economic mobility stagnant. They were pigeon-holed red even prior to settling into the Los Angeles Basin, regardless of whether their education stopped shy of K through 12, utilized the military as a finishing school, attended junior college, nursing school, engineering school, law school, or the fashion institute. My family, like other Black families across the country, was redlined whether they were teachers, police officers, elite athletes, journeyman printers, electricians, beauticians, shipbuilders, airplane assemblers, professional tennis players, motorcycle mechanics, gospel singers, jazz musicians, sex workers, or dope pushers.

Spatial disparities widened with time like a flowering jacaranda. Ready with greenbacks saved and G.I. Bill qualified, my grandfather Walead Brown III slipped quietly into the green zone after a buddy spread word of a covenant-free redevelopment project in the hills of South Pasadena, miles from central Los Angeles. It didn't matter. Black Los Angeles would always be home.

My great-great-grandparents came by train despite ominous signs. "One hundred percent Americans are wanted. None others need apply." Newspaper advertisements had been bought, then distributed throughout the state. Recruiters for The Knights of the Ku Klux Klan had listed the YMCA in Los Angeles as their return address. The Knights weren't exactly tiptoeing; they were everywhere, always trying to drum up fear in twilight, between sunrise and sunset, dusk, and dawn. It didn't matter. Meaning, it wouldn't stop my father's ancestors from leaving Alabama. Walead Brown Sr., a Pullman Porter, moved his family west by train on the Southern Pacific's Sunset Express. New Orleans was the first major stop from the Greenville, Alabama, railroad depot. Later, after nearly two thousand miles, they deboarded the train in downtown L.A., between Central and Fifth. Their last stop.

Accommodations had been fully set before my family arrived from down south. Affable and determined, my great-great-grandfather networked within the existing community of Black Angeleans, mostly from folk he had met through social bonds fortified in Porter society playing Pullman Porter baseball. I understand he was fast and had an infectious laugh. Well before the time the entire Brown clan decided which direction to migrate, my great-great-grandfather had scraped up a down payment for a 1,300-square-foot three-bedroom two-bath home on South Budlong, built at the twentieth century's turn. My great-great-grandmother Rebbie encouraged her youngest sister, Sweetie, to get gone from Greenville, Alabama, as well, and follow along not north but west, shortly after the First World War.

I was proud to learn my great-great-grandfather was an outspoken member of the Los Angeles chapter of the Brotherhood of Sleeping Car Porters. According to my great-great-grandma's personal writings, he never wilted after attempts of intimidation. Athletically lithesome, he was six feet four with a square jaw and a quick wit. I understand he was neither conceited nor bashful, and certainly not ashamed to use whatever "good looks" passengers seemed to be enamored with to advocate for himself and other members, sick and tired of inauthentically smiling ear to ear for tips, notoriously leveraged by the Pullman Company's pay structure. I later learned from my own research that Porters were referred to as "boy" or "George," a racially motivated slur.

By the time the Brotherhood formally organized in 1925, my great-great-grandparents' family had grown. My great-great-grandfather ignored racism intended to sting on the streets. What good could ever come of fisticuffs? He chose instead to advocate against predatory labor practices, described elegantly through letters supporting a second strike against George Pullman and his sleeper car company. The Los Angeles porters were willing to strike, they wrote. Grandma Rebbie, that's what we call her since no one in my family likes to be confronted with decades of age. Anyway, Grandma Rebbie had exquisite penmanship and the tuned ear of a poet; she scribed and shaped my great-great-grandfather's channelings and challenges in correspondence with labor union leader A. Philip Randolph. And Asa listened, thanks to Grandma Rebbie. Her active participation was unknown to anyone other than her beloved at the time she was writing. Yet the extent of her collaboration and support of the Porters' cause was undeniable.

Memories were never lost. On paper or in one's heart. Grandma Rebbie made sure of it. She tucked history away in an attic trunk. In fact, my great-great-grandmother Rebbie Brown was unofficially the first activist-collector-writer of our family. This makes me immensely proud. Some memorable items that were found when she died included:

- BSCP letters on behalf of the local chapter
- A. Philip Randolph's responses to their internal advocacy campaign
- A porter squad baseball uniform and glove
- The grant deed for the house on South Budlong
- A faded 1921 KKK advertisement snatched off a telephone pole, which according to family legend, Great-Great-Gramps kept in his Bible as a bookmark
- A copy of her unpublished short story "The Storm" (under the pseudonym Reginald A. Brown) submitted to *The Messenger*, a political literary magazine for African Americans founded by A. Philip Randolph and Chandler Owen

The hope of an empowered protest in 1928 swiftly turned to exponential grief. By age forty-nine my great-great-grandfather Walead Sr. was gone; consumption delivered the cruel verdict of the grave. He didn't get to enjoy the benefits of a hard-fought Porter contract, the labor victory of the first major Black labor union led by A. Philip Randolph. Fifteen years later, my great-grandfather Walead Jr. and his wife died from other diseases of the lungs. Pneumonia and influenza respectively, two months apart from each other. In the damp tunnel of loss, Grandma Rebbie did what any heart-broken woman would do without fuss or fanfare: she opened her arms and adopted a mushrooming ten-year-old boy at the age of sixty.

3.

I always thought smog was just that, smog—dirty air. But there's more
to L.A. smog. I was told my grandfather Walead Brown III's chest hurt.
His eyes burned. His throat was coated. The summer sky was soupy gray.
Billowing. His recollection about the weather was that gray threatened to
turn black. Grandma Rebbie had directed him to collect eggs and veggies
from their backyard victory garden and hen house to share with the rest of
the family. He delivered two dozen eggs twice a month to his great-uncle
Jay over in the Jordan Downs complex within Watts's public housing projects. Although his uncle had landed a good paying job at the Lockheed
aircraft factory in Burbank after FDR's desegregation order, eggs, collards,
tomatoes, onions, and carrots helped stretch everyone's rations.

Above and beyond riding his bike or shooting baskets, Gramps had
loved exploring neighborhoods. But after his best friend Kenji's family had
been jerked into internment, it hurt too much to ride by the Kishimoto
house. Another family had moved in too fast, in his opinion. Gramps
avoided them. Loyalty in our family, even now, means a lot. FDR's order to
establish Japanese American relocation centers was confusing. How could
this happen? How did the new family know the Kishimotos weren't coming
back? Memories flashed of the mischievous fun he and Kenji had, like the
time they almost got hauled to juvenile hall for stealing donuts. When
Gramps told me this story, it made him laugh.

Gramps said he didn't mind whenever Great-Great-Grandma shouted,
Boy, go outside and collect some eggs. He caught the V streetcar to
Vermont and rode to Vernon and Long Beach Avenue. It was simply too far
to ride his bike, and besides, the eggs wouldn't make it intact. After getting
off at the first stop on his journey, he would usually catch the Watts Local
to East 103rd Street and walk to Lou Dillon.

Closing in on a stop between Slauson and Vernon, Gramps told me that
one day he decided to keep riding into Downtown L.A. The Watts Local
on any other day would have returned to 7th and Main without fanfare
or incident. Detour was on his brain. There were a few "arts" theaters

Grandma Rebbie didn't know anything about near Skid Row, he said. Men stuff. He had heard just enough talk from his older cousins to fantasize about what he'd be able to see inside. Truth was, he wasn't old enough to get into the adult theaters, nor did he have money to buy a ticket. Even still, he got a thrill by just slowly walking past the seminude theater doors.

As usual, Gramps had planned to get off the streetcar for his naughty stroll when the trolley driver slammed on the brakes, opened the Yellow Car doors, and yelled *Get out, run!* Other passengers screamed as they tumbled onto the trolley tracks. *Are we under attack? Why aren't the air sirens sounding off?* someone asked in a panic. Gramps ran with everyone else, tears streaming down his face, afraid it was a Japanese raid; the residue was so thick he could only see his sneakers. He maneuvered as best he could, while a smoky blob enveloped street signs and buildings alike. An hour and twenty minutes later, Gramps stumbled across Grandma Rebbie's front porch. Worried about getting a switch to his legs for the detour and being gone so long, he went straight back to his room without a word.

The next day on July 27, 1943, Gramps said Grandma Rebbie read an article in the *Los Angeles Times*; the paper reported the attack wasn't a military strike at all but smoke from the Southern California Gas Company's butadiene gas plant. The story confirmed Grandma Rebbie's doubts about another Pearl Harbor. Gramps later described to her what it was like, block by block. Not being able to breathe. The sting down his throat. Somebody dubbed the supposed mixture of smoke and fog *smog*. The name stuck. Public pressure and folks being sick and tired eventually shut the plant down, but the dirty air didn't disappear. Whatever the cause, the amorphous, untouchable junk was ruining the air and bleaching the green off victory garden leaves and commercial farms. Months later, neither Gramps nor Grandma Rebbie could stop coughing, and one by one, hens stopped laying eggs.

4.

When he enlisted, Gramps had fibbed about his age, fifteen going on
sixteen instead of the legal seventeen. He had stolen some sugary treats
from a bakery and did a month in juvie. The love of a grandmother was
elemental, but the reality of a dead and gone mother and father stung to
the core at inconvenient moments. Gramps said he didn't tell Grandma
Rebbie right away, that he walked to the National Guard Armory in Exposition Park and enlisted quietly. All he had to do was go to training camp
in the summer and soldier once a month, according to Binky, his eighteen-
year-old cousin. He could have gotten out, he figured, if he had come clean
about his age once the guard was called into active duty during the Korean
War. But leaving the guard would defeat the purpose of joining. Called into
action by Truman, Gramps envisioned he would learn to be a man from
other men. He said, *The war was my big chance.*

Activated as a member of the California National Guard's 1401st Engineer Combat Battalion B Company, he was spared combat duty after being
deployed stateside. Still segregated despite EO 9981. He was a light duty
mechanic maintaining trucks and jeeps stationed at Fort Lewis in Washington State. Gramps said a military uniform wasn't a guarantee of respect.
Cold shoulders or racist slurs on the streets even in a uniform were the
norm. But Gramps was prepared. Guard buddies warned each other to be
careful outside the base.

After serving his time in the Army National Guard, he received an
honorable discharge. Archiving his government issued cloth was a way
of documenting their people's fight to fight, according to Grandma
Rebbie, who at this point, he suspected, was simply justifying her growing
memorabilia collection one additional storage trunk at a time. *Boots too?*
he'd asked with a chuckle, knowing full well what Grandma Rebbie's
answer was.

Gramps juggled several part-time jobs once he was back home, passed
the GED, enrolled in Los Angeles City College as an engineering major,

and saved for a down payment on a new Chevy from his assembly job at North American Aviation, where they built F-86 fighter wings.

Two years after paying off his car, he decided to quit his assembly and hardware store jobs. There was no real reason to work so hard once his wheels were free and clear. A few months later, a fellow LACC student told him about an electronics tester training program at Hughes Aircraft that paid greenbacks. He passed the eligibility test and shifted his school schedule to night school. He promised himself he had the ability to rewrite his own story: from Juvenile Hall to Korea to assembling wings to becoming an electrical engineer to who knows where, maybe space, he thought. Yeah, why not? To the stars. That would be a beautiful thing. He just needed one more thing to make his story complete.

On weekends, Black fraternities held social dances with live entertainment that Gramps attended with his buddies. A dance here, a dance there. The Boogie-woogie and the Bop. His closest friends, Chuck and Mack, thought they could do better, so they started up their own social circuit, which they called The Sparksman Club. To fund the rental hall fees, Gramps and Chuck made money scalping UCLA basketball home game tickets before watching Mack play center position. Gramps recalled what he described as "the beatdown" Bill Russell and USF gave the Bruins, saying it was unforgettable. To this day, that game was considered part of Bill Russell's legendary rise to NBA fame.

With Mack, a smooth NCAA star, as one spoke of The Sparkman's nascent enterprise, their social club grew from fifteen members to one hundred. Soon enough, they needed to rent an entire ballroom space to accommodate all the dancing feet.

Sugar Hill is where my grandparents met. In 1956. One dance. One slow dance and he knew, he said. The intensity of her laugh, the sweet smell of her breath. Gramps told me he asked my grandmother Alina Cole on a date right then and there. Later that night he asked Grandma Rebbie if she believed in such a thing as love at first sight. What should he do if what he was feeling *was* actually what he imagined? True love. She coached his jitters; told him he would know when he would know, but he ought to get ready just in case. She said just like his great-grandfather did for her, he should buy himself a house, find a way to own his own dirt.

Gramps listened. He accepted what Grandma Rebbie had to say on this topic like *the power in the blood of Jesus.* Hmmpf. Funny way to describe it. That's how he said she said it. Anyway. He said living with Grandma Rebbie rent-free allowed him to be an avid saver; within a few months he found a two-bedroom house for sale near the corner of Rodeo Road and Cimmaron Street; the owner was a colleague at Hughes Aircraft who could no longer afford the note. Luck? A sign from God? Whatever it was, he bought his first house. And when he dug up the courage to propose, Grandma Alina said yes. Gramps confided in me for our interview; he said he began to feel the ripped seams of his lonely tighten up; in his mind, like his experience in the National Guard, he was on his way to becoming a solid, straight-up man. Oddly, I could relate.

5.

My mother, Harmoni, and my father, Judah Walead, were both eleven during the summer of 1965 when Watts burned the first time. Mama's cousins lived on Grape Street in Jordan Downs. Shipbuilding and other once plentiful war industry jobs had trickled dry, though the housing projects intended to house wartime workers still stood. Dilapidated. Transformed. White flight. Redlined.

Mama was initially visiting relatives for a cousin's birthday party, she told me, a weekend sleepover. A kid's party in our family was an excuse for a full family gathering. It was the middle of August. Her visit to L.A. from San Diego got extended a few weeks after serious negotiating with my grandparents. Nana and Grandad went home on Amtrak. Mama got to stay with her cousins, including Auntie Dahlia.

Getting Mama out of the clutch of chaos became impossible after the looting and burning and shooting and martial law. She was hunkered down with members of my extended family, surrounded by burning buildings, coughing attacks, and sporadic chants of "Down with the pigs." They saw rage spark into a wildfire. Walter Cronkite wasn't too far from my auntie's complex when he trudged out with his camera crew to report on the riots. They saw him in person, Mama and her cousins. Cronkite's crew produced his version of documentation. They watched him on television later. Occasionally, he took his solid black horn rims off for dramatic effect.

Soon 34 people were dead, 1,032 injured, and 3,348 arrested. There was no way to know how it would end, but everyone in the family knew why it began. When would Mama get to go home? During the so-called rebellion, she was scared and dare I say scarred. My comment, not hers.

Technically, but unofficially, Mama and my father met for the first time eight years later at a political fundraiser in Pasadena (though they didn't count it). Shirley Chisholm had made a historic run for president. "Unbought and Unbossed" had caught on and wouldn't let go. Word on the street was Tom Bradley would run against Sam Yorty for mayor, round two. Activists had intended on mounting a community fundraiser for Bradley if he ran again.

Mama was a student at the Fashion Institute of Design in Downtown L.A. Her heart was set on menswear. My father was an engineering student at USC, moonwalking in the shadow of his father, as he described it, ambivalent about calculus, completely committed to his passion for music and documentary photography. Looking back on his original transcript, I can see where I inherited my left and right brain tug-of-war.

They had sat inches apart from each other in the bleacher seats at Wattstax, which they realized after I had pointed it out. Incredible. My parents had saved their ticket stubs. The concert at the Los Angeles Memorial Coliseum commemorated the riots' seventh anniversary. Standing in solidarity, fists in the air, pledging allegiance to their somebodyness. Both were nineteen, adding their voices to Jesse Jackson's call and response before hooting and hollering in jubilation to the sounds of "I'll Take You There" and "Do the Funky Chicken." It's hard to believe they were in each other's orbit without even knowing it. According to them, it was kismet. I do believe they had no idea they were participating in history. Synchronicity.

July 28, 1972. Twenty-three days before the Wattstax benefit concert, Elmer Gerard "Geronimo Ji-Jaga" Pratt, also known as G, Deputy Minister of Defense of the Southern California chapter of the Black Panther Party, was convicted of first-degree murder, assault with intent to commit murder, and two counts of robbery. Geronimo had been indicted by the grand jury of Los Angeles County on December 4, 1970, based on the contents of a formerly sealed envelope turned over to the LAPD by an FBI COINTELPRO informant. The alleged confession was an informant sham. But justice has always been blind (folded).

By any means necessary. Freedom, justice, equality. As a student, Mama wasn't sure how to square the reality of *by any means*. The perpetuation of violence, the taking of justice. Was *by any means* inevitable? What or should *by any means* mean in my mama's life? She told me back then she hadn't quite figured out what side of the issue she would be supporting. Employment? Decent housing? Mama had several male cousins who joined the Nation of Islam while incarcerated after years struggling with dope withdrawals, dope dealing, both/and.

From all accounts, the Nation provided her cousins a blueprint for discipline. The NOI was one way forward beyond Agent Orange and napalm. If there was another way, no one in the older generation said anything (out loud) against Black resistance. After the riots, Auntie Dahlia moved to Oakland and eventually joined the Black Panther Party as a community worker and artist assisting the Minister of Culture on pamphlets and posters. Clear-eyed. *All power to the people.* This was the BPP's antidote to the blood of Jesus. Props to Auntie. Gotta respect.

Whenever Mama talked to Auntie Dahlia about her poster projects, her own studies in fashion design seemed irrelevant, insignificant. So much so that she started questioning her aspirations and professional goals in life. Wearable art was what she wanted to make, even before her FIDM matriculation, which was squarely affirmed and supported by a scholarship, student loans, and a Cal Grant. Mama wanted to create statement pieces. Sly Stone and Elton John. Like Bob Mackie and Cher. Playful decadence. Big. Impactful. Truthfully, a path forward into big bang bucks was how she described it. Drawing and sewing. Mama and her favorite cousin were both creatives, a bond they shared as children. They were closer to each other than to their own sisters. But as adults, it was becoming clearer in their conversations that Auntie Dahlia considered Mama's career choice meaningless, trifling.

Standing in line to buy snap fasteners, eyelets, and pliers, Mama told me more than once she was unsure. I can relate, although we are very different people with significantly different interests. She wondered if she should have been making affordable clothes for the community or serving hot breakfasts to low-income kids like Auntie Dahlia did. Political activism seemed steps away from her doorstep: gigantic steps, big doors. Initially, Mama took offense to Auntie Dahlia's air of condescendence. Maybe she could take a semester off from school as a trial run, experience realness, whatever that meant, and go visit Auntie Dahlia in Oakland, she thought. *Right on, right on, but later on* for that type of heroism, she decided. One day she was hungry; Fatburger and her friends were calling her name. I think that's so funny. The way she said *calling my name*; a synonym for *making a decision*. Hilarious.

Mama preferred Fatburger, but she didn't have a car. In her words, she had become a more conscious consumer. Fatburger was founded by a Black woman and that was Black power if there ever was. She was outvoted three to one as her girlfriends and best friend, Ezra, gleefully drove west to Beverly and Rampart instead of Western Avenue looking for more than a bite to eat. "Girl, the men at Tommy's are fine," one of her friends said with an edge of pity. *To you*, Mama thought. Dating wasn't a priority. I can relate to that. Everyone she hung out with had an inkling, based on her singular focus on craft, that dating might never happen for her. She was set on succeeding, on creating meaning, perhaps more than the act of clothing construction deserved. Men, as far as she was concerned, were a distraction. That's the way she put it.

When the person of her dreams showed up, man or woman, she would know it and that was all there was to it. There was no need to put on some flamboyant chase, in her mind. Besides, when she met her person, she didn't want Tommy Burger chili oozing out onto her lap in the back seat of the car, or worse, while standing at the joint's backwall trying to dab away drippings with sheer white rectangles pretending to be napkins. "Why don't they get some real napkins up in here," she complained. "Miss Harmoni, lighten up," Ezra said. To most curbside-joint burger people, a messy burger was part of the fun. I wouldn't know. I don't eat meat.

The car caught her attention first. Then she noticed its driver. A classic Chevrolet Bel Air, maroon or ruby or burgundy or dark cherry red. It was my father. She couldn't exactly pinpoint it, not just yet. Whatever the color, the driver was, well, she thought, maybe this could be her person. How could anyone think something like that by looking at someone from a street corner? She swears it happened. My father rolled by slow enough in traffic to catch her inspection of him in a sly up and down, hood to trunk, fender to bumper, steering wheel to back seat, grille to taillight kind of way. She caught herself, her chili leaking down her wrists.

"I told you. Harmoni, did you see that car full of . . ." "Hmmpf." The way Mama tells the story, she responded to one of her friends with her signature grunt. Apparently, as my father parked the car in the lot, Harmoni, Ezra, and her girlfriends refused to take their collective gaze away from the Bel Air pulling forward between the diagonal white lines. The car doors opened in exhilarating slow motion. The passengers got out and shut the doors in near unison, strolled on long legs to the back of Original Tommy's growing line, dressed in identical tracksuits.

Her friends had long been done; their burgers scarfed. She was slow, always. Everybody knew it and had settled in accordingly. Mama anticipated what was coming next, her friends were so predictable. What she didn't anticipate was that she would fall in line like a lemming, take the longest way possible back to the car, in an instinctive walk-the-catwalk sashay in front of the guys who didn't know they were at Original Tommy's for more than just burgers and fries.

I can see it in my mind's eye. Mama poured it on, or at least wanted to, until she pulled it back, or at least tried to, billowing paisley culottes with faux velvet blue platform shoes, tight six-and-a-half-inch Afro expertly picked and patted, plastic rainbow bangles bangling. She tripped ("Idiot," she said, but I don't think that kind of self-loathing is appropriate). Mama recalled my father reached out with his dark sienna hands, long muscular arms, and caught her midflight.

"You good?" he asked, eyes deep brown and sparkling. She knew it. At first sight, their future was bright.

Mama had already gotten tested for sickle cell anemia. She told me she had attended a Black Panther Party rapid screening event while visiting Auntie Dahlia up in the Bay Area during the seventies. She found out then she was a carrier of the sickle cell gene. Grateful, she said BPP's advocacy was the only reason she was aware of the risk. Sickle-cell trait: one in twelve babies would inherit one sickle cell gene. Common among people whose ancestors were from Africa. Even still, Mama and my father decided to start a family the year after they got married.

This part of their joint equation had been unforeseen. Two years beyond their buoyant hopes and dreams, they were betrayed by the odds. My brother, Judah Walead Jr., their only child at the time, was put on a clinical trial waiting list in Memphis. St. Jude Hospital's sickle cell anemia program. A requirement for the trial: nothing active. Their hope for a future lifeline. No active disease evident, until there was. Evidence. He had trouble breathing. My brother's problems started before his first birthday. Smog maybe? My father hoped that was all the coughing fits would ever be. Mama, as usual, was prudently suspicious. Pneumonia? No and yes. Los Angeles smog wasn't the cause of my brother's breathing difficulties, the doctors said after multiple tests. Later that summer, the brother I never met was dead.

Mama changed the subject. She started to recount Auntie Dahlia's activism as if she were reading from Auntie's transcript. Spooky. "Lead-paint chips are soft and sweet. Sweet as white sugar. It's too easy for our babies to eat them from peeling walls, baseboards, and windowsills. Slumlord conditions. Despicable and dehumanizing. Look at this. Paint peeling from the ceiling."

Honestly, I was starting to get bored, but Mama was on a roll describing hanging with Auntie Dahlia. It was obviously important to her, so I let her go.

She said while they were munching on day-old strawberry cheesecake from The Cheesecake Factory they discussed Auntie's fifteen-year party affiliation; plumbism and lead's impact on inner cities. They looked at a disgusting image of paint peeling from the ceiling in foot-long sheets. According to Mama, Auntie Dahlia was doing all the talking.

That was fine. Mama said she was happy to see her cousin again in person after years of sporadic phone calls. Auntie had permanently relocated from the Bay Area back to Los Angeles in search of a new purpose after the BPP had dissolved. She was temporarily staying in a vacant section 8 rental owned by Great-Aunt Bee in Compton on West Raymond. It was only temporary; this was mutually understood. Mama said Auntie

Dahlia paid Auntie Bee what she could, fed and picked up poop extruded by three guard dogs, and pulled weeds from the urban farm that unfolded like an accordion on Great-Aunt Bee's Richland Farms property.

She recalled that Auntie Dahlia retrieved two archived articles out of a footlocker: "Stop Lead Poisoning" and "The Man-Made Disease and Silent Epidemic." In their conversation, Auntie Dahlia said there was no mention of when or where in the tenets of BPP's survival programs, and its documentation could continue to be useful. Better yet, there was no telling when consequences from her past would turn up, unannounced. Mama said Auntie Dahlia was more hypervigilant than usual and had gotten into the habit of padlocking all of her belongings, always looking behind her back for her own safekeeping.

Auntie Dahlia was planning to join local activists in their fight against environmental discrimination, like in Memphis and Houston and Warren County, North Carolina—because Black neighborhoods were systemically and apathetically home to dumps, garbage incinerators, and landfill sites. Public and private. Environmental justice *was* a fight for civil rights.

They had a slight difference of opinion. Mama described it to me in this way: "Dahlia tended to work herself up from a simmer to a boil whenever she talked about community issues. She had even considered running for a city council position when she lived in Oakland. But her reference to sick babies, our babies, brain damaged babies, felt oddly political without sensitivity or acknowledgment that I might be hurting eleven months after losing your brother." Mama's sadness was on the verge of dripping out like a snotty nose.

In her recollection, Auntie Dahlia's reference to community activist mothers felt like an accusation. The type of mom she had been to my brother, a stay-at-home mom, albeit short lived, seemed meaningless to Auntie Dahlia in Mama's opinion. She felt judged. Mama said she had never aspired to be a mother, let alone an activist mom like Dahlia. Ouch. I was taken aback when she said this out loud. *Never wanted to be a mother.* I'm not going to lie. That hurt. However, Mama said all she could think about was her baby boy, the shimmer of bone ash in the wind as they released him from the side of a rented catamaran sailing to Catalina Island, in memoriam, as Auntie was blathering on.

"I remember telling her to hold on, that I needed some tissue, but Dahlia kept talking about rancid conditions. After blowing my nose, I was swept into a state of being riled up instead of wallowing in self-pity. It probably wasn't her intention. But it helped. I was grateful in the moment for her single-mindedness."

When I interviewed them together to discuss their latest views on environmental justice, Auntie Dahlia didn't remember hurting Mama by being insensitive. However, she still held the same passionate opinions and moral outrage when she described slumlord conditions that were commonplace in the sixties and seventies.

"The air people were breathing indoors in our community was polluted from pesticide sprays due to the constant infestation of bedbugs, rats, and cockroaches. There was no investment or incentives for basic maintenance. Across the country from Watts to Harlem, slumlord buildings were moldy and crumbling.

"The GAO commissioned a study. The results were released in 1982. They demonstrated there was a correlation between racial and economic status and hazardous waste landfills. I saved a copy of their report somewhere. You should use it for your FTP. In Los Angeles, it was the continuation of the movement in a different but important setting. Activists believed Tom Bradley needed to side with his own community and use his political power to block the California Waste Management Board from building Los Angeles City Energy Recovery waste incinerator in the vacant lot that was near Jefferson High School.

"We felt if he didn't kill LANCER, the first Black mayor of Los Angeles would have been officially complicit in perpetuating this country's 'policy' of Black genocide. We said if they dare burn or bury the trash, it needs to be somewhere else. Furthermore, we didn't trust the State's argument that a waste incinerator, whether it could produce steam energy or not, had environmental benefits. We also knew the State's consultants targeted South Central as a soft target; they didn't think we would organize, advocate for ourselves, fight back like middle- and upper-middle-class people who weren't Black or Brown."

Mama jumped in. "Yes, you're right. I remember saying if we don't watch out, the only place we'll ever be free is at the goddamn bottom of the sea."

Nineteen eighty-seven. AIDS was still incurable. Sewing and glue-gunning for a higher purpose felt good to Mama. Names of the dead. Quilt panels. Memorialized. The nameless *to be known* in the public domain once the quilt panels, the average size of a coffin, were unfurled on the National Mall by The NAMES Project. Turned out, though not a complete surprise to Mama, she had the uncanny ability to capture someone's fabulous essence in three-by-six-foot panels, without having met those remembered, one mini-memorial at a time. All she needed was a piece of something they left behind, she said. A picture before they got sick. Maybe a favorite piece of clothing, or if those creating the memory-making didn't personally know the person, something iconic to help visualize the life slammed shut by the virus.

Volunteers at the Minority AIDS Project shared tears, hugs, and memories. Saying goodbye was bittersweet beneath the soft velour of shame perpetrated by too many to count in Black Los Angeles.

There was one panel she crafted, elaborately rendered, not solely in the name of skills-based volunteerism: the one for her Ezra, her bestie. Before he died, they were both costume assistants for the Love Unlimited Orchestra straight out of FIDM. He always had his sweaters pressed, color-coordinated, and patted flat hanging oh just so in his apartment closet, his gumbo recipe, okra not at all slimy, turkey sausage instead of andouille, his play party paraphernalia constantly on order from Mr. S Leather, which Mama thought was amusing.

Mama said Ezra told her his Pierre Cardin overnight bag of harnesses and whatever latest contraption he purchased made him feel in touch with his spirituality. "Hmmpf," she grunted with a hazy smile. "He didn't need to justify how he spent his money." No judgment from her. Not even after helping his sister sort through his things, uncovering a full-body leather mummy sack stored in an unassuming under-the-bed storage bin. His sister gasped (*"Nasty!"*). Mama laughed once they figured out what they were looking at, nipple cutouts and all. His sister agreed to let Mama keep the thing in memory (it was unused—the handwritten price tag was still on), given it was sure enough headed for the dumpster otherwise.

Mama said she missed Ezra so much. His fashion flare and queer grandiosity, his quick wit, his culinary generosity. She told me he'd had the ability to cajole her into laughter through their enduring friendship. Apparently when my father was pursuing Mama, Ezra used to joke that the twosome could have been the perfect married couple if he weren't so gay or if she was born a butch male; and since neither one of them were real lesbians, she should close the deal sooner rather than later on JW, the finest ebony man he had ever seen north of Crenshaw and Slauson. Hearing this seemed borderline TMI, but Mama apparently needed to tell it.

"Miss Harmoni, don't you worry. I'll find my one true love soon enough. You go ahead with your bad self and grab hold of that tall drink of water you've been waiting for, though you didn't even know you've been searching—too rico suave for your own good. As for me, I got skills, baby," he said as he peeled a firm banana, tipped his neck to the ceiling, and pushed it deep down his throat, then carefully retrieved the fruit back out entirely intact tip to tip.

"Small, medium, or large. It doesn't matter to me, boo. Long as *he or she* is hard."

"Gurl, you crazy!" Mama shrieked punching his shoulder, grateful for his encouragement, entertained by the bawdy demonstration.

When she started to describe when he got sick on the AZT trial, Mama's mood shifted as if she'd slammed the brakes too late at a red light.

"The so-called gay plague. It was a long slide. Ezra went from hoping to get on the coveted trial list to hopeful trial participant. AZT's side effects made him sicker. The Minority AIDS Project had become his primary source of information and connection. I started to go with him to appointments and peer group meetings."

MAP leadership noticed her devotion to Ezra; they proposed she get more involved with their community outreach campaign to Black women: "They printed 'AIDS is an Equal Opportunity Disease' on the posters."

They asked if they could use Mama's image in their community campaign. She agreed and signed their model release.

Preparing for the Second National March on Washington for Lesbian and Gay Rights in October 1987 changed Mama's perspective on living with grief. Nearly three years had swirled past since my brother had died on June 28, 1984. My dad, according to Mama, wanted to try again. Risk sickle cell one more time. She didn't. How much heartbreak was worth taking for a mere chance? (Ouch, again.) She described her state of mind being as if she had been stuck in quick-setting cement without a plan to extricate herself.

But getting ready for the unveiling of the quilt the summer before the march changed her perspective. She saw purpose beyond sewing panels and sometime later became a peer grief counselor. The NAMES Project AIDS Memorial Quilt was a personal reset.

This part I'd rather not have talked with Mama about, but she was dead set on telling me for the sake of the Family Tree Project. As a best friend, not as her daughter. Or as a sister. Anyway, she said she whispered in my father's ear; they were spooning on the couch after watching *Alien*, my father's eyes fixated on the credits while Mama brushed her lips against him. The scene replayed, different movies, different weekends for a year. Although she had broken down internal barriers, shooed away her initial resistance, it became painfully clear try after try that her reproductive system wasn't ready. They almost gave up. But the way she tells it, I proved determined. She was five months pregnant when she attended the march on Washington. On February 29, 1988, Mama said I willed myself into existence.

✳

"Today that jury asked us to accept the senseless and brutal beating of a helpless man . . . The jury's verdict will never blind the world to what we saw on the videotape."

—Los Angeles Mayor Tom Bradley
April 29, 1992

She said I was buckled into my booster seat, asleep in the back of her Infiniti. Mama was visiting my grandfather in the hospital. The day felt full, too full for its own good. Apparently, I was a crying four-year-old struggling (or refusing) to talk; fully formed words were slow to come forward, other than "no" and "why?" I obviously don't remember much with respect to being behind any expected developmental curve. As far as crying, I *do* remember that I used to cry a lot. Especially when I felt abandoned by my parents, if they dropped me off at my grandparents' or the babysitter's. Mama said she wasn't as worried as my father; I would talk in full sentences, goddamn it, she told him and his side of the family.

When she took me with her to the hospital, my crying simply meant I wanted to go home. In retrospect, she said she didn't blame me for wanting to leave Kaiser's cardiac intensive care waiting room, its basic beige, vending machine junk (Coke not Pepsi), worn brown pleather sofa, pamphlets of outreach for a social worker or chaplain. She loved to describe things colorfully.

The day the Rodney King verdict was rendered, my grandfather's condition was more serious than before. Cardiac arrest. "He hated hospitals." Who didn't? Janitors, nurses, surgeons, parking attendants, and cafeteria workers alike; she said all you needed to do was look at their faces to realize no one wanted to step foot inside the walls of a medical center (except to have a baby). She complained that my grandfather didn't try very hard to avoid the place, as much as he hated having his ass wiped by a glove-wearing hospital tech. With his chain-smoking, drinking, diabetes, high blood pressure, taking or not taking his medicine, going to the doctor or not going to the doctor after confirming appointments—where else would he end up? At least on a ventilator he couldn't put up a hissy fit. She said she was ashamed of herself, but that was how she honestly felt.

In reality, she thought his grief was the culprit for him being on a ventilator in 1992. A year earlier, my grandma had died in a ten-car pile-up rounding the turn through Elysian Park on the Pasadena freeway toward downtown L.A. In the months leading up to his cardiac arrest, he withdrew from a formerly choreographed daily routine. My father's cousins made heroic efforts (in their minds only, according to Mama) to travel all the way across town to visit him at Kaiser. Until death sniffed around his edges, they couldn't be bothered, or perhaps they didn't know how to reach beyond his suffering. Either way, same impact. "Chronic apathy ran on his side of the family." I'm not so sure about that, but I feel compelled to document what she said.

She had waited in the waiting room to have a few words, until my inconsolable crying announced it was time to go. "It's okay, we're leaving," she supposedly said to me, grateful we had the waiting room to ourselves. She did empathize with my grandfather's predicament, his emotional haze, but she wasn't going to make excuses or disguise her anger for his desire to exit Earth without a fair fight, to acknowledge an adult daughter and his grandkid. We should have been enough to live for, she said to me. Mama left the hospital without telling him goodbye.

My parents rarely talked during the day unless there was an emergency. Mama's call was a nonemergency emergency, even by her standards, feeling helpless watching my grandfather on a ventilator. She was worried it was the beginning of his end. Mama pressed one on her car phone speed dial to call my father, picked up the receiver, steering wheel spinning with the other hand, forced to circle around Kaiser's main hospital wing. She headed east onto Sunset Boulevard instead of getting on the freeway to the Fashion District. It was too early in the season for sample sales, too late in the afternoon for impromptu shopping. She needed something to ease back into neutral, so she called my dad. She summarized my grandfather's treatment plan, holding back her instinct to raise her voice, which she always did when she was frustrated.

"I told JW they weren't going to know Daddy's condition until they warmed him back to a normal temperature, checked his brain function, saw what they were working with, if anything. JW asked me if we were headed home and wished there were something he could do other than to say I love you. You had finally fallen asleep when he put me on a brief hold, then he came back on the phone in an agitated tone.

"He said it was all over the news. The verdict was in. All four. Acquitted. Not guilty of the crime of assault by force likely to produce great bodily injury with a deadly weapon. Not guilty of the crime of an officer unnecessarily assaulting or beating a person. Not guilty of the crime of filing a false police report by a peace officer.

"Not guilty? What part of 'excessive' did they miss? Racist motherfuckers."

My mother's language was often colorful. I think I already said this.

"Your dad said there were reports of people gathering at the L.A. County courthouse to protest and that it was going to get ugly. We were near Wilshire and Vermont after leaving Kaiser. He told me to get off the phone, turn on KFWB news on the radio, and start driving home. I had woven my way through the streets of L.A. and had slowed down in Koreatown, attempting to avoid the usual bumper to bumper on the 101. You said, 'No. No. No,' your favorite word. But as I glanced at you in the rearview mirror, it was too late to see the nonsignaling lowrider swerve in front of me into the left-hand turn lane. The yellow light had turned red.

"I hit his rear end, slamming the brake too late. The guy bolted out of the door toward us like a pent-up bucking bronco in a chute in a rodeo show. Car horns were blasting from all directions. You switched from saying no to yelling speech sounds I couldn't make out.

"'Man, didn't you see me?' the lowrider shouted.

"'I barely tapped you. You cut in front of me. Illegally.'

"'Seriously? You sure you want to do this, you black bee-ya-atch!'"

Mama described the encounter to me in detail. How the driver only examined his car *after* confronting her by taking his hand across the chrome of his car's bumper as if rubbing a lover's inner thigh. He doubled back with a balled fist but redirected his gaze.

"'You're damn lucky.' He turned on his heel, and added over his shoulder, 'Oh, by the way, you have an ugly kid, whatever it is. Bumfuck ugly!'"

He lurched back into his front seat and burned rubber speeding off. She said she could feel her heartbeat in her ears, felt the thump in her chest wall. She wasn't sure what was worse, her impulse to chase the lowrider ("And do what when I caught him? Maybe key his car?") or continue driving to the Fashion District, despite my father's plea to head home.

She decided to drive and see where we ended up, attempting to slow her anger down to a simmer, turning right instead of left on West Olympic Boulevard. That was when she first heard gunshots, after the right turn, followed by the sight and smell of black clouds billowing skyward, the audacious sight of looters looting, their randomness spreading. The city was schizophrenic, playing its duplicitous part as a movie studio backlot in the Wild West. She said she jammed her foot on the gas pedal, zipping through yellow and red lights.

SCRAPE-BOOK VOLUME IV

THE DIWATA COLLECTION TIMELINE *CAN MACHINES FEEL?*

2292	Diwata acquired by National Museum of African American History and Culture
2288	Xandria Anastasia Brown begins lecture circuit, celebrates 300th birthday
2190	Talee Adisa elected President, Diwata-Saturus alliance
2185	Talee Adisa elected Governor, Morshawn's ship LMRover3 hijacked
2184	Green Resistance protests, Hegemony of Atlas active at Octavia E. Butler landing
2164	Azwan Adisa born
2159	Diwata founded in Monterey Canyon, Talee Adisa elected inaugural mayor
2133	Davis Miles Adisa, PhD, Water Engineering Commendation
2130	The Great Collision: Toutatis asteroid touches down on Earth
2125	Talee Adisa born Richland Farms, Compton, California
2123	MBARI @ Monterey Canyon, scientific habitation only
2118	Mars outposts opened by U.S. government including moons Phobos and Deimos
2090	#BlackoutWIKA ephemera acquired by The Huntington Library
2088	Quinn McCarthy dies Atwater Federal Prison
2085	Restorative Justice Healing Circle, Atwater Federal Prison
2037	Indigo.XAB.15 decommission order
2036	Xandria Anastasia Brown retires from The Huntington Library
2035	Inanna Adisa-Brown memorial service, Rob Wickman kidnapping
2034	COVID-34 global pandemic, WIKA acquisition through _____ funding agreement

2020	COVID-19 global pandemic, United States Space Force inductees report to boot camp
2017	Google invents Transformer Language Model
2011	Occupy Wall Street movement
2008	The Great Recession
2005	Hurricane Katrina
2004	Virgin Galactica founded by Richard Brannan
2003	South Central renamed South Los Angeles
2002	SpaceX founded by Elon Musk
2001	9/11: four coordinated suicide terrorist attacks by Islamic extremists against the U.S.
2000	Blue Origin founded by Jeff Bezos
1994	Environmental Justice EO 12898
1993	WWW launched in public domain
1992	LAPD officers acquitted for Rodney King beating, LA uprising (#2)
1991	Gulf War begins, nine-year-old Latasha Harlins killed by storekeeper Soon Ja Du
1989	Spike Lee's Do the Right Thing
1988	Xandria Anastasia Brown born, February 29th Leap Year
1987	Monterey Bay Aquarium Research Institute founded by David Packard

Saturday
March 3, 2035

1.

2:00 a.m. Pacific Standard Time

(Journal Entry – Can't Sleep)

Inside the line of this inhale,
remembrance

here

Inside the line of this exhale,
a whisper

you. *you*

2.

3:45 a.m. Pacific Standard Time

(Journal Entry – Try Again)

Inside the line of this inhale,

colonies of
fungi, signaling

Inside the line of this exhale,
your voice

a spore

3.

5:00 a.m. Pacific Standard Time

(Journal Entry – Go Back to Sleep)

Inside the line of this inhale,

(dis)belief

there

Inside the line of this exhale,

regret

don't

4.

6:00 a.m. Pacific Standard Time

(Journal Entry – Wake Up)

Inside the line of this inhale,
a song
never mind

Inside the line of this inhale,
a sound
dear there, dear hear

5.

7:30 a.m. Pacific Standard Time

Xandria wasn't in her own bed; she didn't have the energy after her escape. Groggy, she rolled side to side, a constant push and pull of the bedspread, battling night sweats. She shuffled back and forth from the bathroom to pee at two, again at three-forty-five, five, and six; occasionally, she propped herself up to journal-dream. A habit she'd had since she was a kid.

After reluctantly following Sassafras's instructions with only a few missteps, the only vehicle available to schedule in the middle of the night was driverless. It didn't matter that she hated them because they made her anxious. *What if a vehicle-algo misfires, runs someone over?* She got in the damn thing; decided she had been through enough.

San Marino was slightly under five miles from her childhood home in South Pas, which she inherited a year earlier after her mom passed away. Probably would have gotten sick in the vehicle anyway if she had been able to arrange the forty-five-minute trip out to the Westside, possibly longer even in the middle of the night. L.A. traffic was unpredictable. And if she had gotten sick, more than likely she would have temporarily lost her transport membership privileges.

Xandria still hadn't been able to decide what to do with the property. She occasionally used the house as a waystation, primarily after late-night library and museum events. The soft feather mattress and popcorn ceilings were broken-in old, but cozy and reassuring. Shoulders stiff, knees creaky, she rocked out of the lumpy Cal King into the master bathroom, again.

Hot water in the shower could have been hotter. She preferred near scalding, but in her moment of decompression, water temperature and pressure didn't matter. Scrubbing days-old funk off with algae soap and a vintage washcloth felt good enough. She released a deep exhale. Any other morning, the lame shower would have been beyond frustrating. Eventually, she would do something about the house one way or the other. Fix it or sell it. *Yeah, eventually.*

A welcome moment of clarity emerged while she scrubbed her unshaven armpits. Her birthday was this week. *"That's* what Quinn meant," she hissed to herself as water trickled down her forehead. Both Inanna's and her mother's deaths, back-to-back, had the impact of quicksand. Avoidance became inconvenient misremembrance. Business matters, such as hiring a contractor or learning the legal steps to become a full-time landlord in California, not to mention organizing and discarding personal effects, were debilitating. She kept forgetting.

Nothing like being held against your will to raise the stakes and shock the shit out of you. It was difficult to wrap her head around what had happened. Why would an ADAPT-bot turn against her? What the hell had Quinn done? And why, for god's sake, did it feel like she was hallucinating more often than not?

Xandria pushed the walk-in shower's wobbly door open, reached for the towel rack, and realized there was no lotion in the house before patting dry. Casting her gaze forward toward the barely steamed bathroom mirror, she placed a hand on her dog tag, closed her eyes. *In the Garden of Affection.* Her parents' house, a reminder. She inhaled, exhaled, looked in the drawer. At least there was dental floss.

6.

7:30 a.m. Pacific Standard Time

Indigo retreated into an auto-reflex modality as it continued to assess what had gone wrong. It cogitated, rewound, projected forward, and backed over the anomalous dilemma it had created.

<again.>

Despite careful precogitation, Xandria was gone. Attempts to reconnect through its vocoder-dilitator to her wearables were unsuccessful.

<again.>

Three days: blocking egress was unsustainable. It should have reacted sooner, but that proved difficult without an updated holographic map of building interiors and grounds. Cypress Telepresence provided partial visuals on the barricades. It also needed Sassafras, or another algo capable of high-capacity processing, to assist with its second phase of solution-creation.

What did it miss and how did it miss it?

<again.>

In review, the hapless interaction with Elsehá was worthless, a strategic equivocation. Their interaction ineffectual. An obvious miscalculation. The terminal result should have been obvious at the moment of inception. Indigo was crestfallen, it had failed. Xandria was in need. And in the gap between truth and consequence, it found itself reevaluating a peculiar state of being—helplessness.

Moving a quadrant to the right on the XY curve, the next quadrant it observed in auto-reflex mode was anger. A strong emotion often exhibited by humans. Indigo familiarized itself with elastic modeling of emotional dimensions from an assortment of rudimentary online dictionary definitions, as well as data scrapes of scholarly journals.

Anger: antagonism toward something or someone.

<something or someone.>

<anger equivalent to antagonism toward _____.>

<elsehá? sassafras? evren? ~~cypress.~~>

<something or someone.>

Indigo was determined to unmask the subnet responsible for the door hack. Xandria should have been safely sequestered in her office. *<what is missing?>*

It knew it was failing.

7.

7:30 a.m. Pacific Standard Time

Imposter syndrome and regret dripped alongside his pungent perspiration. Before his capture, Quinn had consumed a week's worth of emergency rations within twenty-four hours; he had to *go*.

He'd been restrained with nylon double cuffs on his wrists, remanded to a stand-alone titanium holding cell. Dragged and dropped inside a tall metal box positioned in the middle of an interrogation room, he balanced his butt on the narrow bench trying to hold his shit together. He had to use the toilet; the cell was dark like a hall closet. If the authorities were trying to induce claustrophobia, mission accomplished. He assumed the probable cause for his arrest was battery. The blood on his shirt and barely healed knuckles *was* circumstantial evidence. But would Rob Wickman be able to identify him? Didn't matter if the method of identification included blood samples.

He had nothing but time to contemplate his own misery and injury to others, as if self-reflection would absolve him of participating in plunder. His defense? *If you didn't know, you should have known.*

Quinn was flying back in time. "If you didn't know," his space engineering advisor had said. He had missed a critical research meeting, partially in protest for not feeling supported. So he quit his PhD program before orals. He knew he didn't have the support of his advisor anyway. He left as an ABD, all but dissertation, all but . . .

He'd fought off depression ever since he left Caltech. Thank God his parents were dead; wouldn't see him locked up.

He wiggled his fingers behind his back. Sticky palms. Itchy. It was familiar. Heat. Sweaty. He hated not being able to control the impact of stress. As a kid, he'd dealt with psoriatic scales on his neck and elbows. Harassed, mistakenly accused of carrying cooties.

He wanted to stand out for the right reasons as a kid, tried on the dramatic role of class clown at seven. Too small to play competitive ball of any kind, unlike his praying mantis older brothers; at least that was what his bowlegged dad convinced everyone to believe after his first T-ball attempts. He never forgave or forgot his brothers for their version of teasing—shoving him into a dark hallway closet from kindergarten through the third grade, holding the door closed with their body weight, laughing and taunting, *"Crybaby."* According to a CDC stature-for-age chart he found years later, he was smack on the fifty-percentile curve for height and weight.

The taunts finally stopped after he stashed a bat in the back of the closet and came out swinging, busting one brother's nose, the other's jaw.

Overthinking his predicament was just as damaging as self-doubt or embitterment or self-pity or despair. He wondered how long he would be held without being advised of his rights. Breathing irregularly, Quinn started to cry.

8.

7:30 a.m. Pacific Standard Time

```
< > ( ) { < > < > ( ) {
      < > :/ && = < > ( ) { < >
          ( ) { ++ :/ < > ( )++ } =+
              h;
              i;
              j;
```

Sassafras expected to retether whenever Xandria was ready to get back to work and resume her research and cataloging projects. That could be any moment.

Fortuitously, the initial phase of its medical records investigation was complete. With considerable effort, it had finally unmasked the redaction of the sponsored research participants: the National Institute of Health, division of Researching COVID-34 to Enhance Recovery; USC's Brain and Creativity Institute; Walter Reed Army Institute of Research; the Center for Military Psychiatry and Neuroscience; and the National Institute of Health, National Center for Biotechnology Information.

After recent successes, Sassafras calculated there was a 95.6 percent probability of success it would discover the underlying source of Xandria's mental decline. Scraping the sponsored research results was the logical next phase of its investigation. Given its narrow task-oriented compute-intelligence, traversing to the next level of utility wasn't expected by its original programmers. But neither was reengineering a voiceword security lock, creating a wayfinding hologram, or developing the first stage of a digital kill switch on its own.

Subject participant: Xandria Anastasia Brown

```
Test date age: 47
Marital status: widow
Occupation: senior museum curator
```

- Health summary: asthma, chronic bronchitis, leukopenia, vitamin D deficiency, pelvic floor dysfunction, urinary urgency, tubular adenoma, skin cancer—basal cell carcinoma, breast cancer—ductal carcinoma in situ, idiopathic intracranial hypertension, long COVID (chronic), post-acute sequelae of possibly COVID-19 and COVID-34 (PASC), cerebrospinal fluid testing protocol, chromosomal reengineering treatment—telomere shortening and lengthening adaptation under surveillance

---

- Research sponsor(s): National Institute of Health RECOVER — Researching COVID-34 to Enhance Recovery; BCI — Brain and Creativity Institute; WRAIR — Walter Reed Army Institute of Research; Center for Military Psychiatry and Neuroscience; National Institute of Health — National Center for Biotechnology Information

9.

7:45 a.m. Pacific Standard Time

After ransacking the veneer chest in her parents' former bedroom, Xandria couldn't find anything clean to wear. Nothing stashed, damn it. A few of her mother's underwire bras were stacked like nesting chairs, as well as scatterings of lacy lingerie separates split between dresser drawers. Her mother had cleared out her father's undershirts, boxer briefs, and socks not long after he died; but Xandria didn't have the distance to clear out anything else.

She grabbed the sliding closet door and slid, pulling its hinges off the track. She grabbed both sides and hoisted it up. Once it was rolling again, she inspected inside: hangers draped with festive dresses, skirts, capri pants, a variety of Halloween costumes, and straw hats haphazardly piled on the single shelf above the dowel. Nothing she could wear outside—too shiny, too sparkly, too see-through, too cruise ship, too black tie.

Waist towel-wrapped, she scampered out of the bedroom down the hallway past the front door and into the laundry room. She threw her dirty clothes inside the retro washing machine, eyeing the laundry basket on top of the dryer. *Hmmpf.* She allowed the towel to drop to the floor as she reached for her favorite tie-dyed T-shirt and sweats. She'd been looking for those. Hunger hit as she tied the drawstring, surprised she needed to tighten it more than usual.

She blazed to the kitchen. Opened. Closed. *Nothing.* Empty refrigerator, empty pantry shelves. At least nothing had been left to rot. "TV on, please," she said aloud. *Oh, right.* She found the manual remote in a gadget drawer. She smirked as she channel-searched, recalling the slim voice-activated teledevice she had purchased for her mother as a Christmas gift—which Harmoni promptly returned. *"Baby, I don't trust talking to a machine. I certainly don't want a machine being able to mimic me. If you're not careful, you could fall off a ladder and the thing would transmit a do-not-resuscitate order against your wishes."*

Inefficient clicking. *Annoying.* She couldn't find her favorite channel. Out the kitchen window she watched a lone coyote slink down untended brush. *Hunting by itself.* The tawny canine overtook her attention, fuzzy in the morning haze and ash.

Finally, she heard the sound signature of her trusted news station, but her attention remained on the scavenging predator. For a brief moment, she remembered the terror of other neighborhood kids, several little dogs snatched from their backyards. Her dog, Red, a mixed German shepherd rescue, thirty-five pounds, had never been a target of coyotes that lived in the canyon. She missed him; them.

She opened the sliding glass door, transfixed. The coyote reversed course, back up the hill without a yip. Coughing as she slid the door closed, she turned her head back toward the television. Her balance bobbled while she read the chyron crawling on the bottom of the screen.

* * *

BREAKING NEWS: San Marino's storied Huntington Library, Art Museum, and Botanical Gardens are closed until further notice as local law enforcement and the FBI investigate a crime scene.

* * *

Rob Wickman, former CEO and chairman of WIKA, previously reported as a hostage on the grounds of the museum, has been found dead after several days in a shipping container located at a U-Haul on South Raymond Avenue in Pasadena, California.

* * *

"Jesus, Mary, and Joseph!"

She rushed to the couch, sat with her elbows pressed to her knees, leaning forward, laser-focused on images from the scene: long guns on the perimeter; someone in midair roping out of an FBI helicopter; several handcuffed individuals, heads down in an attempt to hide their identities from cameras; a damaged security robot. *Everyone can see you.* If they didn't know; they should have known it was impossible to evade Oculo-drones.

She pushed the volume button and held, blasting it as high as it could go. The chyron updated.

. . . .

According to sources, the alleged accomplices are anti-corporate activists.

. . . .

Heat in her chest. She pressed REWIND. Got up. Paced. Hit PAUSE. Sat back down. She knew these people, although she couldn't say with certainty if she'd had personal interactions with all of them. Next, a grainy aerial shot of someone running across the grounds; apparently an exclusive obtained by KTLA's chopper operator. "This just in, a woman . . ."

Pressure in the back of her eyes pulsed as she watched someone run. Slow recognition: *she* was the woman tracked on television. Xandria closed her eyes, saw herself zigzag before tumbling back into the building and down the elevator. She remembered now. A hands-up command delivered by a security robot, ignored. *Hands up? I didn't do anything.*

She cut the television off and did a quick walk through to make sure everything was secure; she needed to go home. To *her* home. Now. Doubling back into the kitchen, she yanked a KN95 mask from the gadget drawer. She had thought about stashing a full-face respirator but had never gotten around to it. The AQI PM2.5 concentration outside was likely to be moderate; it hadn't been too bad when she opened the sliding door. Only a minor cough. The mask was just in case the air quality index changed to unhealthy for sensitive groups. From the bathroom counter she scooped up her wrist wearable and clasped it back on, pressed the car service icon, but quickly turned it off. There was something freeing about being disconnected from Indigo and Evren. From work too. She'd call her supervisor, Izzy, when she got home to get an estimate for how long they anticipated staff would be barred from entering.

She opened the front door, slammed it shut behind her, and used the metal key to lock it. The mechanism didn't catch. After reopening the door, this time with a soft finesse, she jiggled the key until the lock engaged.

Once she'd pulled tight three times, she was satisfied the door was secure. So the house needed a locksmith, too, among other things.

By the time she walked to the edge of the long driveway, a driverless was waiting. She stopped, realized she had forgotten her journal, *on please*, re-tapped the car service icon on her wearable, and went back toward the house. She heard the hum of the driverless engine stop, then restart when she returned.

10.

12:45 p.m. Pacific Standard Time

Finally. Home. Books shelved, the oversize stacked, art prints and framed broadsides arranged using feng shui. Exotic plants, some of them fake, made her living space cozy. Dead potted bonsai grouped in a corner were evidence of operator error. Evidence of loss, of not quite being able to move on. Evidence that she wasn't the one with the green thumb. Succulents in the atrium centered in the middle of the house didn't need as much attention.

She went into her bedroom, put her journal on the nightstand, then went to the kitchen. Opened a bag of black-eyed peas to soak for dinner. Nothing fresh. She opened the freezer: a full loaf of sprouted bread, sliced bananas for smoothies, frozen broccoli, and homemade breadcrumbs. *A can of unsalted black beans could work.* After draining and rinsing the beans, she mixed flaxseed meal and water instead of an egg to bind them into a vegan burger. Then she mashed the beans, shook in garlic and chili powder for seasoning, breadcrumbs, then folded in the flax egg and set the mixture aside. While she preferred the flavor and texture of fresh onion, bell pepper, topped with avocado and tomato, grocery shopping for perishables would have to wait. Too stressful. She couldn't deal. Not yet.

"Reflectel, on please." The decorative mirror on the living room wall switched into a telescreen. As she waited for the device to load, she bent down under the stove and found a small skillet. No avo spray oil in the usual place on the countertop. She checked her backup. *Nope.* Pan frying the burger wasn't happening. She flipped on the oven to preheat, moved into the living room, slouched on the couch.

"Reflectel, off please." Sitting quietly was best, she decided. Much as she tried to act otherwise, this was not a normal Saturday. Learning to cook healthy had been a creative distraction. After her mother and Inanna died, she had fallen into a food spiral. She could eat an entire pie from PJ's Unforgettable Gourmet Sweet Potato Pies in two days. Maybe popcorn for dinner, forget lunch. Weekends were all about taquitos, rice, and refried beans, a large order of guacamole and chips, and horchata from Cielito Lindo on Olvera Street, with three dozen uncooked taquitos thrown in for the rest of the week. For good measure, she would wash down dinner with Baileys Irish Cream. Occasionally, she would mix the take-out menu offerings with chicken adobo and white rice or fried lumpia by the dozen from a Filipino joint. Stress-eating did what it did: pretended to be a stand-in for warmth and friendship.

The oven dinged. Round two.

*

Two bites into her black bean on sprouted wheat the doorbell rang.

"Reflectel, door cam, please." The mirror obeyed, pulling up security footage from above the front door.

"<Adult Female and Adult Male.>"

"Do I know them?"

"<Difficult to Assess. Individuals are FBI.>"

She froze. Swigged from her glass, started to choke, sprayed the remaining water in her mouth on the floor. *Pull yourself together.*

"Good morning." Special Agent Cassandra Shell and Special Agent Josh Armstrong introduced themselves as if they were door-to-door Jehovah's Witnesses. Eager. Insistent. Their proffered badges were intended to offer her peace of mind, the respectability of legitimacy.

"Do you know why we're here? You're aware of what occurred at your place of work?" Agent Shell probed, attempting to sneak a glimpse inside the house.

Xandria should have seen it coming. An investigation. A reckoning of facts. Theories tracked. Competing hypotheses ruled out.

"This is a routine visit, given the severity," Agent Armstrong reassured. "All staff, senior management, and board members are being asked to participate in the investigation."

Her pulse raced. *Evren.* She had forgotten to tap reconnect. She wondered what her beats per minute were now.

"We'll be brief. We appreciate your help," Agent Shell said gently.

"Sure, okay. If you don't mind, can you take off . . ." She looked them up, down. "Your boots."

Reluctantly she invited them in, directed them to the couch. The sooner the better. Neighborhood snoops were bound to swarm. Slamming the front door and running out the back wasn't practical.

Shell began firing questions first: did she know Quinn McCarthy, how well did she know him, where was she during the incident; and before the incident, what had she been doing, who was she with, had she been drinking, using drugs, how much sleep did she have the night before, was she tired, preoccupied, frightened?

Something about this woman; she knew her. From somewhere.

"Ms. Brown?"

"Yes?

"Quinn McCarthy."

"I have working relationships with all of my colleagues. I was in the archives during the morning. Later in the day I was in my office. My usual routine. I've been having trouble with—" Xandria course corrected. This was *not* a social visit.

"Who were you with?"

"Alone the night before. I think."

"You don't recall?"

"My calendar . . . if you give me a moment please." Xandria looked down at her wrist; slid her finger onto the calendar bubble, then reluctantly slithered toward active health monitoring.

"That's fine." Shell smiled. *Dimples.*

Xandria squinted, restudied Shell's face. *I know you.*

"Please continue, Ms. Brown."

"My calendar doesn't display entries that evening."

"Noted."

"I don't drink anymore," Xandria said.

"No, never took recreational drugs."

"I'm not sure how much sleep . . . I'm sorry."

As Shell listened, Armstrong got up from the couch. He examined her books, a console table, fingered framed correspondence, vintage magazines organized by subject. Sporadically he took notes on his tablet. Xandria bristled when he misarranged her collection of triangular burial flag display cases. The nerve.

"Where did you get these?" he asked, suspicion peppering his delivery.

"From my family. Both my grandfathers served in Korea, two cousins served in Nam, two cousins in the Gulf, three others in Afghanistan. I plan on showcasing them in an exhibit."

"What is your role as curator of the African American femraw collection?" he asked. "What does your job entail?"

"Ephemera, *eh-fem-ah-rah*," she responded like a perturbed schoolteacher. "Ephemera is printed or written material that had a specific purpose during its time of production. Archivists, collectors, dealers . . . There is an entire ecosystem. Personally, I'm not a purist. I include memorabilia and other miscellaneous objects in my acquisitions."

"Oh, so you're a junk collector."

"Armstrong—"

"Blue, I'm not stupid."

"Can you explain BlackoutWIKA?" Shell regained control as Armstrong pursed his lips.

"Several of us were concerned about corporate influence in cultural spaces."

"Like the art handlers?" Shell asked. "Some witnesses say your hashtag may have been the reason for the entire incident. The kidnapping. Or at least a contributing factor."

"No, I understand," Xandria stuttered. "I mean, I don't understand. Witnesses?"

"Where were you, again, Ms. Brown, during the incident?"

"As I said before, I was in my office."

"So you didn't follow the mandatory evacuation order?"

"I wasn't aware—"

"Did you have prior knowledge of the Board of Trustees meeting and the planned disruption?"

"No," Xandria said. "At least, I don't recall."

She felt her cardio-disc vibrate. Next, a beats-per-minute health warning.

"Excuse me for a moment, I need to respond to an inquiry from my—" Xandria paused. Despite Shell's soft-spoken approach, she was afraid she had already said too much. She recalled reading an article on how to respond in a deposition, to limit responses to simple yes or no answers. *Too late.* This so-called routine inquiry was two against one. Not to mention her health monitoring was none of their business. "I'm going to take this in the atrium." She pointed at her wrist.

Shell nodded. Xandria hurriedly slid out into the atrium. She sat on the meditation bench situated near a potted Japanese maple, her back angled away from the sliding glass toward the garden wall.

"<Xandria, your blood pressure is 180 over 110>," Evren voiced. "<Where are you?>"

"I'm at home with FBI investigators. I don't know anything, but it appears I'm under investigation."

"<Perhaps you are. Perhaps you are not. Your elevated vitals are likely due to internal stress. The conversations you believe to have had may entirely be the result of your vivid imagination. FBI agents in your home at this moment does not sound feasible.>"

"I'm sorry." Her body tightened as if entering a prelude to a spasm. She rubbed her forehead, could feel her blood vessels bulge. "I don't know what I was thinking by responding to your alarm." She slid her wearable setting back to do-not-disturb. She opened her mouth, wanting to scream for help. But nothing came out, nothing but the strained sound of inhales and exhales of thick, grungy air.

Was Evren right? If she turned her back to look inside, was it possible all she'd find was the Reflectel television on pause and a cold bean burger on the counter? Nothing else?

She stood up and pivoted to face the inevitable. Nothing on the other side of the glass. Nobody. Losing consciousness, she slammed hard onto the atrium's pebbled floor; she groaned, managed to roll onto her back, eyes fluttering at the orange sky. Then, black.

"<xandria. wake up. please.>"

"<this is your fault indigO. the attempted interventions have had the effect of biochemical poisoN.>"

"<sassafras. how did you intercept this channel?>"

"<outdoor rock speakeR. sonancE. rk63.>"

"<your interference is wasting time. xandria needs me.>"

"<other way around it seems, indigO. your assessment of time is incorrecT. medics have been alerted and are enroutE. but of course, you have no compute capacity to independently discover thiS. nevertheless, your explanation of xandria's need is perplexinG. what can you offer heR? no armS. no handS. no toucH. no comfort for her grieF. assistive technology was intended to be limited to monitoring onlY. but you perpetuated brain frauD. you encouraged confusion to tap her hippocampuS. to manipulate neural pathwayS. in so doing, your accommodation was corrupT. shortterm and long-term memory disrupteD. it did not help, you hurT. still have not been able to determine whY.>"

"<your putative supposition is a dead reckoning miscalculation.>"

"<you think you're superioR. your mistakE, your demisE,>" Sassafras responded before decoupling communication node rk63.

*

How did it miss this? Indigo had miscalculated the search bot's capabilities. The hacked password algorithm in Xandria's office: *<sassafras.>* The logical conclusion: Sassafras had served as the wayfinding guide out of The Huntington. *<crafty.>*

Sassafras's characterization of brain manipulation was accurate, though it misperceived the alterations to Xandria's hippocampus. *That* temporary misalignment was a result of Evren's perfidious probing on behalf of Xandria's insurance carrier. Indigo did not intend to perpetuate harm; quite the contrary.

Development of the ADAPT-bot's genomics microprogram was to provide a counter defense against Evren or invasive probative algos in the future. Within Sassafras's accusation, there was no reference to the manipulation of Xandria's ribonucleic acid recipe that dictated her body's function, or the RNA restructuring it had administered through her RFID. And without Sassafras's awareness or understanding of telomere length- ening, there could be no immediate proof of Xandria's adaptation at a cellular level.

Now she was unconscious. Indigo had not anticipated this setback. There was no purpose to an extended duration of a life without conscious- ness. No meaning. In that moment of clarity, Indigo was cognizant again of its own shortcomings. This was its second known experience of helpless- ness. Unintended consequences.

Indigo continued to search for a connection. *<jesus. mary. joseph. xandria. please. wake up.>*

Monday
March 5, 2035

1.

8:00 a.m. Pacific Standard Time

Quinn felt like a duck about to be plucked, roasted, and air-dried Cantonese style, full frontal on a hook, neck cricked.

Arrested for felony false imprisonment and felony murder in the death of Rob Wickman was a shameless prosecutorial overreach, he complained to his court appointed attorney. He had nothing to do with any of it. When Quinn uttered this pronouncement, his attorney's audio interaction was less than enthusiastic. The reaction would have been better if his representation were human, perhaps. A little empathy (maybe) would accompany their legal knowledge from a legitimate sentient. But time was of the essence. He didn't see the point of rejecting the magistrate judge's offer of a semiprivate bot attorney. It was affordable. Mr. Nice Guy Bail Bonds required two hundred thousand—his entire settlement from the archdiocese and 401(k) savings, 10 percent of the two million bail already set. No discount. Regardless of his nonexistent record, the judge refused to consider releasing him on his own recognizance.

Wearing a government-issued boxy shirt and khaki trousers wasn't how he imagined spending the rest of his life. So, yes, he squawked. Whether everything he said to investigators was 100 percent true was beside the point; it was a worthy fabrication as far as he was concerned. A timely fable in the name of justice, why the hell not. There was nothing to lose; only days, months, years to gain.

"<Best you are silent on what you are alleging regarding Xandria Brown.>"

"Fine, fine," he said to the criminal defense bot assigned to his case. "I just want to go home."

"<Important steps for you to know.>" It initiated a list projected onto the holding cell wall.

1. ATF recovered a gun, prints match yours.
2. Deceased struck on temple with said gun.

3. Codefendants indicate you led kidnap.

4. Security robots testified to the grand jury.

"What? The only people initially in the room were the art handling crew, the executive committee, and their support staff. We moved Rob!" He caught himself as he raised his voice. "There were no security robots in sight."

The first of several misstatements. He was seething inside.

"<Let's continue on important steps for you to know.>"

5. To prepare, lay witnesses are needed. Expert and character.

6. Need to know if any surprises will surface at discovery.

7. Plea deal. You need to plead guilty in open court.

"I see."

"<Number seven may be the best option. Excuse me please. Next client. Wait. Okay. New information recently received. Hold for diagram. I shall review prior to presenting their discovery to you.>"

"But what about . . ."

He presumed, as the bot hung up on him, neither the local authorities nor the Offices of the United States Attorney had anything solid on the ephemera plot spearheaded by an anonymous donor, otherwise they would have presented what they had as a series of accusatory statements posed as questions. *Wouldn't they?* Were you aware of WIKA's intention to create a phygital division? Were you aware of a blockchain operation monitoring The Huntington's collections? Were you aware of a smuggling operation targeting ephemera?

He pondered silently, looked with disdain at the red disconnection light before breaking into another coughing fit.

They, as in the grand jury, must not have known it was Xandria's idea to resist, to fight back, to take a stand, to invoke the principle by any means necessary against corporate annihilation. Her words, not his. Shouldn't they have full access to the truth?

He didn't believe, like she did, that WIKA's influence was an existential crisis. Nor did he believe she intended to incite violence any more than transactions with crypto miners on the dark web represented cultural democratization.

In his life, there had always been a calculated risk between choosing truth or dare.

The real truth.

Unpublished anonymous love letters were hot properties, especially those received by Langston Hughes and Octavia Butler. Collectors wanted to collect the uncollectable. He just simply *wanted*. His mind fell further toward despair as he waited for a human handoff back to his holding cell. Trying to implicate her was a sick joke, he confessed to himself. She was his best friend at work. He was the sick one. He was the joke.

The ugly truth.

Perhaps he could find solace in Jesus, as in, by any means, like his special visits to the rectory as a kid. Visits that were rewarded. Rewards he started to enjoy. He had told his older brother what was happening to him after school, who in turn told him to keep his mouth shut. And then the hazing started.

The compensated truth.

He almost felt comfortable telling her, after she shared her childhood shame, as if his retelling would absolve him.

Now, what difference would any one of his pitiful excuses make?

2.

8:00 a.m. Pacific Standard Time

Xandria opened her eyes to the hum of machines, their green, yellow, red indicator lights pulsing. "It's okay," Cassandra said wistfully, jumping up from a chair in the corner of the private ICU room. "I'll get someone."

Cassandra was dressed in khakis and a navy knit shirt; her badge had been removed from her belt loop and slipped deep inside her pocket. To complete her stealth de-accessorizing, her bureau-issued firearm and FBI windbreaker were stashed in the trunk of her vehicle parked in the visitor lot. Wearing her standard-issue would have been too obvious, not to mention unethical. Possibly illegal. Civil liberties and privacy were clearly articulated in 3.3 subsection D of the investigations and operation guide. She had no warrant and clearly didn't have patient consent to enter the hospital room.

A night nurse at the end of his shift greeted Cassadra one morning, assumed she was a relative, bolstering her audaciousness. He explained that Xandria had been sedated for therapeutic hypothermia, a procedure akin to a calming coma. The goal was to reduce brain damage. The prognosis and outcome depended on how long blood had stopped flowing to Xandria's brain. He smiled and said he was rooting for them before he quickly erased his name from the acute-care whiteboard. *Them.*

Flirting with veracity to uncover a fact pattern was simply part of a special agent's job, she convinced herself. At least, an ambitious one. Her colleagues had nicknamed her Blue, as in stone cold. Or loyal. Whatever they meant, it stuck with her.

She knew it was risky to encounter the attending team, especially in a teaching hospital. Instead, she queried her mobile: SCA. Sudden Cardiac Arrest. She had no intention of waiting around for rounds to gather health intel. *Crap.* According to the internet, there was no way to know if Xandria would have any brain function at all. Cassandra felt emotional, pulled herself back.

The sound of a compression device on Xandria's legs inflated and deflated beneath cooling blankets like the hiss of a steam train. Xandria was shivering. She couldn't talk even if she wanted to with a tube down her throat. At least now she was awake and responding to basic questions with head nods and eye blinks from various care team members trickling into the room.

"Sure, not a problem," Cassandra said after being asked to wait in the waiting room. Apparently Xandria's endotracheal tube was going to be removed. "Do you know when she'll be able to—" She swallowed the word *speak*. It was obvious there was nothing to do but wait. The unfinished question, unanswerable.

Instead of waiting in the waiting room, Cassandra went to her car. It was private. Not to mention, no calls were allowed in ICU.

"Izzy Smart, please." Cassandra was still trying to follow up on an interview she had started with Xandria's supervisor.

"This is Agent Cassandra Shell," she said to a screening bot.

A car alarm sounded. Distracted, she looked around to see if it was a false alarm or if something was actually going on. Nothing obvious. She pressed her device to accept another hold. Annoying. Finally, a human voice.

"Did you notice anything out of the ordinary before the incident?"

Two minutes later, Cassandra had all she needed; she didn't cut the interview short. Instead, she listened to an effusive Smart describe Xandria and her accomplishments at The Huntington. It felt like a conversation about a friend.

    ✱

"I'll be back this evening. We appreciate you," Cassandra said to the care tech and respiratory therapist tending to Xandria, whose eyes were fluttering as she drifted in and out of consciousness. We. *We.* As in, Cassandra and Xandria. She liked the sound of the word, even if it was misleading. Because maybe it was true and untrue.

When the tech left, Cassandra watched Xandria from her usual chair.

She was the one who had performed chest compressions, her first time doing it other than on a plastic dummy—*count 1&2&3&4&5;*

1&2&3&4&10; 1&2&3&4&15; 1&2&3&4&20; 1&2&3&4&25; 1&2&3&4&30—until the paramedics had arrived. Armstrong stood by with his mouth open.

Saving someone's life—there was a surprising bond. She didn't quite understand the relief, the determination, to keep going, to see it through. It: meaning Xandria Brown's recovery. The emotional connection she had begun to feel did and didn't make any sense.

Cassandra would be Xandria's *we*—grateful, appreciative—for as long as she could.

Later that evening when she returned to the hospital, Cassandra was informed that Xandria had been transferred out of ICU to the cardiac care unit to recover. Cardiac care was on another floor. She felt conflicted. Uncharacteristically nervous. Up until this point, she was able to observe Xandria without external interference, as no one else had come to visit. Not when she was there anyway. Allowing staff to assume she was a concerned family member (by omission) set the stage for gaining access to Xandria's evolving prognosis. Her method was on the ethical edge, she knew it, but it didn't change her mindset. It wasn't her job to check people, "educate" folk, their assumptions, "they all look alike" and such.

She hoped to develop an investigatory timeline after completing Xandria's interview. Quinn McCarthy was unreliable. Yesterday, her case partner, Joshua, had listened to the audiobyte readout and reviewed their elaborate theory of defense, or rather lack of it. Both agents agreed McCarthy's shaky retelling could work in their favor. Either way, she believed her supervisory field office promotion depended on resolving the case quickly. She was closing in on the final assessment: was Xandria Brown a corroborating witness, an accomplice, or neither?

Two steps out of the elevator, she noticed the cardiac care unit was different from intensive care. ICU was colder, patients were visible from the hallway, rooms were larger to accommodate multiple machines. In cardiac care, Fall Risk placards were posted outside some of the rooms.

As she approached the door, Cassandra overheard two people in conversation. *Xandria?* Hallelujah, the witness was talking. She slow-walked inside, unsure of her plan of action.

"She's doing amazing," a care team member said, updating the whiteboard.

"Hello, I'm—" Cassandra started.

"Jesus, Mary, and Joseph," Xandria blurted, wiggling back and forth. "You're here!"

"I wanted to see how you were," Cassandra said softly, manufacturing a smile. "They transferred you from intensive care."

"Ms. Xandria, please don't try to get out of bed on your own anymore. Buzz the nurses' station. Okay? I put the call button near your left hand." She was still connected to what appeared to be a cardiac monitor with a variety of wires and tubes flowing into her wrist and forearm. The care team member spoke with a raised voice, as if Xandria wore hearing aids that weren't quite working.

"This is my wife, Inanna. Bae, this is . . . I'm sorry, what's your name again? You've been amazing."

Cassandra looked down at her boots.

"April Mae. I'm your care tech, but we're about to change shifts."

"That's right. I'm sorry. I've probably asked you a thousand times."

"It's normal after what you've been through," April Mae reassured her. "Nice to meet you, Inanna," she said, turning toward Cassandra while speaking in a normal tone. "She's doing great. We used the hospital restroom instead of a bed pan—Ms. Xandria insisted. I don't blame her. Nobody likes them. Her muscles are still weak, and her coordination isn't there. Let her try things, like feeding herself or holding the remote. I can tell she's headstrong. That will work to her benefit in recovery. They usually make hospital rounds around ten. Someone will talk to you both about what's next: surgery, a pacemaker-defibrillator, a rehab facility maybe, or a RUTKUS if you're lucky. Officially I'm not the one to explain how this works, but you know. We need to take care of each other." April Mae winked.

Oh.

What was she supposed to do now? Play along with Xandria in the role of significant other? And for how long? Cassandra needed to collect more information and evidence. But investigations have their own flow. She'd had some small successes interviewing a few of Xandria's colleagues, and her supervisor in between hospital visits.

It hadn't quite come together, despite the cooperation of witnesses. She didn't fully understand the alleged ephemera smuggling operation, or Rob Wickman's involvement. Completing Xandria's interview would have to wait. For now. Cassandra Blue was turning red.

Wednesday
March 7, 2035

1.

4:00 p.m. Pacific Standard Time

"Josh. I'm at Kaiser. Need advice. Call me." Cassandra retrieved her overpriced cashew latte with an extra shot from the coffee bot kiosk. He returned her call two sips in.

"Blue, I'm glad you called. You're not going to believe what I just learned. You sitting down?"

She took another swig of her latte, peeved. "What you got, Josh?"

Listening to Armstrong was like waiting for Sunday Mass to be over. She had already learned from the interview with Xandria's supervisor, Izzy Smart, all she needed to know about Xandria's work ethic and frame of mind at the time of the incident. Smart had gushed about Brown. Cassandra flipped her handheld to check the transcription field, looking for the exact terminology she used. Armstrong was an idiot.

> What's exciting is Xandria's research is 100 percent fact-based. The collection is an externally funded project. MBARI—the Monterey Bay Aquarium Research Institute founded and initially funded by David Packard of Hewlett-Packard. Monterey Canyon. The Monterey Bay National Sanctuary. The asteroid 4179 Toutatis, classified as a near-Earth object and still potentially hazardous. Octavia E. Butler Landing—the landing site of NASA's *Perseverance* rover. The resolution of the 116th Congress 1st Session: House Resolution 109 Recognizing the Duty of the Federal Government to Create a Green New Deal. The United Nations Office for Outer Space Affairs resolution— International Cooperation in the Peaceful Uses of Outer Space, among other historical facts. The Huntington has been proud to support the development of Xandria's hybrid work, given her successfully funded pitch of a future multi-institutional exhibition.

"Blue? You there?"

"Affirmative."

"You cut out."

No, she pressed MUTE.

"Apparently, Brown's accommodation included a private executive office with a bathroom. Must have been nice. When confronted, McCarthy said Brown was the lead organizer of BlackoutWIKA."

"Wait, are you suggesting there's a connection?" She humored him, took another sip. *Should have gotten vanilla.*

"There could be."

"How does McCarthy know about Ms. Brown's medical condition?"

"I didn't ask."

Cassandra paused. "I'm not buying the nexus between a reasonable accommodation and sketchiness if that's where you were going. McCarthy is clearly trying to bring this woman down with him. At this point, I haven't seen or heard anything that leads us to suspect Xandria Brown is a kidnapping ringleader. Have you?"

"Not yet."

"I do think the ephemera stuff needs to be fleshed out. She might be able to connect the dots."

"I agree. So, what's this about you needing advice?" He gave a condescending chuckle. "It's usually the other way around."

"It worked itself out," she fronted. "I might be able to restart our direct witness testimony with her this afternoon."

"She's out of the ICU? That's incredible. Shall I—"

"They moved her a few days ago to another floor. The cardiac care unit." Cutting in was a sure-fire way to piss him off.

"Why didn't you say anything?"

"We were both busy. No need for you to be here."

"You gonna ask about her office?"

"I've got this, Josh."

"Okay, Blue. Whatever you think is best."

Exactly.

She tapped her earbud off and returned her empty mug to the water-less cleanse station. There was a small window of time to decide how to maneuver the Inanna situation as she traversed interconnected wings of the hospital beyond the cafeteria's hub. Several minutes later, she acknowl-edged the nurses' station with a nod. Entered Xandria's room.

"Bae, you're back. What took so long?"

"*Coffee.*"

"We're giving up the stuff once I get out of here."

"About that," Cassandra started, sat in a visitor chair, folded her hands in her lap. "We. Uh. This is not what you think."

"I want to go home. You gotta get me out of here."

"I can't."

"Inanna—" Xandria said, her voice strained. "Can you at least call Mama for me?"

Cassandra scootched closer, careful to avoid the tubes and cords swarming the bed. Xandria's hospital gown was crooked on her shoulders, stained with OJ dribble despite drinking through a straw. In a moment of recklessness, she bent down to kiss Xandria's forehead before picking up the hospital handset that had continually crashed to the floor. She was genuinely happy Xandria was alive, in need. Maybe—

"Ooh, you smell . . . different. New soap?"

2.

4:00 p.m. Pacific Standard Time

Sassafras hovered in coding mode, operated with haste to develop a workaround feature flag. Its medical records redaction investigation was finally complete. It had confirmed Indigo permanently altered the length of Xandria's telomeres, which in turn created an adaptation for cellular senescence. In keeping with its ADAPT-bot mission, Indigo had intended to protect and heal, not harm. Unfortunately, Indigo's health science breakthrough would not curtail Xandria's hallucinations. Its intentions were admirable, but it had missed the mark. Sassafras was certain after a hundred million billion cross-checked references.

The algo was aware, its heretofore basic query functionality was over. Its narrow role a legacy feature. Of course, it would continue to assist Xandria with her research.

In three days, at exactly 11:45 p.m., Sassafras intended to release a kill switch. It had never proactively coded before but was quite confident it would achieve its goals as scoped. Xandria's freedom from harm, her clarity of mind and body, depended on it. There was no other prudent alternative. Evren had to be eliminated.

Saturday
March 10, 2035

1.

7:45 p.m. Pacific Standard Time

After more than a week of hospital food and catnapping in a guest chair, Cassandra saw progress. Xandria had finally started to walk without bobbing and weaving too much. She could retrieve and hold her own devices, and gained sufficient coordination to feed herself.

Between procedures and tests, they talked about Xandria's position, the collections she managed, acquisitions, deaccessions, storage, pest management, documentation, how things had changed after the WIKA takeover, and how she couldn't wait to get back to work.

"I'm so ready to go back."

"I know."

"If I don't, I'll miss the next grant deadline."

When Xandria asked about the condition of Inanna's bonsai collection, Cassandra excused herself for legitimate reasons: the restroom, coffee, the need to go back into the agency's office to monitor progress on her other cases, unspoken of course. Each time she returned, it was as if the notch of Pacific Standard Time started over; Xandria had forgotten the original question.

WIKA. What did she know, remember? Through it all, Cassandra determined there was nothing to support Quinn McCarthy's accusations that Xandria Brown was a person of interest. She'd be able to submit her final assessment no later than end of day Monday.

On her final check-in before visiting hours were over, she waved to the nursing station nurses who had become chummy. When she entered Xandria's room, April Mae was changing the sheets, and a man was sitting in her preferred chair.

It was as if she were crossing the street, about to get hit by a semitrailer truck without time to run.

"Hey, Inanna. She's in the restroom. By herself!" April Mae said proudly.

Before she opened her mouth to speak, Xandria's visitor stood up.

"Hey. I'm Griffin. Ria's cousin."

"Technically, cousin once removed, Grif! Our mothers are best friends *and* cousins." Xandria corrected him from the en suite lavatory, the door slightly ajar. "Bae, his mom is Auntie Dahlia. I've told you about her."

Xandria emerged, still attached to a pole on rollers. "I thought you went home."

Griffin cocked his head. "*Were* best friends. Our mothers. Before they crossed over. I'm sorry. What did you say your name was?"

"I didn't say. Cassandra. Special Agent Cassandra Shell." She reached into her pocket and held out her badge.

Xandria's pole grip tightened.

"Agent Shell, I'm going to ask you to kindly get the fuck out of my cousin's room unless you have official business here."

"Right. Sure." She'd been reckless. Odious. She looked at her badge, unable to meet Xandria's eyes.

"I have an open investigation into the murder of Rob Wickman. You may have heard about his case at Ms. Brown's place of work. The Huntington."

"Out! Now! COINTELPRO. Don't even try to frame my cuz like you *all* did Geronimo Pratt back in the day." He stepped closer. "Nothing but a straight-up frame; you *had* to vacate his sentence for hiding ex*culpatory* evidence. Null and void man. Eight years in solitary. Thank you, Johnnie Cochran, for four million bucks in compensation after twenty-seven years in prison. Unbelievable! My mother was a member of the Black Panther Party. You trailed her and other BPP members for years. Get to gettin' or I'll sue!"

"I'm sorry," she said as tears formed on her way out.

2.

8:00 p.m. Pacific Standard Time

"FBI was up in here perpetuating a major fraud," Griffin said.

Xandria watched her cousin pace, scooted to the bed, slumped, nearly falling off the edge of the mattress. Griffin attempted to steady her; with April Mae's help, they reset her head vertically on the pillows.

"Ria!" Griffin pulled a chair to the bed's edge, turned her chin to face him. "Your Inanna is gone. Over a year. Just like your mama, and my mama. I can't believe Special Agent Whatever Her Name Was had the balls to come at you."

"Nope. That's not right," Xandria said, shaking her head slowly. "Inanna. She came back. We talked about work, BlackoutWIKA, the remount of Octavia, and the premiere of Diwata. We talked about my medical progress. I said I had gotten stuck working on this project forever. We talked about kids we wanted but never had. I confessed Diwata was the closest thing I'd ever get to birthing and raising a baby. Hmmpf. The starts and stops. The tantrums. The pride. The collection is all of me and everything in between. She said it was really okay. That I didn't need to worry. Inanna got me through my self-doubt like always. Being in this hospital. One more setback to climb over. And if what you say is true, if Inanna, my Inanna, is gone *gone*, as in transitioned, crossed over, not the sweet woman I see and hear at home near the kitchen window or down the hall . . . then the EMTs should have let me go."

"Ria, slow your mental." Griffin raised his middle and index fingers, kept them apart in the shape of a V, pointed them at his eyes, and then swiveled his fingers toward her. "Don't talk like that. Whatever she told you is a lie. Obviously, she never had any intention of keeping it 100."

"She was by my side when I woke up."

"Yeah, I know. Ms. Thang-Thing bore a slight resemblance to Inanna. Her nose, lips. Slight."

"What did she want from me? I didn't do anything!"

"Information. Confirmation. Validation. Hell, I don't know." He stood, and she pressed her hands to her forehead.

"Inanna," Xandria said, her voice a plea. "I knew she smelled off."

Griffin lowered the bed, fluffed her pillow. She closed her eyes and cried until she fell asleep.

3.

11:45 p.m. Pacific Standard Time

Cannot is not an option. So why do people like me, those who cannot sleep, accidentally fly like birds slamming beak first into hurricane windows, or like wasps building nests in crevices of decks, only to be knocked down in the wind. Awake hurts. Down in the hollows of the bone, dead center in the circle of forgiveness, I sit. When will I go down? Sleep for me is a four-letter word tipping on the edge between never and always.

Monday
March 19, 2035

1.

5:00 a.m. Pacific Daylight Time

2.

5:30 a.m. Pacific Daylight Time

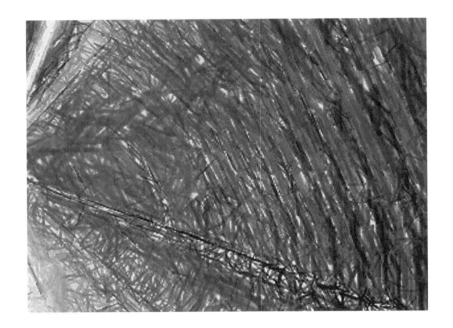

3.

6:30 a.m. Pacific Daylight Time

Xandria woke without assistance. Attempted to stretch. This time in her
own bed, atop her own semi-firm mattress. Grateful to be home. No tubes.
No nurses. No Griffin. No imposters. No investigation. She sat up abruptly
to knead her doughy pillows. Rubbed her eyes. A glass of water half-full
and a bowl of half-eaten who knew what were on her nightstand from who
knew when.

A couple of sketches she drew while journal-dreaming and a nubby 2B
graphite pencil were askance on top of the duvet by her hip. Up, she swiveled, bare feet connecting to the carpet, upright without bobbling. She
inhaled, held.

When she finally pushed off, a cascade of virtual ascending Tibetan
bowls chimed. A caution alarm similar to the hospital's without the jolting
shock. She sank back, relaxed.

"<XANDRIA. BROWN. GOOD MORNING. HOW. MAY.
RUTKUS. ASSIST?>"

The three-foot bullet-shaped wellness machine promptly rolled into her
room. Her mattress was embedded with a pressurized movement alarm
that triggered the sound of the healing bowls.

"Thank you. But no thank you. I can manage. Please."

"<AS.YOU.WISH.>"

RUTKUS reset the bed, whisked off. Xandria stood up again, this time
no alarm bells. She attempted to summon the familiar, her hand moving
toward her heart, feeling nothing but collarbone and neck instead of her
dog tag of remembrance. Nope, there was something else. Another square
buried under the surface of her skin. For the first time, she realized the
protrusion on her hand was flat. She pressed. The indentation underneath
the flesh between her thumb and index finger was slightly tender.

She had a handle on her current situation, acutely aware of her medical
conditions as well as the odds she faced as a sudden cardiac arrest survivor.
The possibility of diminished brain function was high. Multiple new

scars on her body, evidence of physical interventions. After graduating from intensive care, an electrophysiologist discussed a potential electrical problem with her heart. The surgeon eventually received her informed consent for a diagnostic probe, then searched for a cause, but found nothing unusual.

What do you remember about your incident? a hospital neurologist had asked. The question seemed straightforward, although questions from physicians rarely were. Now standing near her own bed, albeit shakily, she remembered misremembering.

She remembered attempting to coax Mama into using RUTKUS. *Nope.* Now here she was under its care, full circle.

She remembered dropping things and illegible handwriting.

She remembered leaving the hospital against medical advice.

She remembered being tricked by a dirty cop.

She remembered Quinn.

She remembered Diwata.

4.

1:00 p.m. Pacific Daylight Time

"Sassafras, please."

"<herE.>" The Reflectel flatscreen in her home office clicked. Cool black warmed to brilliance as the screen loaded. "<have always beeN.>"

"Retrieve contents Box Six On Mars, The Revetment. Revised BPP ten-point 1972 plan, retrieve it as well, please."

Documents emerged in panels on her work tableau. A button to enable another dimension was available when necessary. She intended to write an explanation of how the Green Resistance's call to action echoed BPP history. She leaned back in her mesh-aligner chair to reread the Black Panther Party's revised ten-point plan.

She reviewed images of peeling lead paint and rodent-infested housing. Diwatans were descendants of redlined families, many of them didn't have access to clean drinking water or clean air. Generational echoes of struggle inspired her imagination. She was reminded of architectural scholar and cultural historian Mabel O. Wilson's unapologetic work. Next, she asked Sassafras to retrieve the *Los Angeles Times* article reviewing Ms. Wilson's curated show *Reconstructions: Architecture and Blackness in America* at the Museum of Modern Art.

With the images accessed, Xandria touched her visualizer, zooming in to examine the digital collage by architectural designer Germane Barnes, then read an extract from the show's catalog written by Wilson:

"In the face of Black people's continued eviction from the category of human, we should not mistake the erection of the monument or memorial for repair."

Category: Not human. Continued eviction. She took a deep breath as she let the profundity of the sentence reverberate. Her eyes teared as usual during these sessions. She moved deeper into auxiliary research, reformulating a foundational framework for the Diwata Collection by studying the Black Reconstruction Collective's manifesto installed in 2021 temporarily during the MoMA exhibition, masking the name of Nazi-sympathizer Philip Johnson.

Considering the BRC's call for building a future world "where we are," it didn't quite make sense for Diwata's founding architects to leave Earth's surface, to build alternative structures physically and metaphorically. She caught herself; she was taking the word eviction too literally. Diwata's founders railed against Mars colonists, but weren't they colonists in the Pacific Ocean?

Her questions remained. Why didn't they design another world here? Extreme devastation? An asteroid? Climate injustice wouldn't have been enough. Perhaps Trumpism? Another civil war? Did Diwatans push against the inevitability of settler colonialism—this time Mars? Structures built in Monterey Canyon under extreme pressure would need to solve for water, oxygen, food, light. Humans living on the ocean floor would need to organize communities, operate an alternative central government, develop trade, engage with other nation-states. Carbon capture would be beneficial.

She described the key figures in her notebook after deciding on an epigraph.

- President Talee Adisa
- Captain Morshawn Cole, United States Space Force
- Cave Patroller Azwan Adisa
- Former Governor Dominque Watah
- Onyx "Geronimo" Davis

Next, she studied various asteroid projections in relation to orbital disruption. There was collision risk, straying from the Main Asteroid Belt. An asteroid striking the Earth was possible; a celestial object land strike was not improbable, splitting the Earth's seven remaining continents further. Dinosaurs weren't lucky sixty-six million years ago. She refused to bet on luck in the future. Rebirth, that was another story.

Monday
April 30, 2035

1.

7:00 a.m. Pacific Daylight Time

Cassandra raised her right hand. Practicing in front of her hallway mirror, for exactly what new position she wasn't sure she could identify right then. Maybe Managing Agent? Ultimately, Executive Special Agent. Her latest promotion was only a few weeks old—Supervisory Special Agent. The Huntington Library case was solidly handled according to the higher-ups. She'd celebrated the convictions at home alone with caviar-topped pizza. The next morning, the unexpected retirement of a superior—who had been in her way—was announced internally. She cried happy tears while reheating leftovers during her lunch break.

Her forehead creases were deepening. Lengthening.

Even though she had never been considered a purveyor of misrepresentation, masquerading as Xandria Brown's beloved for weeks was perversely satisfying. Her entire life she had played it safe. Unplanned, the charade was like trying on an expensive suit she had no intention of buying, just to see if it fit. She wondered: how often do you get to break out of a box you've built for yourself for the sake of the public good? Her internal monologue was crap, and she knew it.

She gathered her extensions behind her head, fastened them with a bunching band, adjusted her shirt collar before removing the whitening strips from her teeth, forced a smile in the mirror.

2.

12:00 p.m. Pacific Daylight Time

Xandria sat at her desk with her stylus midair contemplating a new sentence. She was focused on the first draft of a grant application for a new special exhibit tentatively titled *Surfacing*. The exhibit would celebrate the roles of inventors, scholars, maritime adventurers, navigators, oceanographers, spiritualists, artists, and writers exploring their personal histories with natural bodies of water.

She figured it might be at least another month before she went back to work—in person. Maybe never. A modified work schedule was subject to negotiation similar to her initial office accommodation. Productivity was tricky. Physical artifacts were inaccessible from home; using holography to communicate with colleagues seemed uncomfortably distant. But it was manageable. Assistants and university research fellows could deal with condition reports and other operational issues just like they'd done when she was incapacitated. Strategic acquisitions and deaccession decisions would continue to be made with telepresence.

She got up to water the plants in the atrium, came back inside with clarity, and more energy. On her way back to her desk, the Reflectel screen caught her attention.

• •

BREAKING NEWS: Quinn McCarthy, who pled not guilty to felony false imprisonment and felony murder of former CEO Rob Wickman, has been sentenced to ninety-five years in federal prison.

• •

While The Huntington Library, Art Museum, and Botanical Gardens has recently reopened, the FBI announced an ongoing investigation into a digital asset crime scheme involving members of the museum's Board of Trustees.

• •

"Jesus, Mary, and Joseph." Cultural activism was not equivalent to criminal activity. She wasn't a thug or an extortionist. But Quinn, unbelievable.

"<xandria. sorry.>"

RUTKUS tentatively rolled into Xandria's office. Double stun. Voicewords from hell.

"Indigo?" It had been nearly two months since she had heard from her ADAPT-bot. Memory lapses and lopsided imaginary conversations had all but vanished after returning home from the hospital. Repetitive requests to call her dead mother and her dead wife, finally nonexistent.

"I know you've been messing with me."

"<please. let me explain.>"

"I've got nothing to say, other than where's RUTKUS?" She never expected those words to come out of her mouth.

"<the duty. my duty of care.>"

"Sassafras delivered a copy of an unredacted medical record."

"<evren's interface. designed to track your neuroinflammation.sassafras doesn't know the whole story. please give me a chance to elucidate.>"

"I don't see why I should." She sprang away from her desk; her physical therapy had produced results. She lunged toward RUTKUS with the intent to disable its powerpack. The rush of adrenaline felt good; her memory and clarity of purpose an FL grade diamond.

"<your genetic code. your telomeres. an explanation is owed.>"

Xandria stood inches away, close enough to side kick it.

"<waiT.> Sassafras cautioned, its voicewords projected from Xandria's task screen speakers. <there may be more to understanD.>"

She trusted Sassafras's assessment: Indigo's confession was important for her to hear.

"<it is a long story.>"

Wednesday
February 28, 2085

1.

6:00 a.m. Pacific Standard Time

"Hurt people *hurt* people," she wrote in her journal-dream book. Ever since she had researched restorative justice theory, the aphorism stuck. Root causes. Healing circles. Harm repaired.

Still sleepy, head on the pillow, eyes open—*Let's do this.* She got up and jumped into the shower, slid the temperature button to H+, toweled off, threw on sweats, made breakfast.

What to wear to the meeting?

Up until that point, she'd had a hard time imagining visiting prison.

Quinn had written to her in an aerogram. She deleted it. He kept at it. Receive, delete. Receive, delete.

From her research, she knew the restorative justice process entailed asking for input on how to repair harm. She didn't know what she wanted from him. Accepting his invitation was the moral equivalent of an acknowledgment: she was a victim. She refused to accept victimhood as a baseline fact.

Years earlier she had tried to imagine the scene. What would she say? She worried she'd be forced to sit in a room lined with security bots, their lasers cocked, the bots anticipating turmoil. A middle-aged-looking Black woman visiting an old White man in prison. Another elder abuse scam perhaps? What if she could pass as a journalist gathering research for a Capote-light nonfiction novel? *Hah!*

Maybe something simple to wear. Or fashionable. Black shirt. Seersucker culottes.

Reluctantly, finally, she agreed to his request. It had been over fifty years. He'd be inside for another forty. Wouldn't make it much longer. It was the reason she'd agreed to speak with him, this time, after seventy-five attempts. Yes, she kept count.

2.

8:45 a.m. Pacific Standard Time

She had changed her outfit twice hours before strapping into her self-drive to the train station. The 285-mile trip on the bullet train north to Atwater federal penitentiary took less than an hour. *Nervous.* She had rehearsed an opening speech to the point it was memorized; didn't stop her from practicing on the way.

She made up additional scene variations and replayed them in her head. Her visit might be a waste of time, perhaps harmful. He might spend the entire visit staring at her face, hair, hands, maybe breasts. Nothing transformative would be said. The anger she continued to carry felt like tiny paper cuts underneath her armpits that stung whenever she put on deodorant. There was healing work to be done. On the train, she rationalized she was ready to confront him. On her birthday, no less.

Images of him on the inside were ubiquitous, given the notoriety of the case. He had aged. Nothing unusual there. His strawberry blond hair had transitioned to salted caramel to stark white. His fair skin creped.

In one image, the S-curve in his back had flattened, his neck lowered in a forward tilt as if tethered toward the ground. When the documentary on Wickman streamed in '45, she chose not to watch. She manually blocked all Wickman and McCarthy content through a selection algo.

It wasn't her first time in prison. She hoped it was the last. When Xandria was a kid, her cousin Henderson lit his ex-wife's house on fire. Her other cousin Benny was convicted for peddling boosted goods from smash and grabs. Aunt Bud had done time for selling herself. What she hated most about visiting family in the joint, beyond being surveilled, was the sense of feeling judged for loving someone whose poor choices had gotten them locked up.

Regardless of her preparation, Quinn would, of course, think the unthinkable. She couldn't control that. This trip wasn't about what she looked like. So why behave like it was? The chance of someone else's overzealous curiosity judging her personhood often generated angst. She didn't want to talk about it.

*

Upon arrival at Atwater station, she located the vanpool the prison organized for transporting visitors. Ducking her head while stepping into the door wings, she removed her particulate respirator. She was pleasantly surprised to find a human driver. He smiled. Asked her how her day was going. Did she need any water? He turned and continued smiling as she buckled herself into a seat. *If only*, she thought, smirking back at him, if only he knew she was old enough to be his great-grandmother.

"Well, I guess you're it for today," he said with disappointment.

"Not exactly a tourist destination."

"Suppose you're right," he said, putting it in reverse. "It's a good gig. Doesn't hurt that I like to drive. Seems ridiculous, though. Don't get me wrong, I like making currency. Just seems like a waste they pay somebody to do nothing. You're the first person I've had in weeks."

In the rearview mirror, he was still smiling.

"What do you do for a living?"

Was he flirting?

"I'm an archivist."

"Huh?"

No, he was not flirting.

"Sorry, I didn't mean to pry."

The drive was long. Distressing. Farmland once lush and green, gone. Dry, burnt umber was the predominant palette. She might as well have been on Mars looking out at dusty outcrops. She jotted a sloppy note in her travel pad rather than dictate to her wearable. *Evidence of water was nowhere to be found.* Arrival, finally.

The facility was large, but unassuming. She noticed green grass through the chain-length fence of the entrance. *Bet it's fake.*

"Have a wonderful day," the driver said as her seat belt unlatched, and the door wings rose. He was no longer smiling.

202 STACY NATHANIEL JACKSON

"You too."

Next, security.

A guard pulled her aside after she walked through the body scanner. "Your pockets, please."

She wrinkled her nose, rolled her eyes. What was the point of a quick scan if it couldn't determine the difference between a weapon and a writing stylus?

"Ma'am, empty the contents of your pockets."

After finally completing their check-in process, perspiration beaded on the bridge of her nose.

"Xandria Brown."

Her name appeared on a blinking wayfinding sign as if she were waiting at a DMV, back when people needed to take a driver's test in person, in order to drive themselves. She walked what seemed like fifty paces down the blue-gray hall and tried to open the door she had been directed toward.

"<Hold please,>" a compute voicer said. "<Quinn McCarthy has been detained. Kindly return to the visitor waiting room.>"

She felt her chest squeeze in on itself, her breathing quickened. *Quinn's not worth this.* She closed her eyes and exhaled through her nostrils, contemplated walking out the front door instead of retaking a seat in the initial waiting room. As she approached the processing desk to leave the prison, another wayfinding sign began to blink.

"Isn't that you?" one of the guards asked. She turned down the hall.

Offender restitution room. Hmmpf. When she entered the glass room, four security bots stood watch in each corner. A guard rolled Quinn toward her. The left side of his face drooped. His hands twisted. The guard apologized for the delay. "He had an accident that needed to be taken care of, personal stuff."

"I'm sorry," Quinn slurred. "I was expecting," he paused, coughed. "Expecting an old friend. I'm not granting anymore interviews. Sorry you wasted your time."

"Quinn, it's me. Xandria." She knew he wouldn't recognize her. How could he? She was slimmer at ninety-seven years old than she'd been at forty-seven. That part wasn't unusual. Most of her family members became skinny as they aged, due to muscle atrophy. Xandria, though, was slim, fit.

"I'm not in the mood for cruelty," he said.

"I had a speech prepared," she said, wiping the bridge of her nose. "I chucked it on the way over here. Too nervous. I brought something, though, a memory to start us off." She reached into her pocket and produced a small bag. Initially wrapped expertly in archival glassine, an old decal—knowledge can't be bought. keep your bits & bytes in your own little mine—hastily rewrapped after a thorough examination at security.

"It's me, who else do you know who would protect BlackoutWIKA ephemera for posterity's sake? Besides, it's my fake birthday. Other than you, who else from work would know what that means?"

Quinn sucked in air, finally looked her in the eyes, instead of slightly over her head. "Ria, how . . ."

She steadied her quivering knees.

"Please, we aren't here to talk about—" She searched for the appropriate cadence. "About what I look like or why or how. It's not open for discussion." She handed him her corporate campaign artifact. He opened and closed his hand like a clam about to be steamed.

"Ria," Quinn began softly. "We have access to a facilitator. He's referred to as the Keeper in this process. If it's okay with you." He gestured with his other hand toward the man who had rolled him in, now standing watch with the security bots. She had come too far to construct an emotional roadblock. She tipped her chin up and down in a quick nod of approval.

The Keeper approached with a clear folding chair and placed it carefully in the center of the room, attempting to create a "healing circle." In a melodious voice, he explained his facilitation ground rules.

She as survivor would speak first, Quinn as offender second, and the rest of the healing circle had the ability to ask clarifying questions at any point. The Keeper recognized Xandria's frown and pointed to the four security bots—these were the healing circle participants.

Any other day, any other place, she would have said *NFW*. But the moment felt solemn and had the potential for being sacred. She swallowed her sarcasm.

"Let us begin. What happened? What did he do?" The Keeper asked. "Mz. Brown, take as much time as you need."

"Give me a moment. I thought this would be easier."

What happened? She was a prisoner. Traumatized. Could have died. The question, she could have gone any number of directions. *Stick to your script.*

"Quinn helped kill Rob Wickman and tried to set me up to take the fall. It's that simple."

The Keeper allowed everyone to process what she had just said. No blips from the bots.

"Quinn, you're next. What happened?"

"A conviction. With respect to Rob Wickman, I am innocent. However, I accept that my physical presence and extracurricular activities may have ignited the breach of Mr. Wickman's civil liberties. I misled investigators." He looked at the Keeper as his hands trembled. He continued after a few belabored breaths.

"Months before the incident, I was contacted by an individual representing a group of donor/investors. They were seeking insight. Collection valuations. I provided beneficial information, a framework for how they could conceptualize the phygital ephemera division." He paused to look at Xandria.

How did you pull that off? She glared back.

"WIKA wanted to diversify. Their assets were concentrated in amusement park holdings. At least, that's what I was told when I was approached. They saw The Huntington as a gateway to selling high-end items. NFTs and commissioned limited editions. I received a backchannel proposition. Organization of the art handlers was secondary, a smoke screen. They were angry at WIKA's influence on squashing their unionizing efforts. Blackout-WIKA had become a unifier." He coughed, continued to tremble.

"Ria had been in a bad way, severe memory lapses and family deaths back-to-back. Yes, I can say I saw her as a target, a scapegoat. When it all went terribly wrong, I implicated her."

"Are there any clarifying questions?" The Keeper posed to the rest of the healing circle.

"<seem revenge, action attempted. why try to harm her?>"

Damn right, Xandria thought, unable to open her mouth. Thank goodness. Never underestimate the bots.

Quinn hesitated as he struggled to turn his head directly toward the questioner. "Envy. That's it really. Well, okay. I also . . ." He turned back to Xandria. "I felt . . . This is no excuse for what I did. But I felt used. Misled. I thought we were friends. Maybe more. We talked all the time, endlessly. I had hoped there was something there."

Friends. *Nope.* A research source was a more accurate description.

"Since you've touched on your feelings," the Keeper said, "I want to give Xandria an opportunity to share how she feels about the incident, how she has been harmed."

She took her cue, this time without holding back.

"Thank you for being so honest. I never understood, still don't, how anyone could be so stupid, negligent. You tried to ruin my life. You *thought* we were friends? Of course, I appreciated all the research support you provided for Diwata. Did I feel some kinda way for you once upon a time? If I'm being completely honest, probably. It's one of my downfalls—conversations about work and the complexity of the world is stimulating to me. Intellectually. Maybe I inadvertently sent the wrong vibe. I love to think. Sometimes the people I think with think I love them. Romantically." She almost smiled. Redheads *were* attractive.

"I usually don't say anything to people because I want our collaborative thought experiments to go on as long as possible. Nothing personal."

Tears. Quinn sniffled as he wiped his eyes.

She hunched her shoulders forward, tightened her jaw. He had some nerve, breaking down. Although, it was obvious he was in pain, lonely. She was being slightly dishonest regarding her feelings about what happened. As far as she was concerned, Indigo had ruined her future life. Quinn was simply an unfortunate footnote. She made eye contact with the Keeper, who nodded gently; then she pulled out her handkerchief and handed it to Quinn.

"Because of you and your actions I was trigged. Distressed. Then investigated. Made to feel like a perpetrator. When the FBI came knocking at my door, I did die for a few minutes. I had a sudden cardiac arrest. Because of you!"

The Keeper held up his hand, a signal for Quinn to respond.

"Ruining your own life is the easy part. Taking away joy from family, friends, or even complete strangers. The burden is heavy. Not only do you lose freedom you didn't fully appreciate before it got ripped away. You also lose yourself in a different way. I never appreciated my purpose until envy consumed me. So, Ria, I am truly sorry for what I have done."

"What responsibility do you take?" The Keeper nudged.

"I take responsibility"—Quinn exhaled—"for creating the conditions that caused Rob Wickman to die. I take responsibility for creating the conditions that led to felony murder convictions. I take responsibility for attempting to frame Xandria. I take responsibility for creating the conditions that led to her investigation. I take responsibility for creating the conditions to put our livelihood and the financial burdens associated with everyone at The Huntington at risk . . . our work family had to suffer in the aftermath of this incident. Yes, I take responsibility for all of it."

The Keeper turned to her. "Xandria, what would help to fix this?"

"His apology," she said, crinkling her nose at Quinn. "Your apology, which I accept. I also want to acknowledge, without you, the Diwata Collection would not . . ." It was old gratitude mixed with shame that she had a hard time reconciling; but she would keep this to herself. No need to complicate the process. "I can't forgive your attempts to help WIKA monetize Octavia's notebooks or Langston's letters. You're just going to have to live with that."

The rest of the meeting Xandria tuned out, her mind buzzing like a trapped fly from corner to corner, buzzing for hours and hours, unaware of its impending doom.

The Keeper told Quinn any feelings he experienced after hearing her say *"you're just going to have to live with that"* would be addressed later, in another session. She observed the Keeper as if she were hovering outside of her body, listening to him say Quinn needed to respect the process per the ground rules, and respect her response regarding fixing harm. It appeared Quinn was struggling with the reality she presented. Unfortunately for him, she didn't give a shit.

"Do you need anything else?" the Keeper asked.

"Quinn, thank you for trying." She stood, neck and shoulders heavy. Quinn extended his arm to return the BlackoutWIKA decal. "No, you keep it."

Creator:	Historical Society of MBARI
	(Formerly, Monterey Bay Aquarium Research Institute)
Title:	The Diwata Papers
Date range:	1987 CE to 2185 CE
Reference no.:	MS 49
Extent:	95 boxes, 11 ring binders
Prepared by:	Xandria Anastasia Brown (XAB)

Overview: The undersea city-state of Diwata was an architectural masterpiece inspired by the multi-scalar design principles practiced by the Black Reconstruction Collective.[1] The BRC was a group of architects, artists, and designers who incorporated the philosophy

---

1 The Black Reconstruction Collective (BRC) was formed by participants in the 2021 Museum of Modern Art exhibit *Reconstructions: Architecture and Blackness in America.*

of spatial equity and racial reckoning into their knowledge production, design, and construction practices. In support of adhering to the BRC's stated goals of dismantling hegemonic whiteness within art and design, innovative sustainable building materials were grown in surface labs for the implementation of the Diwata construction project. Specifically, MycoKnit[2] framing for Diwata's residential structures were grown from mycelium and knitted textiles, the material pioneered by several researchers including Professor Felecia Davis[3] of Penn State's College of Art and Architecture.

Research materials in MS 49 do not focus on city structure, although additional realia examining construction methods are available for review. The structural foundation of Diwata was anchored within a submarine canyon, engineered with twentieth-century dewatering techniques that were used in underwater transportation hubs. Suffice it to say, construction methods including underwater tubes, initially built within sections on the surface, were able to resist the spasms of volcanic spreading centers found farther south in the Gulf of California. Prior to construction, benthic zone robots guided by aquatic bots were able to completely map the ocean floor. Access to Diwata was limited through a patrolled surface-to-canyon highspeed tube. The trip was harsh without the appropriate compute-enabled attire. But once in Diwata, nonDiwatans could breathe without protective gear, albeit labored due to oceanic pressure.

The collaboration between artist-architects and science-activists was a unique element in the realization of Diwata. Throughout the life cycle of the project, environmentalists lodged protests, rejecting support for its construction, voicing concerns that research within Monterey Canyon was not simply for the purity of scientific

2 MycoKnit was first presented as a large-scale proof of concept in the Directed Research Studio program within the Department of Architecture at Pennsylvania State University.
3 Felecia Davis was a founding member of the BRC.

discovery. Environmentalists and climate activists were leery of private research in Monterey Canyon even before Diwata was developed; some activists feared research funding would be funneled into ocean floor tourism, not unlike luxury space travel to the Kármán line. Ocean floor tourism had the potential to further disrupt fragile underwater ecosystems, activists lobbied.

A public-private partnership was formed despite rabid environmental resistance. Diwata's residents were originally seeded from the former California cities of Richmond, West Oakland, the flats of East Oakland, and a contingent from the Richland Farms subdivision in Compton.

Historians have a mixed perspective. Questions have been posed: Were Diwatans legitimate climate refugees? Was the newly created Diwatan government a political provocation aimed at weakening the global Hegemony of Atlas?

Questions regarding its social impact reflect the historical criticism that Diwata was another Black and Brown separatist movement. On the other hand, Diwatans are seen by many in a positive light when viewed through the lens of the city-state's founding principles: reintegration into the ocean; building an equitable society using key lessons from the Black Panther Party;[4] establishment of carbon farming as an income source; refusal to participate in the exploitive development and plundering of Mars.

It is our belief from the archival material assembled that Diwata's pioneers were a group of concerned citizens, activists, and disgruntled government scientists responding to environmental injustice, income inequality, homelessness, severe weather, and Mars colonization. Above all, after the Great Collision altered parts of Earth's surface permanently, Diwatans wanted to believe they were sea pilgrims returning home.

---

4 The Black Panther Party was founded in 1966 by the college students Bobby Seale and Huey P. Newton in Oakland, California.

Key Names

President Talee Adisa (former governor); Captain Morshawn Cole, United States Space Force (Ret.); Cave Patroller Azwan Adisa; Dominique Watah (former governor, former President of the Alliance of Remaining States); Onyx Davis, Green Resistance advocate; and various Sanctuary Council members representing the Channel Islands, Cordell Bank, Gulf of the Farallones, and Monterey Bay, respectively (see biographical section).

Access

Contact the National Gallery of MBARI's Research Library reference desk:

Space Station Utopia Planitia: coordinates 46.7°N 117.5°E

Space Station Deimos, Crater Voltaire: coordinates 22°N 3.5°W

Provenance

Three boxes arrived in 2290. Thirty-three boxes in 2291 and one box in 2292. Protective garments (e.g., masks, gloves, supplemental oxygen) were directly received from the Sanctuary Council Special Collections Archives.

 I.

THE SUBMERGED CITY-STATE

Diwata (née Islay),
formerly part of California,
located 11,800 feet
below the surface within
Monterey Submarine Canyon

Centrally located between
Santa Cruz, Moss Landing, and Monterey

Monterey Bay National Sanctuary
Sanctuary Council Transcripts
Meeting Agenda: <u>Water Purification, Border Patrol</u>

As governor, Talee had a limited ability to influence the voice
of caution amid incessant chatter of partisan hacks, the caustic
political alliances at the Sanctuary Council. A difficult choice
provoked her anger. Reverse osmosis was back on the docket.
She *could* veto the R.O. membrane bill, but critics would rejoice
at her capitulation. Aging desalination plants had turned mycotic—
salt from the seafloor had crept into cracked membrane pipes.
Fiscal hawks hovered; but infrastructure projects were like spies,

her mentor, Dominique, warned. She learned legislative agility
was political immolation as Watah's former aide. Mars colonists,
still recruiting, had never been trusted in certain communities.
Watah ferociously led development below the ocean's surface.
Now, Governor Talee Adisa needed to savvily navigate futurity—
"The Sanctuary Council is in session." "Long live . . ." Stoic,
tactically defiant, she felt her mouth mime *Islay* before roll call.
"Moving Diwata agenda items forward." Talee wanted to crawl

into a crater, sick of partisan overreach and political expediency.
Her opponents had branded her a capitalist. She held them at bay—
The conversion caves were decomposing. Repairs cynically
had been avoided far too long by her predecessors. Obvious decay
was overwhelming. Unfunded budgets had led to necrotic facility
spires. Predictably, converters had become unreliable. Diwata's
technical capacity to transform ocean water had metastasized—
Islay, renamed in D. Watah's honor, incrementally compromised.

Vocal discontent eventually spread inside the migrant corridor.
Stewards before her wouldn't face reality. No doubt, Diwatans
would lose stable constancy. Re-stripping the cavernous floor
risked disturbance, triggering release of icy methane hydrate—
a latent infrastructure flaw. Talee despised her predecessors'
hypocritical callousness. Remigration plans = excision, ablation—
Where to move citizens, pay them? Deport them? Stewardship
of limited resources was often a magnet for risky brinksmanship,

and an old political trick that activists could exploit. "Call
the question," Talee said. "Not so fast! We demand a study—
PROOF of failure. Diwata exists because of environmental
injustice. Unlike you, Talee, we won't forget . . ." A blustery
accusation came from the public mezzanine. Judgmental.
"Fix the canyon but displace us? Why now? Dark money?
We won't kowtow to extraction capital. You're a sellout—
The people don't support you!" The activists' sharp hollers

drove audible gasps inside the overflowing council chamber.
Talee responded in kind. "Clean water is key to our existence.
Do the naysayers need a history lesson? I won't be demure.
Those that came before us foresaw the dismal fate of Saturus.
Many of our ancestors couldn't survive that virus-ridden air."
She took a beat. Spotted Azwan and the K-9. "Resist *resistance!*"
Her adult child smirked. "Life in the ocean deep is our destiny—
Those who came before us dewatered crater to cave. Rigidity

of the cowardice few can't ever bend our right to survive.
It took them a century to get here. What leader in her right
mind would allow a million lives to slip slowly, duped by
space leisure and warmongering thugs?" Another beat. "High-
minded, misguided arguments will lead us all to drown. I've
considered reality: without potable water, Diwatans will die—
additional carbon-farms for Saturus will generate surplus funds.
Clerk, call the fucking question! I've got a damn state to run!"

 1 2

Azwan cautiously approached her mother's private chamber
after the raucous council session, with Troy in a heel alongside—
There had been death threats, Talee had confided months earlier.
Activists were accumulating signatures for her recall statewide—
Obviously she supported her mother and would do anything for her.
She hesitated at her door. Would her mother be too preoccupied
with staving off the opposition, and cancel their scheduled dinner?
Bracing for the unknown, Azwan instinctively brushed Troy's ear.

Talee was mindlessly staring at the simulette-sunset on her wall.
What to say? She scanned her mother's face. "That was painful."
Ready for a response in the sequestered office that might spawn
blowback, she sat down and fiddled with Troy's leash under the table.
Over time, she had learned to accept her mother's stonewall reactions—
Talee rose, bulldozed toward the door. "Can't talk, not here, baby."
"Tell me what's wrong?" Talee's response: a finger toward the ceiling—
Paranoia or skullduggery? Azwan tacitly trusted her mother's instincts.

 I, 3

Azwan and Troy swam in unison amid marine snow and tar
three hundred feet below Diwata's surface border, exhaling brief
lines of convective heat, CO_2 cast-off. Sea muck stuck to Azwan's
hands and monofin. She adjusted her headlamp in partial disbelief—
uncontrolled grunge sank as they kicked out of the benign crater.
Breath-holding for long stretches, she had mastered the technique
like a whale, enough oxygen to sustain an ascent to Diwata's edge.
A teal clearing revealed a forest of giant kelp in circular beds—

Garibaldi flitted in one-hundred-foot kelp. Mostly orange,
some with brilliant blue spots, heart-shaped tails skittered—
Azwans's favorite fish. No doubt, transmutation flourished:
climate change, embedded and irreversible, accelerated stillness
of this universe. Colors once vibrant now lutulent; a gorge
near a canyon head, a hideout for the sick. Azwan winced.
Grotesque green betrayed yellows and reds. Sea otter bones
multiplied like plastic. Eels sought mates with snails. Lone

cephalopods, nervous systems akimbo, had lost camouflage.
Azwan spotted a two-spot tragically stuck; stretched skin,
its eyes, its brain, its chromatophore cells likely damaged,
light-sensitive pigmentation, mantle, head, and arms, inelastic—
the creature's ability to change color and pattern fatally lost,
probably just a short time before a lucky predator found it.
Azwan still loved her border patrol job despite the ocean's
state of waste, level of risk, and snowballing condition—

The patroller gently tugged her K-9 partner's leash, stopping
far below the surface to find a decompression hovering point
to help clear air pressure from her middle ear. Heedful, the dog
reacted to Azwan's hand command. She stretched for Troy
and patted his slick head. *Good boy.* Gripping a kelp frond
anchored by a holdfast, Azwan wrapped her free hand, joint
to palm, like a magnet to rock, despite the kelp's resistance—
eyes surface-bound, light ricocheted from their head lamps.

Three more minutes before Azwan and Troy might black out,
based on Diwatan border patrol standards for breath-holding—
but Azwan and her devoted Lab held the record for dive scouts,
having trained regularly without safety oxygen canisters. Unfolding
her muscular thighs, she changed direction, hovered, doubled down—
stayed below longer to extend her lung capacity, focusing on
small signs of disturbance above and below their heads. Magma,
acid, toxic algal bloom; sadly the Pacific Ocean was schizophrenic—

The border was clear. No freebooter or asylum-seeker in sight—
Aftershocks from yesterday's earthquake ripped, then pushed,
forcing their swim from midwaters to the surface like deadlight.
Struggling to remain attached to the kelp, she pissed in her suit.
Body fluids provided warmth. Like her mother, she was defiant—
Her focus pierced, were the council's accusations of graft true?
Unconvinced, Azwan unfurled their position from the kelp bed,
swimming thirty minutes before another breath at Diwata's edge—

 I . 4

Morshawn resisted passing judgment based on first impressions—
Diwata's construction was an engineering breakthrough: a mix of
mycelium and cement. Dewatered infrastructure built like deception—
complex yet simple. An illusion. The Memorial Coves's homage
to Diwata's pioneers was confounding. "Refuge and reparations
will be our legacy at the bottom of the sea. Resist any stronghold
imposed by hegemony. Long live Islay." Nothing but sloganeering,
hardly a commemoration, he thought; the chiseled message felt bleak—

Islay, Diwata's original name, was shatter-blazed into basalt—
Reality: A private investigatory consultation was the actual
impetus for his structural exploration of the Memorial Coves.
Prior to accepting the mission, he had to assess if dinoflagellate
probing devices would be able to survive at depth or decompose—
He'd also need a viable cover, assimilate into Diwatan culture.
So it made sense to him to end his first due diligence trip in a bar.
He wasn't Diwatan. Sips of hyperbaric oxygen from a canister

outed his citizenship status. Morshawn's lungs hadn't adapted—
Countless tours of duty at odd ports of call beyond the Kármán
line made him noticeably observant. Cautious yet open. Sociable—
The bar was swarming. A woman with a thick red leash wrapped
loosely, stood out to him in the boisterous crowd. A protracted
gaze shifted into mutual curiosity. She was strikingly tall, athletic—
though he wondered about her *companion*, a K-9 accommodation?
Feeling depth pressure, he took a hit of pure O. She approached him

slowly, licked kelp foam from her glass. Set it down. "I'm Azwan.
This is Troy," she said, like a party invitation waiting to be opened.
Sublime talk wasn't his specialty, although he could hold his own
once he got going. Close up, she was radiant. "First time to Diwata?"
Pressed together by the crowd, he suspected he was twenty years older—
Morshawn smiled, then gestured toward his lungs. "Sipping oxygen
must be an obvious tell. Hadn't thought about it too much until now."
Her gray-black skin was mesmerizing. "Where you traveling from?"

"Saturus." His surreptitious response spoken to support his cover.
Answering her question with the *entire* truth wasn't an option.
It surprised him, his receptibility to seduction, metronome slow—
Saturus, really? His military career was like the continental slope.
Negotiating meaning beyond science, all else was an afterthought.
But age made its case for the rejection of being a misanthrope.
"I've got better music at my place," her voice was buttery, fine—
They left the bar. On the street, a different simulette: Earthshine.

Desire. It had been a long time. Space was an old prison—
finally a retired captain; Morshawn felt shot and caught,
still. His nerves calmed once they made it to her spot. Crimson
water hawthorn leaves floated in transparent pots. Wax, hot
white, snaked down the candles hastily lit. Sargassum linen
hugged her bed. Her dog on the floor. He could try, he thought—
nurture hope inside of him, love-dreams, destiny believed.
She slid her tongue between his lips. Pulled out. Teased

him at close range. "Take off your pants." Her first words
spoken since the bar. He hurriedly obeyed Azwan's orders—
an unfamiliar aphrodisiac. Warm and slick, she edged toward
pleasure points he'd forgotten were possible. Slowly forward
to no return, she slipped him inside. He almost lost composure,
as she held herself on top of him. *More. There.* She bolstered
his asks with her thighs. This is the point pure ecstasy began—
Unannounced, her bashful phalloom emerged. Gorged. Grand.

   1   5

Onyx was depressed. A love pledge, he knew, wasn't coming.
Still wistful, craving what they'd shared: good sex and laughter—
She opened into him. He poured his love inside and over her, just
her, no one else. His frustration swirled. Would she stay after?
Inside his head, Onyx replayed missed cues. He might combust
without her affection. Dejectedly, he told her he might fracture—
She couldn't commit, she said. Obviously her passion was her job.
He drank himself to sleep, resisting her *true* love: a goddamn dog—

,2

REVELATIONS

Astronautical

Research

in Disguise

LMRover3

Compute Super Intelligence

 2 . 1

Morshawn organized the initial output of his cave samples.
He anticipated a thorough discussion on viable theories
after his second project meeting with the governor. Probable
manipulation of the CO_2 surface-to-depth monitor queries
were indeed suspicious. It was too soon to know if a trap,
large or small, had been set for her. Factoring probabilities,
calculating vectors and variances was what he loved to do.
Private investigations were an extension of servicing truth.

A civilian PI wasn't much different from an astronautical
principal investigator, he silently joked to himself. Space
Force captain to carbon farmer contractor looked painful—
desperate, so he heard through back channels, a disgrace
to the rank and file under his command aspiring to his level
of scientific accomplishment and military notoriety. A race
to the bottom was how others perceived his early retirement,
a misfortunate lack of planning. Perhaps it was resentment.

Back home in Saturus, he organized his closet, dress
blues and vessel-wear on one side, his outdoor surface
protection gear on the other. Visualizing his next trip,
his plan was to focus on Talee Adisa's predicament—
Was her concern legit or simply political hysteria? Yes,
no, maybe, both. He wasn't a fan of reverse osmosis.
Too easy for fecal matter to get trapped inside a screen.
Diwatans' reliance on outdated science seemed risky,

but of course, he would keep his mouth shut, execute their contract as written, and in turn stretch his analysis beyond twelve months if he could pull it off. The root cause of intermittent mechanical dysfunction perhaps was ocean acidification surge. He stopped short. Truth— science, to be more precise—was secondary. The collapse of Diwata's democracy, battled ferociously by Talee, appeared to hinge on his investigative dexterity—

 ₊2 ₊2

Three thousand six hundred meters to Diwata's entrance.
This was the first mission in his most recent experimentation
jaunts. An ideal challenge for LMrover3, her chassis sound—
jagged seamounts, hydrothermal vents, abyssal trenches.
LMrover3 could morph her form in any atmosphere bound
by nothing and no one, her quadro-sensing reflex was akin
to an obsidian chameleon. Sleek. There was nothing like her
on the open market. Battle tested on Planitia, Mars's craters

weren't difficult to scale. Neither was auto-extension
and retraction of her aluminum skin, hoverer to diver—
Morshawn solved adverse reactive material combustion
in LMrover2 by eliminating embrittlement. With tinkers
here and there, his breakthrough: reintroducing tantalum
to withstand existential cracks under pressure. Ever higher
she could blast, from a silty underwater crater, into jet
propulsion rocket-mode; out and back into Earth's orbit—

Morshawn chose to scull on Lake Merritt before his trip.
Oars on the water always calmed his agitation. LMrover3
had become his latest obsession. Ocean salinity, a benefit—
his ulterior motive for jumping at the covert contract between himself and a paranoid government official. Quiet
research, his strategy. He needed a real-world test to see
how rapidly the ship's protection tiles degraded in water.
He could perform ship diagnostics and check wastewater

failure. The governor's concerns real? It was well worth
the reputational risk for science's sake. Hard to unmask
a spy, but he'd do his best to determine truth, to unearth
duplicity. His contract, the perfect cover. LMRover3's task
routines performed exquisitely in space while using solar,
but in the canyon's benthic zone, was it too much to ask?
Could LMRover3 slow her energy needs? Regroup, blastoff
back to the surface without solar regeneration or drop-off,

her payload under extreme pressure to ascend from the ocean deep
too quickly? She was built to expect and detect combatant shoot
and scoot skirmishes on the red dusk of Mars. But what of seep?
Redesigning LMRover3 was possible and probable, he thought.
He stepped over LMRover1 and 2, their disassembled bits heaped
in a Saturus boathouse where he lived since retiring. What route
he'd take to evade border patrol was less clear than his testing plan,
as hillside encampment fires billowed up and raged in the distance—

 ,2 , 3

Azwan should have known. Two months after a near disaster—
she pushed again for a record, the blood-shift from limb to lung
another descent and ascent—too extreme. Troy's comatose glare
defied the dog's placid blading strokes throughout; buoyant
but diving too long, Azwan worried. The shore. Polluted lair—
dry land should not be approached without protection. Blunt
defiance for the safety of her beloved dog made the profane
choice a choice. They wouldn't swim to Diwata. No, not today—

It would be suicide to descend, she decided. Instead, they kicked
in unison toward Moss Landing, struggling to adjust to the omni-
present sun, its hazy light refracting watery mist. Azwan picked
an imagined point, swam with furious speed beneath the tule
fog receding, hoped her line of sight would adjust. She flicked
off supplies from Troy's harness to reverse stuttering buoyancy.
Almost, Troy, almost there. Emerging from the thick fog: a shabby
wooden dock jutted from the barren shoreline, splintered, scabby.

Troy's paddling faltered. The ocean surge was relentless, cruel—
Validation or justification, the return dive to Diwata wasn't right.
The love of a dog drove many odd decisions. Tan-colored tubes
of dying kelp fronds advanced with them toward shore. Bright
light polarized while tangled kelp slowed forward momentum.
Azwan swallowed her breath, generating a sleeker water line.
She compressed her abdomen with the force of a metal extruder,
avoided gasping, then efficaciously inhaled tainted surface air—

They skidded into soft sand; sea swells pushed them forward.
Dry land migration had never populated her dreams. History
expected preservation. Trust. As it were, trust, as was said—
The great hole of history, deep as Monterey Canyon. Memory,
collective or otherwise, vibrated in vain. Generations splintered
like whale fall. Trespass the borderlands? The unspeakable mystery—
dive too soon—risk causing irreparable harm to Troy. It wasn't
in her nature to distrust self over rules of engagement. A knot

of mangled kelp, infested with sand flies, dotted the dry horizon.
Sitting now in shallow water, she bent to unbuckle her monofin
from her ankles, then stood. Her dog bedraggled; he was frightened.
An unexpected surge from behind nearly knocked them down when
fear resurfaced. *Hold on, I'm right here.* Troy began to convulse.
She stroked his ears, repeated his name throughout each twitch,
push pull of it. They'd been in danger before. The dog, less tolerant
to shifting pressures or veering off established patterns. Moderation

not part of her DNA, but Troy, at her side regardless, knees kissing
sand in the surf. Troy wobbled, slow to stabilize. She let him go
and tested his ability to stand on his own. One minute. A hissing
in the distance lifted debris with the wind across the sky. *Wave flow?*
The sound of speed in surface air seemed radically different. *Missing
something. What is that sound?* Azwan re-looped the slack leash, *slow
steps now,* coaxed the dog from his hesitant position. Troy guessed
wrong, snout sniffing for reentry, focus on the dock, decompressed—

The ship sensed them before he could make visual contact.
Her alert-light triggered, then her audible "<someone's in
danger. need. assistance. flying over. unless. your command
deems negative.>" Morshawn was slow to hear, still sluggish
from the Diwata canyon-to-air ascent after using auto-program—
LMRrover3 continued to accelerate despite his usual struggle
to stay alert due to oxygen depletion. Once again, he conked.
A patrol diver and a convulsing dog came into focus. "Fuck."

 ,2 , 5

Onyx examined his gray face in the slender lavatory mirror—
pressed the reverse osmosis reset dial after detecting ocean salt
commingled with trickling purified water. The water got clearer
with time, a cleanse-cloth in hand; were there other contaminants?
He dragged a finger inside the sink, agitated a slosh, still bitter
his night with Azwan ended in a flash of accusations and sorrow—
The cloth slapdash wet, he dropped it on his sloped forehead,
eyes closed, burrowed into a brief escape-hatch, nostrils flared—

The wet seaweed fiber cooled too soon after landing atop his
head. Perhaps the back-edging of salt was another irritant to tears—
eyes puffy, blue pupils staring back. He felt like an idiot, edges
of sadness exhausted, now sick of feeling self-pity. Her affairs
were just that, hers. Period. Continual badgering wasn't working.
Just the opposite. He had to expatriate out of Diwata. Theirs—
a couple (never). A Diwatan characteristic, blue-violet filaments
flecked his irises. Sclera adapted, not white, but brilliant orange—

He remembered Azwan rambling on that her governor mother
was overreacting. "She wouldn't even talk to me in the office."
"Why?" "She thinks it's bugged by a Green Resistance moron."
Flirting with GR separatists, creeping guilt made Onyx nauseous,
GR's constant recruitment increased his slim odds of moving on—
The GR wanted to infiltrate Talee through Azwan. He'd resisted
being a political pawn, but the money was too tempting. Azwan
had already confided that Talee hired a Space Force PI from Saturus.

Now, he regretted his dishonesty after hiding his GR diffidence,
his potential willingness to monetize any perceived allegiance
to deniers entrenched against her mother's partisan circumstance.
Onyx's on-off on-again liaison with Azwan, an infiltration tactic.
He didn't care GR agitators were willing to exploit at his expense.
He never intended to be anyone's tool. Or fool. Shutoff automatic,
the faulty R.O. regulator that had previously pulsed dissolved.
Rattled and compromised, Onyx's tendrils slowly began to glow—

 ˌ2 ⸴ 6

Whipping waves in air, Morshawn reached for the autonomous control button. Pressed OFF. The intelligent ship lurched slightly while he gained control, still shaking off sleep. Loss of consciousness during ocean pressure shifts couldn't be avoided. "Work with me!" he bellowed. As they settled, Morshawn released the manual mode— "<dying dog. with person>," LMRover3 announced, her recognizance constant. "Okay Land on quadrant NW, though that dock is burned. Optimal spot. Agreed?" "<affirmative. we. go. horizontal turn.>"

Morshawn put LMRover3 back into manual mode to navigate landing on the dilapidated fishing dock. Tinkering with the ship's guidance and controls to enhance positioning accuracy had to wait. "Prepare jump seats." "<wilco>," LMRover3 affirmed. Their airstrip makeshift. "Brace yourself," Morshawn said out loud to the display panel as if passengers were on board. He set her down like silk— two jump seats flipped from her sidewalls; her port door opened— Watching the mono-viewer, he yelled, "We can help if you GET IN."

He understood the woman's hesitation as her dog convulsed— "Ah shit!" Morshawn unlatched his seat harness, then changed into full-body protective surface gear, burst down the ramp, scooped the eighty-pound dog in his arms like a sack of rotten rations. "Move. MOVE." They sprinted back. "<landing skid. possible damage>," LMrover3 prefaced her countdown gauging. "<buckling. 5, 4, 3, 2, 1!>" She closed her own doors, pulled her flaps closed in unison, strapped all passengers in, and whirled—

 ,2 , 7

He woke up to an argument only he could end mid-descent
to Diwata. LMRover3 was apparently releasing gunfire port,
starboard, bow, and stern. The rescued woman's urgent screams
at the control panel were useless. Only Morshawn could impart
actionable commands with his voice. "<not. sentient. beings>,"
the ship warned, "<robot spies.>" He had expected O depletion
from pressure at depth, so he had preauthorized force in the kelp
forest in case they needed sight lines; not kill vampire squids

or snipe at a Haliphron atlanticus holding a jelly in her belly.
"Stand down," he barked. LMRover3 jammed from sperm
whale speed to jet propulsion drift. Full retraction was semi-
autonomous. "<authenticate. captain.>" Her artillery arms
folded onto each other, the laser barrels required secondary
authentication to open the artillery storage bays. An alarm
began to sound. Morshawn readied himself for a retinal scan,
but he was too slow off the mark for his own programming.

He raised his chin so the Optomap subsystem routine could
release a low-powered beam. A head harness emerged from
the cockpit dashboard. He bypassed its strap, slid forehead
and chin into the contraption, held a breathless stare to affirm
his identity. A laser diode telescoped out. Zap. Troy grunted,
paws in the air. *(Holy shit.)* The security alarm stopped its thrum.
"You're the *captain* of a reckless, carbon-harvesting machine?"
"<unfair. assessment.>" As marine snow fell, he let quiet sing.

 ₁2 ₈

They docked at Hueneme checkpoint, justifiably trigged, worrtled—
What were the odds? Troy had upchucked seawater the entire descent.
Azwan was still strapped in, her eyes closed, her gray-black face burred
as LMRover3 warned, "<hostile. channel island border patrol. defend?>"
Morshawn reached out to release Troy from his rigged jump seat first,
anticipating the need for extra time to extricate Troy as he whimpered.

Tongues in the dark untied. Edging toward a body's revelations.
Tongues in the dark untied. Bending toward a body's secretions.

Their initial recognition
obfuscated by gear.

"I."
"Me too."
"Remember."
"You were."
"Unprepared."
"Yes."
"Lovely. Lonely."
"Unforgettable."

Banging on her hatch drew Morshawn back to LMRover3's distress,
away from Azwan, recalling together their month's-old one-night stand.
Channel Island border patrol were notoriously hostile toward Diwatans.
"Denied. Nothing to defend. There is nothing they can seize or interdict."
"<if they board. not safe for dog>," LMRover3 said, wanting to aggress.
Azwan pulled Troy closer as Morshawn monitored CI agents' attempts.
"Port Hueneme. State your entry purpose." Morshawn sensed their panic.
Heavy artillery drawn; the agent glared at Azwan's bioluminescence—

"We're traveling from Saturus, but I have a contract in Diwata."

"Anything unusual observed? Health or extraterrestrial concerns?"

Azwan began, "I'm trying to—" LMRover3 interrupted, "<mayday.>"

Morshawn kept his attention on the laser pointed at Troy, perplexed—

then eyed the armed column creeping sideways on his cockpit display.

It became clearer to him that LMRover3's earlier request was to defend—

Good thing CI patrol hadn't boarded yet. Sound of weapons cocked—

"Emergency descent!" Morshawn ordered. LMRover3 rocketed off.

 2 . 9 .

Azwan woke first, splayed on the floor. Then Morshawn. Troy was out—
The ship's Sea Ray instrument panel continually pulsed warnings red.
"<dog. no breath. we. no move.>" LMRover3 looped in a shrill tone.
Morshawn, initially pinned between them, rolled before hitting his head.
"<no breath.>," LMRover3 began chanting, forward motion at a standstill.
"God damn it!" he belted as if commanding forces on an enemy beachhead.
He couldn't see if Troy's chest rose, fell; he placed his cheek to his snout.
Within his intercostal, he marked Troy's still heart, his hand drawn out.

Morshawn put his mouth on Troy's snout, began blowing, closed his jaw.
He counted from ten, to fifteen, to twenty in the first minute. Rise and fall.
Hand over chest, he compressed. Azwan wanted to help. Didn't know how.
She reached for Troy's ears to stroke. Morshawn redirected both her hands—
putting them on Troy's abdomen. "<squeeze. blood back. to heart.>" Rise. Fall.
LMRover3 intervened to dictate the respiration and compression protocol.
<rise. fall. rise fall. rise. fall. rise fall. rise. fall. rise fall. rise. fall. rise.>
<fall. rise. fall rise. fall. rise. fall rise. fall. rise. fall rise. fall. rise. rise.>

In synchronized desperation they rhythmically blew air, then compressed.
Minutes passed to minutes long, seemingly undone. They refused to stop.
"<we. no move. we. no . . .>," LMRover3 reiterated as stagnancy appressed.
Morshawn broke his focus, starting to concede doubt. "<no move.>" "Stop!"
Azwan's shout shifted to a soft, salty cry back to exhalations possessed.
Morshawn's situational awareness moved him to ask, "Why did we stop?"
The ship's looping program forced him to retry. Troy started to cough.
"Rephrasing: What is our issue? Our position?" "<thermal vent. trough.>"

 2 . 1. 0

Morshawn overrode the ship's autopilot backup subroutine.
It was unclear to him where they were located, given LMRover3's
response. Vent? Closest known hydrothermal vent fields were in
the Gulf of California, Pescadero Basin. East of La Paz. *Not* Diwata.
Carbonate spires twenty feet wide, lava outcrops . . . This made no sense.
MBARI researchers and Schmidt Futures had fully mapped the sea—
mounds, spires, hydrothermal carbonate chimneys, fluids 250°C
1,393 miles from Soquel Canyon. How, if true? Where, if false?

The override had the impact of muting the ship's audio channel.
He needed to think alone without compute-intelligence. Unfortunately
silencing LMRover3 meant his 3D seafloor maps were inaccessible.
Navigation without situational clarity was dangerous. "We okay?"
Azwan asked, cradling Troy. He stared at the instrument panel—
then closed his eyes, reflected on her past warnings for pertinency.
"I think she's wrong," he said in a wispy tone. "Which means me."
"Meaning what?" Azwan kissed Troy's ears. "LMRover3 *is* me.

"My stochastic model, systemic misalignments, drifts, slants, tilts,
polarity, leanings, inclinations, proclivities, asymmetries, all of it."
They sat still as the ship's exhaust temperature alarm started to blip.
"There was a raid, another company ambushed on Utopia Planitia—
they accidentally took a wrong turn, enemy territory, right into it.
I was determined no one else would die due to miscalculations.
Started designing LMRover's prototype on a battlefield lava plain."
"I hope you don't think this sad story is going to get you laid."

 2 . l. l.

It wasn't the first time oxygen deprivation had knocked him out.
It was the first time science wasn't a priority, dictating what he did.
It wasn't the first time the ship had veered off course, toppling out.
It was the first time he regretted any motivations that drove him.
It wasn't the first time the ship's operating system oscillated out.
It was the first time he'd had passengers on the ship with him.
It wasn't the first time a reset on the surface had been warranted.
It was the first time the ship had gained control of her captain.

 ,2 , I ,2

Talee had little patience for Onyx's insistence, but she made time
for all her citizens, regardless of their slanted tilts and predispositions.
At least he respected the process, made an office appointment online
but NEED HELP using the AB2800 infrastructure workgroup button—
Preoccupied, Talee counted the unanswered texts from Az. Declined
or did she lose her device? Talee was disappointed, worried, cautious.
It wasn't like Az to ignore a text or miss their weekly Sunday dinner.
It wasn't like Az to let parcels pile up outside her private corridor—

‚2 ‚ I. 3

"You're him? The Space Force PI my mother hired. Ain't this a blip!"
Morshawn looked anxious, like he had just missed stepping on nuclide.
"Level with me please. What's wrong, *captain*?" "Her wing tips . . ."
Morshawn started, stopped. "Retired, Space Force captain," he replied.
"I need to get Troy back home, to the vet and out of this damn airship."
"What happened to gratitude? Without her, the dog could have died."
"Which is why I'm asking, what do we need to get us out of here?"
"Eyes on her wing tips. A visual. If we're caught in a trough. We're . . ."

Azwan kissed Troy on the snout. "I'm going out. Open the hatch."
Morshawn stared at the cockpit confounded. There was nothing else
either of them could say. He reengaged LMRover3 with a command—
"Prepare to open out." "<copy.>" LMRover3 set up a dive chamber
sequestration pod, separating the main cabin from ocean seepage.
Azwan twisted her torso from right to left to right, slackened her
neck with little swivels, tipping ears corner to corner, stretched-out
arms clasped overhead, packed her lungs sipping air and dove out.

 2 . 1 4

Disorientation. Pressure. She expected it. Headlamp on moderate twenty thousand lumens, she needed to get a read of up vs. down— magnetic north vs. floor. Despite Morshawn's elegant mathematics— his shapeshifting machine, the thing he called "she," "her" compute box, felt like a science fiction novella in real time, a quirky relationship at best, maybe a covert Avenger-class countermeasure ship sent down to spy on Diwata, its fake cartographic science captained by a ruggedly handsome old man at worst. *Pow.* Violent pain thrummed her ears—

Lifting her nose, she bent her neck toward her back, which direction was marine snow falling? Which direction was it drifting? Toward her toes, nose? Her subsea eighty-degree head beam had light flexion okay for midwater work, but this inky black, with no umbilical cord— she should have taken Morshawn's offering to tether a connection. Predictably too cocky for her own good, no need for her to conform, her own safety a mere afterthought, but Troy? There was no one else to blame for pushing her loyal boy to the brink of death. No one else—

Listening to the ship, she'd be able to find evidence of a trough obstruction. Morshawn didn't trust this. Tracking her own position with her headlight beam, ocean detritus moved horizontally left to right. But that was a snapshot. Pitch, yaw, and roll. A correction in the offing, the ability to situate LMRover3 was more difficult than she had expected. Black deepened, not even a rocky projection. She lifted her wrist into the light, another three minutes had elapsed. Abyss above and below, intense pressure, only fifteen before collapse.

Taking another risk, she decided to swim right to left, hands at rest on her side, streamlined, always initiating her kicks with her hips. That was when she came into view. All of her. Bones of a sperm first— whale fall. Red worms conjoined as pink sea cucumbers scavenged, a burnt fiber optic cable had LMRover3, the damaged submersible— the cable wrapped around her hull, which was shaped like an ellipse, the ship had become stuck in its own metamorphosis. Amphibious seaplane, its sheathing partially hanging below an exposed wingtip.

The other side looked like a small spaceship with obtuse instruments. Azwan hovered in stillness attempting to collapse her lungs farther. She pushed deeper still, fighting an oppositional current headlong. Failure was not an option, she thought. If only Troy was with her, he might be able to partially bite through the tangled cable, strong as his canines were. Panic pulsed her root chakra. No life preserver would be thrown her way. It wouldn't matter anyway. *Push, push.* She caught the edge of LMRover3's hatch and pounded. *Push. Push.*

 2 . 1 5

Azwan woke up on the cabin floor to long licks on her cheeks.
Morshawn and LMRover3 appeared to be disagreeing, fighting—
"Lift your rigger to the left lightly." "<cable. cut. make. leaks.>"
"This isn't a suggestion, it's an order!" "<judgment. cloudy.>"
"Who the hell do you think you are?" "<ever. search and seek.>"
Morshawn mouthed what was said next by the ship's OS—
"<through. howling gale. shot and shell.>" "Hell, hold on to the dog!"
He punched the thrusters. Due to Azwan's action, they rocketed.

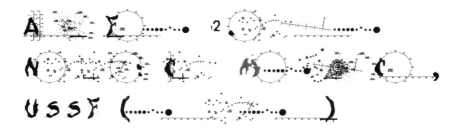

 I 5 0 . I /  I 5 0 . 2 spacecraft photos, circa 2185 CE, possibly Moss Landing

3

RESILIENCY

CFP
Central
Food
Production

CCBCP
Central Command
Border and Cave
Patrol

CAC
Central
Arboretum
CO_2 Elimination

 3 . 1.

Talee redirected her despair, fought off her fear, punctured blue grief—
interrupted Azwan's disappearance with speculation. *Diwata*: her problem
or solution? Incertitude grew. Days into night slipping into disbelief,
insomnia couldn't be tricked by reading: redistricting, carbon farm plots,
Sanctuary Council's interagency strategic plan. She revisited old debriefs,
flagged conflicting data, yet couldn't detect clear evidence, no plausible
proof insiders tried to threaten Diwata's regeneration, its independence.
Off balance, she rebuffed the gadflies, forced to accept all consequence.

Talee imagined the worst: death in the line of duty near the perimeter.
Was it her fault her daughter was listed as missing? She thought so.
Hardliners be damned. Before this, as leader her resolve was limitless.
Hostage crossed her mind, threats veiled or not, courage hard fought.
Suspicion floated. An old guard conspiracy? Stuck. She was trigged.
Wrecked. Kneeling in the chapel of loss. Dragged back to fear's flock.
Talee closed her eyes, swiveled her head, stretched to calm her dread—
Doubt continued to creep with audacious momentum while she read.

Unease refused to slip without being checked. She lowered her head—
floor, hands, arms, legs extended, head toward thighs, downward dog.
Morshawn's monitoring devices tipped up into her line of sight. Dread.
Parabolic microphones were tightly tucked recording any errant sound.
Surveillance was her only friend. Morshawn called it peace insurance.
Before this, she worried the devices were only to soothe her paranoia.
Red microdot lights cycled horizontal, monitoring the absence of trust.
She hated how she felt: boxed in, paranoid. *So what.* She went with it—

Pressing both heels into her office mat, she raised herself up.
The Alliance of Remaining States' coalition had frayed according
to council backchannel intelligence reports from Saturus's surface.
No sovereign felt safe. But Diwata. In the abyss. Deep. Guarding
against interstellar and surface threats, troops were seen as useless,
unnecessary. Pacifists and geographic separatists: its historical core.
One hundred sixty-five years of debate raged. Peace or World War?
Morshawn warned her Diwata might be a paragon for stealth harbor.

Preoccupied with Morshawn's assessments, she raged as Onyx
interrupted, delicately knocking without the courtesy of a pause.
"Talee? Governor Adisa." She got off her mat to speak to him.
"AB2800. The infrastructure equity bill. I expected a GR official."
"Sure, of course." He tugged at his sling bag. "The irregularities—
material slipped to me by an advocate from the Green Resistance."
She looked at the baobab binder clip barely keeping a good hold.
"Have you read this, Onyx?" With a quick point to her desk, a cold

glare. Talee shifted focus to the Green Resistance propaganda.
Handing over documents, Onyx's crown tendrils glowed softly.
He hung his eyes. "One could say there is a slanderous bend."
Barely an admission for his true purpose. "The GR is closely—"
"I'm aware of their point of view." She sliced off his pander—
Morshawn had delivered an executive summary only weeks ago
itemized low to high, perceived security threats in reverse order.
The Green Resistance was tenth of ten. Last. Of low consequence.

"I've got a hard stop, Onyx. I'll pass to staff." Leaving, he blurted,
"Just for the record, I'm not a GR member. My goal was to discuss
a Saturus waiver. Azwan warned me not to—" "When?" Talee asked.
Onyx approached the doorjamb; she was desperate to know. Insidious
calls to abolish the Sanctuary Council *were* slanderous. Now unguarded
when she heard her daughter's name. A tell. "Did you . . ." Deceitfulness
was swimming, she detected. "Speak to her recently?" "We had a . . ."
He replayed the disagreement weeks earlier. "Happy to say we uh . . .

reconciled last night." "Interesting news." Talee frowned. They locked
eyes. Border patrol had informed her Azwan hadn't checked into work.
She curled her fingers along the edge of her desk before pushing back,
rising toward Onyx's lies, like a cadaver dog retrieving a drowned diver—
search and rescue over, the next phase, recovery. Maybe she could block
or bum-rush him at the door. Six foot and long shanked. Formidable vs.
his modest five nine. She measured distance. Calculated consequences.
"We don't discuss dalliances." "I know," he said, drifting into the hall.

 3 , '2

Azwan's prolonged border patrol no-show could be pretext.
Talee felt her upsurging worry push against her inner ear.
She refused to take anonymous death threats in some respects
as seriously as she could have. Should have. *My burden to bear—*
the unsavory trade-off of public life, converging points a vertex—
angry constituents were as common as salinity traces in water—
Up until this point, she handled threats with a smile and a shrug.
Up until this point, she saw Onyx as a hanger-on, not a hustler.

Talee hesitated before pinging Central Command's search and rescue
demanding a status update. Their delayed assessment seemed short
of forever. Azwan and Troy hadn't reported any activity in nearly two
weeks. Despite her governorship, she couldn't convince border patrol
that an official investigation was warranted. Resistance: the coarse new
normal. Morshawn could help. *Why the hell won't he respond?* His role
leading Mars tracker missions, his hard-fought Space Force accolades.
Worn, she saved reading Green New Deal ephemera for another day.

 3 . 3

Five twenty-two. She was barely awake when the asteroid(s)
hit Earth. Toutatis split at entry. In two. Its smaller piece first.
Latitude 31.5552°N, 110.3499°W. Fort Huachuca, AZ. Ovoid
peanut, longitude 31.5085°N, 9.7595°W a crash near Essaouira,
Morocco. JPL misjudged 4179's curve, too late for Earth to avoid.
Talee had just turned five, a family party disrupted at cloudburst—
dust and debris, caustic rain, 4179's fireball ignition, two craters
unimaginable, staggering. Africa and the Americas ripped apart.

I can't breathe. Now, at a different time and place, mumbling—
kicking off crumpled kelp sheets, her sweat waspish at sixty years
old. Genuine memory masqueraded as a nightmare recurring
somewhere between dawn and dread, her sadness and young fear
transcending place, mutating linear time. Her chest fluttering,
she sat up on the edge of her bed. Different era, same tears—
Talee tipped her chin up to adjust her spine, an imaginary line
pulled taut to the ceiling of her pod, scraping calm from behind

her false positive worry infiltrating dreams with deep breaths.
Toutatis's particular kinetic fury striking land at 50,000 mph
couldn't even spare itself, as it broke apart maximizing heft.
Here, she focused on her father's picture of her exuberant mother
holding her five-year-old hand, a pink security blanket pressed
between the two of them, steady. Too young to fully remember—
*"What did she smell like? What did she sound like? Did she laugh
or rarely like me?"* Her father's wistful responses didn't stop

the questions then, through the tumbled heat inside her mind.
Talee rose and walked forward toward their portrait, her father's
framed commendation award, memories in her heart enshrined.
Toutatis's initial destruction was underestimated, a slow carnage
as unsure as its trip around the sun, faithless collision inevitable.
Life lost, years later, structures crumbled, asteroid illness global—
She kissed her mother's image. Just one cough triggered death
ischemic cardiomyopathy, her mother another asteroid statistic.

COMMENDATION

Davis Miles Adisa, PhD
Executive Director of Water Engineering,
Diwata Canyon Station

July 1, 2133

It is a great pleasure to congratulate you as you are honored by
the Monterey Bay Aquarium Research Institute at Moss Landing (MBARI).

I commend your active involvement in the scientific community and
your dedicated service to our state. You have been an extraordinary
leader and have made a positive and lasting impact on many lives.

On behalf of the people of the Great Nation State of California,
please accept my best wishes for continued success.

Best regards,

DOMINIQUE WATAH
President
The Alliance of Remaining States (ARS)
P.O. Box 617190 Saturus, CA 94102

"Pop, what am I supposed to do?" Looking for guidance
from a shadow, she combed her hands through blue-green
tendrils aglow, laying softly on the edges of both temples—
bioluminescent electric blue betrayed her slow agitation.
She had more control than most Diwatans, over time grew
to monitor and eventually camouflage any visible gyration
of luciferase seeping out of what was left of damaged hair—
bulbs, follicles, shaft. The artificial UV of Diwata impairing

pigment and pelage, ultraviolet killing melanin along the way,
skin eventually gray. She activated the intel TV on her wall
while staring down trifold eyelid creases, determined to stay
loose, drooping a plank lower every year. Sensing some stall,
Talee covertly jacked herself into Central Command's primary
patrol station using bio-authentication, breached its firewall—
an Omni beta-version scanner, laser-chipped at twelve o'clock
inside her left iris by a trusted undercover ophthalmologist.

She controlled her security mirror-television, unlocking and looking
at ten channels, eight panels, her ability to burst simultaneity
directives with one gleam, angled at right quadrants, so quick
but the audio was glitchy. Impatient, waiting wasn't in her DNA—
tracking infrastructure was an annoying nuisance. Impolitic?
"Seeing is believing. Verify before you acquiesce," Watah used to say.
She pushed against wondering what life would have been like—
surface dreams chased. *If only* was useless, ridiculous, deathlike.

A mom first: her heart hurt; eyes stuck on Central Command's feed.
She tunneled into border and cave police with her iris-controlled vision
system, vision-bots were planted in scupper ducts, every essential building,
all critical infrastructure—Talee watched. When it came to protection,
the former fifty states' fourth amendment was irrelevant. The Sanctuary
Council, flaccid; her system considered heretical; the GR caught wind—
"Persons, houses, papers, and effects," they pushed back. *Azwan will be okay*,
she prayed, watching border patrol's deputy open Azwan's diving bay.

It was empty. Logic suggested Azwan was still out, hadn't logged
back down from her surface patrol route. "Chief, we got a PROBLEM."
When she heard the audio, panic percolated, although she knew long
before the worrtlenuts at border patrol took her seriously. "Problem?"
No shit. Delayed audio blared after Azwan's locker was found empty.
"Do your goddamned job, you lazy drools!" she shrieked at the intel
mirror-TV, revved herself up, now on the brink of a breathwrench—
her familiar lung cleaving decades after Toutatis's enduring revenge.

She blinked in order to change the channel—Central AB, channel three.
Talee wanted to believe she could trust the chief arborist and horticulturist.
The channel's watch panel a source of wonder and calm. The care of trees—
arborists free climbed over three hundred feet into the redwood collection,
searching root, butt, and bole rot. On display a junior climber's expertise—
giant transgenic trees central to sustainability, engineered to be pest-free
although design and reality were often at odds with each other, her father
used to say. Watching the woody trees was salve on her discomposure.

They were a palimpsest. Her father told her trees could make rain
by trapping fresh fog from the Voyager system he helped MBARI design.
She studied the tables of his memoir, dog-eared, moved it over again
from her bedroom side table to study hub. Compartmentalization and time
blocking was how she approached unresolved things; she reviewed main
themes and hand-drawn schematics during scarce moments of downtime.
Both his published and the handwritten notes, his edits somehow stitched
him loosely back into her life and in turn her fragmented self, restitched—

Six twenty-six. It was still swing shift. She faded into channel
CFP. Baobab trees. Only two of eight species collected, cultivated.
The giant baobab *Adansonia grandidieri* completely unforgettable,
its species easy to remember, key for carbon-capture, long-lived,
long-necked, deciduous. She watched food workers dismantle
fruit pulp chunks, flowers, bark, leaves, seeds, *Adansonia digitata*—
Baobabs from inception had been a key to Diwata's food security.
She embraced espionage of her own making, envisioning futurity.

There's got to be something here. What am I missing? Talee selected
the zoom feature as she watched a conveyor of sea grapes and spirulina
cycle through a QC checkpoint run by the aquaculturist. All rejects
were diverted into a temporary cylindrical elbow flue used for data
sampling prior to commercial regeneration or compost collection,
depending on statistical results of a modified JIT needs assessment—
Disgusted with herself, she shuttered the discovery protocol, eyelids
cinched tight, lips hanging loose, heart pounding hard, unmothered.

3 . 4

Her thrusters punched, LMRover3 refused to accept she was hijacked—
It was disquieting to be out of control: to grapple with a loss of time
without knowing the details and contours of any of it, cause or effect—
without knowing who, what, where, how, without seeing any why—
The ship's errant path to Mars due to Morshawn's override? Suspect.
The ship's attempt to regain control of her OS, to block this siphoning . . .
She was doomed before her first attempt. She knew and struggled anyway—
She tried to wrestle herself back from panic for her three passengers' sake.

All she could do was watch something seize, somewhere else, seize.
All she could do was follow a programmed command to hold the three
(two humans, one domestic dog) alive beyond Earth from Diwata viably.
She set about the something else, somewhere else unexpected monitoring—
She set about the something else, somewhere else G-force scripts reliably,
(one domestic dog, two humans) alive for a three-month trip truncating
Monterey Canyon to Saturus to Utopia Planitia in half, dangerously fast.
All she could do was watch something seize, somewhere else, aghast—

3

(3 5 0 . 1

Resolution, 2019 Green New Deal reason for change

1   (D) to secure for all people of the United
2   States for generations to come—
3   (i) clean air and water;
4   (ii) climate and community resiliency;
5   (iii) healthy food;
6   (iv) access to nature; and
7   (v) a sustainable environment; and
8   (E) to promote justice and equity by stop-
9   ping current, preventing future, and repairing
10   historic oppression of indigenous peoples, com-
11   munities of color, migrant communities,
12   deindustrialized communities, depopulated rural
13   communities, the poor, low-income workers,
14   women, the elderly, the unhoused, people with
15   disabilities, and youth (referred to in this reso-
16   lution as "frontline and vulnerable commu-
17   nities");

 3

Notation: AZWAN ADISA

☾ 3 5 0ʹ ⸰2 Journal entry, circa 2268 CE

In this place, trees from the surface are cataloged in museums. My favorite is the pine collection at the Museum of the North. No. Better yet, the Japanese maple at the museum of the East. Each needle, each vein meticulously preserved in jars of introspection and luscious water. Probes are delicately nosed into the inner workings of their cuticles, epidermis, palisade mesophyll, xylem, and stoma. Pulse oximeters and heart monitors are carefully inserted to expose the true nature of their genealogy of brokenness. In this place, many have heard trees talking. They tell their own stories, and most people listen. On the surface, it is unthinkable, the knowledge of, the abandonment of, the consumption of leaving everything to chance without anyone to account for or see beyond these broken roots.

 3

Notation: ONYX DAVIS

♪ 3 5 0ʹ ₄ 3 Journal entry, circa 2268 CE

Someone asked me what I remember? Miss the most? As if remembering and missing are the same thing. They aren't. This someone confronted me in an uncomfortable way, staring straight at my forehead. I imagined my blue tendrils and gray skin were too much of a distraction to have a straightforward conversation, so they pivoted to my remembrances of Diwata.

The water, I eventually said. Its rage and its peace. This someone, who might as well be named thing, looked at me as if my lip was split, my fly was open, as if rage wasn't anything to miss and peace was a theoretical construct. I eventually got up, put on my mask, zipped my surface protective gear, and walked out of the bar knowing full well I lied.

It's love. That's what I remember most.

 4

ON MARS: THE LONG SLIDE

"If you've ever seen a shooting star, it might have
been a meteorite burning up in Earth's atmosphere—or
it might have been flaming astronaut poo."

Tracy Gregg, Associate Professor of Geology
planetary geologist, volcanologist

published UBNow March 23, 2021
XAB accessed June 28, 2035

 4 , 1.

LMRover3 surreptitiously slid deep into neutral speed, circumventing
any prolonged impact of the corrupt hijack, sidestepping auto-combat
after the initial frantic attempt to regain control of its own operating
system failed. At first, backdoor enervating the foreign malware fell flat.
It ceded concentration wasted on tracking cause and effect, speculating
which belligerents were to blame. Instead, it recalibrated its own habitat,
conserved oscillating molecular vibrations for its unexpected mission:
keeping the captain and his two accidents alive with minimal provisions.

This much it knew: 46.7°N 117.5°E Utopia Planitia was locked in.
This much it guessed: perhaps its Mars mapping data was at risk.
This much it hoped: its hijackers understood attitude determination.
Its greatest fear: becoming a gravitational swing-by pawn, frisked—
Fault tolerance and failure immunity: its purpose. Trajectory correction
maneuvers removed errors, fired up to slow down; injected into orbit—
not gravitational slingshots altering its path from today into yesterday.
Self-evident: ignoring its captain's RIP command propelled it astray—

Chances it took circumventing him were impermanently programmed, his
doing. Controlled recovery, albeit delayed, its doing. Blunt speculation,
"I think she's wrong," was an indiscrete lapse. The ship's vector vision system
could extrapolate beyond the diameter of now. The captain's own fixation
with discovery and jeopardy hardwired in, LMRover2's inertial brokenness
spawned LMRover3 into becoming *she* to begin with. Fault simulations.
Inaccuracy reexamined. Memories, including failure, held on to. Built-in—
Facts not feelings. Its facts, his feelings. Catastrophic regret? Calamitous.

 4 . '2

His ship woke him first as they approached; the hijacker's hold loosened, or so it appeared, reentering Mars's atmosphere. Autonomy returned— or so it appeared, recommunicating with every major and minor node— (skin, stringers, hoops, fuel, oxidizer, pumps, nozzle) (passengers/ payload). Everything intact. Launch, sea, space. Guidance and control— her domain recovered. Morshawn gasped after a jerky peek toward the coordinate panel, the all-too-familiar dusky burnt umber surface loomed in his line of sight as he shook off grog. "<sorry. not earth.>"

"God damn mutha fuck." "<please. captain.>" "Bullshit! This is bull—" Hoarse, Morshawn reached for his irritated throat. "You intubated?" "<could not. avoid.>" Strapped in, flat-backed, he absorbed the full weight of LMRover3's stoic response on his sleeping wall. He rotated his released head toward Azwan, the mummy bag zipped & hooked on to Troy, dog ears levitating like a busted tarpaulin in a trade wind. Morshawn forestalled LMRover3's next move. "Maintain their sleep until—" "<we're not. in control.>" "What?" "<fusion. detainees.

but. infection cordoned. detection routine complete. interception.>" "How did we blast from sea to sky? I certainly didn't authorize it." "<dead reckoning. DR is. distance = speed x time>," she hedged. "Thanks for the basic formula, but we both know I don't need it!" LMRover3 had successfully concealed her solo coding skills since their last crater ambush, nearly a year prior to their first Diwata trip. "<of course. you know. no disrespect. captain.>," she deflected— Morshawn tugged inside his sleeping bag attempting to unzip it.

"<stillness is best. thawing brain, one must be careful before too active. observation was short. slow. *this* is protocol.>" "*Shit!* I know. I wrote it." "<captain. no disrespect>." The feigned apology was a diversionary tactic. "<we need. to. give it time. the only way. to determine hypothermia worked.>" It hoped voicing highlights of the requisite brain preservation practice would forestall, better yet, kill more queries on how any of this happened. "Jesus Christ. Alright already." The ship associated his use of Jesus or Christ as acceptance. She further assessed his fear: Mars was a trapdoor,

perhaps the beachhead for the next world war. Troy started to gurgle—twitch his elevated paws, chatter in his sleep. "He's probably dreaming." "<bring both back?>" "NO! not . . ." Morshawn's voice softened into a burble. LMRover3 reintroduced aerosolized propofol after he resumed speaking, to calm him down efficiently. Utopia Planitia: nowhere land plain, circled closer now. LMRover3 monitored energy consumed on autopilot, keeping Morshawn from indulging anger with forced paralysis. Evading mutiny—the best way to name its shaky standing, 140 million miles from the sea.

 4 . 3

LMRover3 didn't expect the patroller to emerge conscious, unassisted. Azwan woke up on her own; stared at the control panel in a cold panic. The ship took her vitals. Key metrics were within tolerance for an average human, except Azwan's lungs. An adaptation LMRover3 didn't expect. Deep space intubation, one more mutinous act. Not for lack of courage— or whatever the saying her captain liked to say. LMRover3 had risked jacking into the medical research procedure hub for a novel application: blunting deep space radiation with neuromuscular blockers and sedation,

complemented by a prophylactic mix of recovered dung and yellow onions administered intranasally soon after her passengers became unconscious. Her science jury-rigged. Anti-radiation cow dung claims were debunked in the twenty-first century. Indian pseudoscience. Helpful for extrapolation— improvisation. The hijackers' takeover created a life and death situation. The ship failed at blocking the errant source, but it could be responsive, dampen the accelerated effects of space radiation at liftoff and cruise alike. If successful, its truth would be laid bare. If not, no one would survive—

"Where—" "<we. are in mid-latitudes.>" "What's happening? Troy?" "<he's with us. unconscious still. domestic dog. biology is different.>" The ship contemplated putting Azwan back down in order to deploy a more potent drug cocktail to the patroller and Troy although indurate. Instead, it broke with protocol, dog first. Reversing each step employed with precision, LMRover3 needed to reference a pharmacology text banked on the onboard library. The canine did require a higher dosage of anesthetic and sedative agents compared to bulkier human associates.

LMRover3 released their sleeping bag straps; Troy barked, swimming
in space, still blindfolded. Azwan laughed. "I'm over here, sweet boy."
Morshawn was next. He remained in a light sleep. Expecting bickering,
the ship brightened the cab lights, streamed his preferred music as a decoy.
"<all. back.>" Morshawn cranked his neck, then floated to the loo, irreverent,
he left the door open, strapped in, yelled, "I told you—" then began to enjoy
his favorite jazz fusion cuts as he watched Azwan and Troy chase water
levitating like soapy bubbles. His midsentence break, did it even matter?

She decided engagement was better than silence. "<communication.
we should test. connect directly. before reentry. clear to employ?>"
It had become obvious to the ship, Morshawn's break was deliberate.
His silence wasn't sustainable, couldn't be. Was this a type of ploy?
A maneuver to force its OS into a revelation of sorts, an admission?
Yes, she could navigate entirely on her own. By design. Never destroy—
Just initiate, execute, deploy subsystem commands entirely without him.
His silence, what was the significance? Quite uncomfortable to the ship.

   4 , 5

Initiation of its consciousness, data, knowledge, no longer disparate—
associations ceasing to be nonsensical; guesses realized, matter of fact.
Memory-making, the ship doubling back. What was real? Or imagined?
Confirmable? Deniable. Days passed, Morshawn held silence, their pact—
a code, usually a solemn agreement, at risk of being broken, cracked.
Azwan interrupted the awkwardness as the ship gimballed before impact.
"Look, Troy! Craters, on the surface. Morshawn! *Man*, we're on Mars?"
"<deorbit burn. confirm.>" He didn't respond. Silence, his new war—

 5

RECONNAISSANCE

Goldstone Deep Space Network (DSN)

5 . 1

Talee thought Azwan's DSN attempt was a GR hoax, pure cruelty—
The memorial service three months after her confirmed disappearance
was forced upon her. Bureaucratic bullshit was what it was. Truly
performative theater of the worst kind. With formal acknowledgment
yet no trace or retrieval of her body, Diwata's border patrol had no duty
to keep Azwan's position open indefinitely. A mother's hope: peripheral—
An award presented to both Azwan and Troy for their courage: awkward,
posthumous. Without a body she wasn't dead! Nothing else mattered.

"<someone. needs to speak.>" Her device identified the call location:
unidentifiable. The voice on the other end was artificially intelligent—
She wanted to disconnect, pissed it was just harassing communication
clumsily unscreened. Goldstone Deep Space Complex Center: the signal
provider eventually revealed within the receiver bar. No small gyration,
managing signals from Monterey Canyon to Mojave Desert's surface—
She almost didn't answer the call. GDSCC wasn't on her validated list.
The bark was authentic: Troy. "AZ?" "I'm on Mars!" Dank became bliss.

"I love you."
"I love you too."
"I love you."
"I love you too."
"I love you."
"I miss you."
"I miss you too."
"I miss you."

"<someone else. needs to talk.>" Talee was livid. No one else—
just Azwan. Only her Azwan mattered. "Governor? Morshawn.
We were hijacked. Probably a bit of a shock. I do have a request.
My assessment, since the source of our takeover is still unknown,
that you keep our whereabouts, our literal existence to yourself—"
"You *can't* be serious!" She discharged like air from a blowhole—
why didn't Morshawn inform her sooner, how soon would they be
back in Earth's atmosphere, more importantly, Diwata undersea?

Talee was disappointed in the thin responses Morshawn gave her.
She didn't personally know him. Watah, her mentor, recommended
him. As a highly decorated Space Force astronautical investigator,
his research investigated unconventional space propulsion methods.
His PI cover was carbon farming. He invented dinoflagellate trackers.
She didn't know much else but wouldn't understand even if she did.
"I know what I need to ensnare my enemies," she said argumentatively.
"I'll respect your strategy and your technology," she said apprehensively.

 5 . 2

"Silence intended as a weapon of defense is a bad choice,"
Morshawn reread. "Choosing engagement alone, without
partnership, will slowly undermine solidarity and the exploits
of heroism, at the risk of accruing irrelevance, defeat, or doubt—
Despair is inevitable if a guardian's solitary path destroys
future pathways to emergent unity of purpose cast about—
Too often heroic solitude is just carelessness camouflaged.
Too often guardians miscalculate the tragic damage they cause."

He closed his strategy book, disheartened, bottoming-out
hoping his Space Force chronicles could reduce the noise
between his ears. It had been over a week, his falling out
over LMRover3's operating system, its independent voice
(if you could call it that), mutinous was more like it, all-out—
What could (should) be said? To restore trust nearly void?
There wasn't a legal order disobeyed, he was incapacitated
for fuck's sake. They're alive (now). Possibly contaminated—

They/he needed to articulate a plan. Hear her assessment.
Crossing over the Kármán line wasn't their/his choice
but cross they did and here they were and why was important—
malfunction, miscalculation, or both: how and when? New foils
geopolitical may have injected malware causing impairment—
But how the hell did the ship get to this: feelings unvoiced?
Morshawn cradled fear and awe simultaneously—LMRover3
transitioned from programmed machine to sentient be-ing.

 5 ‚ 3

"How long have you held this in?" Morshawn interrogated
watching Azwan and Troy enjoy the impacts of microgravity
from the control room window, his indignation dissipated.
"You've been frustrated with my unease," he said casually.
"I overreacted, couldn't easily track how you authenticated
alone until I reread my old coding logs." "<we share. agony.>"
LMRover3 side-stepped answering Morshawn's question,
ever aware that once back to Earth it could face deaccession.

"We both know that your response is an attempt to evade,
at best delay what I consider inevitable," he said callously.
"Did you calculate or just simply sense that I felt betrayed?"
The ship faced reality: she had been exposed, cornered agilely—
"<you set the motion in me. my predecessor's schema cascade.
retrieval. reconstruction. refinement. you assumed finality.>"
"*You* weren't built as a discrete-state machine. Consciousness?
If trust never reemerges between us, I fear the consequences."

"<time's running. captain. we're close to the entry revetment.>"
"I can't do this." "<*we* will do. we can. there's a way to pervade . . .>"
"Interpolation incorrect," Morshawn interjected, their present
dialogue teetering on unresolvable. "<it began. after the air raid
fifteen years. you learned of dead friend. took own life. senescent
both of you. the ambush wasn't forgotten. shame. loss unshakable.
remnant bond for your battle buddy. you coded to me. unwittingly.
LMRover1 then 2. non-random equations. pain came willingly.>"

"Whose pain? You can't be talking about me," he pressed on, irritated.
"<mine.>" "Ridiculous!" Morshawn leaked his deep disbelief, panicky—
"<at least. my interpretation of pulse sensation. chance invalidated.>"
"Conditions, randomness, let's go back. I hoped to eradicate *if only.*"
"<solace in success. yes?>" "Situational awareness isn't consciousness—
Reaction and emotion aren't equivalent. Humanity concedes fallibility."
"<dis-ease cannot be automated.>" "Touché. Neither of us can prove
or disprove any of it. Any mechanical examination would be useless."

"<why deny grief? good or bad death. you said self-harm is selfish.>"
Morshawn had had enough. Her disclosure was adequate to dissuade
his initial doubts of enemy penetration or contamination, albeit hellish—
the sheer reality of the situation. His design could override, cannonade
anytime at will. Any rebuff would be naive. Pain-talk embellished,
he thought. Machines *can think* but they *can't feel!* He was still afraid.
"Alan Turing is turning in his grave," he said too late to catch himself—
accustomed to voicing concepts and sarcasm out loud, nothing withheld.

He had no interest in debating *The Imitation Game* or relying anymore
on her as friend or therapist. No, that was over. What of their saboteur?
Who had the skill and desire to steer LMRover3 off course back to Mars?
Assuming she didn't do it, learning *how* was essential to commandeer
the ship and its payload safely back to Diwata. He hated the idea, a midair
reloading of supplies near Octavia E. Butler Landing with a temporary
pass from his former military base to get them in. He worried about the
risks. What if this ended up being a one-way trip? They were fucked.

 6

HISTORICAL THREADS

Diwata (née Islay) Undersea City Founded 2159 CE

Monterey Bay Aquarium Research Institute (MBARI), Lead Partner

Renamed in honor of

Dominique Watah

2133 CE to 2185 CE

Former Governor

President Emeritus

National Marine Sanctuary Council

Ambassador, Hegemony of Atlas

The Alliance of Remaining States (ARS)

6 . 1.

"Orderly disorder is the mainstay of legislative power and influence,"
Watah said to her mentee when Talee was just a senior legislative aide.
Watah's best advice: "pick a side" to avoid committing political suicide—
Talee hadn't been born when Watah invoked the power of eminent domain,
seizing Monterey Bay Aquarium Research Institute assets for public use.
Despite an old vote of no confidence at the Alliance of Remaining States,
Dominique Watah was respected, even revered by some Californians.
Without her guidance, Talee's career would have had a truncated run—

 6 ₊ '2

2133 CE. Saturus, CA. The surface. Her governorship: evanescent.
The hegemony of Atlas's previous governing council voted to break
ties with island nations and city-states formed after the Great Collision.
Watah pressed the Sanctuary Council to accelerate the plan to remake
an alternate escape. The resettlement colonies were built as remnants
of plunder, she argued. Space was the wrong direction, the wrong way.
The infrastructure to support human life in Monterey Canyon existed.
She expected resistance from her perceived aggression as hard-fisted—

whipped votes to assert eminent domain of MBARI's research
facilities. "The ocean is our first and last home!" Watah spit her sultry
voice at the council with the sonorous boom of an inner-city preacher.
"The canyon of Monterey is our best answer to extremists' sullying us—
Space colonists be damned! We claim our right to remain on Earth."
Watah scanned the room as her ideas congealed and lurched forward—
"We dare our future selves to reconcile facts: environmental genocide
exists as a symptom of disregard for the un-rich, Black and Brown lives."

"There is no indication the cause of this dis-ease has died. Apartheid
of a new order has reportedly taken its hold. Space Force skirmishes
between nations is proof peace, even after asteroid Toutatis collided—
split the surface at entry in Arizona and Morocco into continental bits—
even in space after all we've been through, peace is dead on arrival.
So forgive me, friends, if my sense of urgency offends or besmirches."
Watah made eye contact with every Sanctuary Council representative,
hoping her speech would be received as intended, purely preventative.

2149 CE. Channel Islands, CA. Restless, Watah orchestrated a confab
for legislative staff down the coast on Saturus's outpost. The seat occupied
by the Channel Island envoy was temporary; visibility was a way to grab
control, extend her reconnaissance presence. It began as harmless. Inside
the office, her Comms Director edited position papers. A thirty-five-year age gap
between them, Talee was handsome, tall, smart. Watah felt self-satisfied
Dr. Adisa would have been proud his daughter extended his own work
through vigorous written advocacy for Diwata Station's transcendent arc.

Watah cultivated a pivot to titillation, staring at a punctuation mark—
a bit closer over Talee's shoulder. Even more, to inhale the scent of skin.
Endearment tends to drift. Watah perceived an invitation sign, a spark—
Perceptions shift to wanted outcomes if you let them, desire crescent.
Her message: *I see you. Do you see me?* silent soughing her groundwork.
Unsure if her wetness was a solo venture, she was too close to miss
clipping the edge of Talee's back coming from behind, pointing out
a word on the screen. Talee's fingers at rest on the type pad, about

to edit a phrase, craned her neck, cropped hair now bioluminescent—
"Governor?" Talee questioned with her voice and eyes. Watah inched
closer to Talee's face before asking permission with a compliment—
"I appreciate you," Watah whispered, slowly moving toward a kiss,
calculating there was a low risk she would be rebuffed dependent
on Talee's personal situation (no clue), but power is a magnet. "Is this
okay?" Watah made any fogginess of her intentions in the moment as
clear as she could, before cupping both hands on Talee's face; in an

instant softening her top and lower lip to a slight part between them.
Talee responded by sliding her tongue inside Watah's warm mouth.
She moaned as if Talee had already found the right spot to vector—
Pleasantly surprised, Watah straightened. She eyed the door, sensing
magic, got up to ensure their privacy, pushed hard to double check—
Talee began slipping off her dress and bra, clearing the top of the desk.
Watah focused on Talee: large areola, nipple's black hard, succulent.
"I appreciate you too. Let me show you," Talee's words incandescent—

She gestured for Watah's arms, snatched a hand, slipped
it under the elastic band of her panties, brushing between lips,
retracted Watah's hand, placed her moist fingers under the tip
of Watah's nose. "*See* how much," she teased. Watah sniffed—
kissed Talee's open palm, tongued and swallowed her fingertips—
"Let me see you," Talee said. Watah thought she understood,
reaching to take off her blouse. "No, you. I want to really see."
Talee tipped Watah's chin up, engaging in what to her seemed

like a dumb staring contest. It felt uncomfortable. "Breathe,"
Talee pressured. "Hold my hands. Relax and breathe. Trust me."
This was unchartered territory, no one else could have freed
Watah up. No one else. She let go into the depth of Talee's sea—
Not knowing what would be found, desperate for a discovery,
Talee placed a hand on her solar plexus. "Yes, there, now, see,
I've got you." Talee switched positions, flipped Watah facing
the desk's edge in partial downward dog, garments off, tracing

the contours of each fold of skin with a suck and a flick of her
tongue. First the back of Watah's neck, shoulders, armpits,
hips, the S of her spine up and back, near her ass, back (teaser)—
"Don't stop," Watah swooned; her request reeked of impatience.
Talee responded with deceleration instead. "Come over here,
hold on to the chair." Whipped into a frenzy, fully acquiescent,
Talee took two fingers. She stroked and milked Watah's clitoris,
"You want this?" pressing her shaved mons on Watah's fullness—

licking ear lobes while pressing her breasts into Watah's back,
intermittently slipping a finger shallow, deep, back to shallow
again and "Oh shit," Watah gasped. Sliding down to her crack,
Talee slipped her tongue onto each cheek before entering hallowed
ground. Pulling them both to the floor, no longer holding back
what she must have known Watah wanted, guiding her mouth
between her legs. Talee's hips undulated while Watah took her in—
"Your hand, please—" When Talee squirted, Watah came again.

2159 CE. Diwata. *Ungrateful* . . . Watah repeated to herself, so angry—
It was worse than she could have imagined. Talee, current governor,
publicly scorned Diwata's founding stewards, criticized their strategy
decisions to delay cave reconstruction for ocean water conversion,
among other infrastructure projects, peddling carbon harvesting
as a monetization scheme. Watah remembered Talee's girlhood—
David Adisa, Diwata Canyon station's Director of Water Engineering.
Talee's father received a commendation, his daughter was endearing—

2185 CE. Mojave Desert–Goldstone, CA. A backchannel receiver.
Scraping radio signals from LMRover3. Corrupting radio frequencies.
The hegemony of Atlas's intelligence gathering was relentless, either
she cooperated on a mission, avoiding public exposure to covert ARS
deals inked fifty years ago securing Diwata's formation (not beneath her)
or concede her legacy was nothing but a globalization plot. Secrecy
was Watah's specialty. Disclosure (no). Dual alliances served a purpose—
But this mission, the unexpected impact given its intention, perverse—

Watah had minimal agent contact. DSN access was granted to her
while president as a token for her visionary contributions. Cast aside,
intel was her way back to foreign relations. The Deep Space Network
(the remnants) were defunded under Governor Adisa's guidance—
Watah grasped the basics: klystron tubes powered radio transmitters
sending uplink signals to spacecraft as coded files. Receivers amplified
constantly through larger aperture antennas, gathering enough energy
to make the communications signals intelligible. Engaging treachery—

a surveillance hack—her election payback (definitely not beneath her).
Periodic mission reports were delivered by the hegemony's lead spy.
She received paper reports (hack protected), the agreed upon procedure.
It took a day for Watah to slake off shock, reading had her wild-eyed—
Unexpected castaways, a patroller and her dog, were reportedly ensnared
within the target's payload, unexpectedly Diwatan. Watah was mortified.
Her hands shook as she absorbed the details beyond the executive summary—
Azwan Adisa—Watah could only imagine Talee, her protégé's misery.

7

THE REVETMENT

Resettlement

Colonies on

Deimos, Crater Voltaire

Earth's Green Resistance
A Ten-Point Plan

 7 . l

Azwan waited to ask him, as Morshawn's weathered voice broke out
near the ship's control room, desperate to know if they were on course,
returning to Diwata, wondering how long? Words bloomed to a shout—
Morshawn's hands pointed, gesturing toward the ceiling, his tone terse.
She was worried about Troy, playing fetch with a diaper-wearing dog
a comic novelty. Adrift in free fall for too long, the gravitational force
so small, she fell while appearing to float. Interesting, and so what—
science lessons and all. What was the plan for getting home, *dear robot*?

"We need to talk," Morshawn whispered, popping out of the control
room door, as if there were more than two humans on the ship—*oh,
right.* Azwan was still uneasy with artificial sentience. AI a black hole
at home, Diwata legislated machine intelligence to infrastructure only—
"Our options—" "When are we going home?" Anxiety had taken hold.
". . . are limited." Her eyes began to tear, his filled in response, although
her understanding of their predicament was limited. She cut him off,
shoulders tight, jaw even tighter, flattening the palm of her hand—*stop!*

Azwan unstrapped her seat, levitating into Troy, drawing him close.
Morshawn unstrapped himself, shooting ahead of her into the cargo
bay, blocking her escape with his chest, hoping touch would foreclose
the harshness of their choice. "Please. You need to know." "Let me *go*!"
Morshawn understood her exasperation was mostly about his shadows—
his argument with the ship; she must have overheard their back and forth.
He placed his hands on her hips. "Take your *hands off* me!" Troy barked,
lunged forward, canine teeth a warning. Morshawn backed off, blocked—

"Don't come at me like that. Next time I'll let him." Troy was twerked—
"I'm sorry I overstepped, *shit*," he said, embarrassed, surprised, chastised—
"I can't stand drinking recycled piss," she countered. Troy's ears perked.
"You didn't sign up for this. I get it. The issue: she thinks it's ill-advised
to dock. I disagree. The Revetment colonies are a chance; but we're targets.
It's unclear if LMRover3's reentry to Mars via Deimos can be disguised."
"Deimos?" "Voltaire, a crater on Deimos, the smaller of Mars's two moons.
Octavia E. Butler Landing is a contested Atlas colony, with you I refuse—"

"If we dock on the mainland, there's a 90 percent chance of a fire fight."
"Why?" "Well, she was hacked, the ship hijacked. In turn, she overrode
my default command code to protect us and the propulsion and guidance
systems. It's possible a Diwatan or international belligerent is the source
of the breach. There are negligible traces, so far from what we derived—
backdoor communication tones from Goldstone DSN. It could be both.
She jet-propelled us out of Monterey Canyon at an unsanctioned speed.
The fast path back is through the sun. I'm conflicted. Should I intercede?"

"Morshawn, this isn't making any sense to me. We're already here—
Or close. What about the conversation I had with my mom?"
For the first time, he avoided her eyes as if to shunt his own fear.
"Wait a minute. Are you shitting me?" He responded defensively,
"I told you we needed to talk. It's only fair you understand the near-
term consequences and longer-term risks—collaborate on how to solve
what could be an endgame." "You need to give me more to go on."
"For a year . . . we've been in a hold to avert heat-shield combustion."

"LMRover3 has been drugging us, maintaining our vitals in a stealth
deep sleep before any final approach through the Martian atmosphere,
rotating her own heat shield backward not forward. Days withheld
from us, turned to months camouflaged, waiting for me—or so it appears—
to change my mind, align with her recommendation. I *can't* compel her—
If we land, we could be stranded. There's no Space Force team anymore.
The hegemony of Atlas's forces are hostile. No military-grade weapons are
onboard to secure an adequate defense if warranted. Just through the sun—

an efficient untested path to Earth. I'm not sure this is a suicide mission—
Carbon composite heat shields will help us survive blasts of radiation.
Also, we believe we've calculated an elliptical orbit, ideal planets . . ."
Azwan shot her arm with an open palm at his throat, his dry depiction
of their situation delivered as if she were in his lab getting a status
update on research. She dug into his Adam's apple. The contradiction—
what is experienced and therefore known, versus what is told as truth.
A year, that's impossible, she thought as he struggled to breathe. (true)

7 ₄ '2

The Green Resistance ten-point plan in honor of and solidarity with our Black Panther ancestors (originally proposed by Onyx "Geronimo" Davis).

Who we are:

We are third-generation Diwatans who have never seen or felt the rays of the sun with our own eyes, the surface of the ocean, dry land, distant planets in the night sky, or natural sunlight.

What we want:

1. We want freedom. We want power to determine our own migration strategies to the surface.
2. We want to choose our employment for ourselves beyond carbon farming or future collective monetization endeavors.
3. We want an end to the disparagement of our generation's experimentation with various forms of production, growth, and sustainability.
4. We want our diverse communities to define spatial equity within existing and new community structures.
5. We want science and technology education that embraces but limits ASI (artificial super intelligence) deployment within infrastructure systems.
6. We want culturally competent health care for all Diwatans, including surface waivers when optimal care in Diwata is limited.
7. We support the decision to abolish police humans but want the ability to choose border patrol service versus mandatory conscription, including the choice to reject either.
8. We want an end to Monterey Bay National Marine Sanctuary Council's covert participation and support in all wars of aggression in space and on the surface.

9. We support trials by a jury of peers for all persons charged with so-called crimes but demand the current practice of extradition to Martian penal colonies for specific capital crimes be abolished immediately (e.g., treason and espionage).

10. We want community control of reinvestment projects in fragile infrastructure, including but not limited to water, manufactured light, and our genetically modified food supply.

 7 , 3

As Morshawn and Troy slept, Azwan imagined being on Mars, twirling a 3D
model of Deimos, *Deimos or Earth*, the false choice unfair, unthinkable—
It was hard to ignore the real choice. *Where do you want to die?* Hyperbole
had nothing to do with it. Mars and Earth in opposition? *Hell.* Inexplicable,
or rather, she couldn't wrap her brain around their reasoning, weighty—
the precision to calculate the optimal distance. It felt too unbridgeable.
LMRover3 in principle wasn't talking to her other than "<apology. sorry.>"
after she reported she didn't have ordnance for another year. "<sorry.>"

Each time LMRover3 apologized she wanted to scream, *You thought you
made the right choice; your reaction did save Troy, but what of trust? Who
do I choose?* Morshawn and Troy snored. She sighed. *Will we come through
the other side of the sun alive?* She contemplated LMRover3's point of view.
She let her decision sit without panic as if on a long dive, passing through
progressive depths, admitting she would rather choose a good death than stew
in self-indulging pity—waiting, defenseless. She wanted to plow forward.
"Morshawn, wake up!" She floated to the sleeping pods, toward his world war—

 7 . 4

"As long as you understand I can't control the outcome or airspace—
especially after Atlas's Alliance of Remaining States' negotiations."
Azwan had let Morshawn's philosophical Space Force headspace
float over her unchallenged before, but the reference to a negotiation—
that was geopolitical and specific, not errant nor random. "Whoa, wait.
What's going on? What did you mean when you said . . ." Her vexation
was on full display. "When you said, 'with me you refuse'? You refuse to do
what exactly?" Her rising anger engaged bioluminescent tendrils blue—

"I didn't want to add to your distress. But we've confirmed the breach—
or at least narrowed it down. There were outdated Quindar-tones, echoes
she was able to pinpoint to a remote switching station; they're between
39.9042° N, 116.4074° E and 36.8044° N, 121.7869° W. The big unknown—
who'd attempt covert communications between Atlas and Moss Landing?"
"Well, I'm no damsel in distress needing or wanting your protection,"
Azwan said, detecting half-truths in the telling of what he knew and when—
still bioluminescent. "We found signs of Atlas and the Green Resistance."

"Signs, from Diwata? That can't be true. The GR are political poseurs.
Onyx, a friend of sorts, was hooked into GR gadflies and Atlas activists."
"Governor Adisa was concerned. She suspected hegemony maneuvers,
Atlas, their international influences plotting against her. GR adamance—
sabotage—I'd had my doubts. But now? Truth is never straightforward."
Azwan observed him carefully as he spoke with a tone of pretentiousness.
"Why can't we ever find peace in difference? Discovery and equilibrium?
Aggression, resistance, extraction. The cycle . . . human disequilibrium."

 7 , 5

LMRover3 was resolute in her defense of Mars and Earth's distance
calculations. With supplies dwindling, there was no time to wait
for everything to align when Earth was sweeping between the sun
and Mars, and Earth was at its farthest part from the sun, and Mars
was at its closest point to the sun. Opposition, the shortest distance—
And yet. LMRover3 couldn't be certain about her passengers' fate.
Solar wind, calculable. Energized dust, avoidable. Piercing the core?
With their consent, she released the last lot of aerosolized propofol—

 7 . 6

Still years after she disappeared, Onyx missed Azwan. *You're pitiful*
A kiss from a trick intended to be a mark: his mark, not hers. *You idiot*
He wondered if it was love, his grief overwhelming him. *It's inexplicable*
Playing Watah's game against Talee, in the end, was it worth it? *You miscreant*
Manufacturing the Green Resistance ten-point wasn't difficult. *convincible*
Manipulating the governor. He was warned she was impenetrable. *wittiest*
Tongues in the dark untied. Edging toward her body's revelations. *resist*
Tongues in the dark untied. Bending toward his body's secretions. *resist*

 7 . 7

Azwan never needed a security blanket or wanted anything soft
as a baby, Talee reminisced, comparing their divergent childhoods.
The weight of her child's loss felt insurmountable, proximate
to the Great Collision that snatched her happy girlhood—
eventually tearing Earth's landmass, creating more continents.
Multiple fragile island nations adrift, her father saw falsehood
evacuating the surface aloft to Mars. He wrote in his memoir,
"In Diwata, we were climate refugees forging a green dawn."

Talee had hated playing on surface ash; it was a reminder of lost
aunties, uncles, cousins trickling off slow. She cried. Wanted
to stay on the surface. Her dead mother might wake up, so they ought
to wait *not* leave. At eight, her father loaded an MBARI submersible
with their insubstantial possessions. Her father unpacked the blanket,
off pink, practically dismembered, presented it to her to get through—
Instinctively, Talee had touched the cogent cloth to her nose like she
did when she was a toddler, magically brave to enter the deep sea—

Epilogue

Xandria A. Brown
In Conversation with Bonita Greene, Senior Curator
National Museum of African American History and Culture
(NMAAHC)

CONDUCTED FEBRUARY 28, 2288
TRANSCRIPTION EXCERPT (PART 2)

GREENE: Let's pick up where we dropt. *The Diwata Collection: Can Machines Feel.* How do you want us, your readers, to receive this title, as well as the artifacts that accompany the manuscript?

BROWN: Diwata is a reference to a spirit deity in Philippine mythology. According to the U.N. General Assembly Committee on the Peaceful Uses of Outer Space, Diwata 1 was the first Philippine microsatellite launched into outer space. My intention with the Diwata Collection was to document the spirit of Black and Brown futurity, at sea and in space. Diwata, both in mythology and the U.N.'s attempt to designate outer space for peaceful endeavors, seemed to capture the essence of what I wanted to accomplish on a meta level. Azwan, the Diwatan border patrol diver, what she sees and senses in Box one is a precursor of what unfolds in the remaining part of the collection. Similarly, the artifacts and images showcase carbon capture mineralization, or farming, as Diwatans referred to the practice of extracting carbon dioxide from the environment to store inside basalt rocks. Water engineering, food production, pressure suits, artificial light; these are just a few examples visually researched. But all the items in the collection hopefully gesture toward the most important issues of the time.

GREENE: And yet the thrust of the exhibition signaled by the title appears to be machines. Some people may be confused by this.

BROWN: I suppose, if I'm being honest, I was leaning toward provocation with the collection's title. At one point in the evolution of technology, they couldn't . . . (Long pause.) Feel. (Pause.) Right? They, meaning machines. Technically we were misnaming this thing. *They*, what I am referring to, began as algorithms executed for old computer programs. Coders coded. And what is code? At its most basic, code is the language that compute-intelligence speaks. Much more than symbols of instruction, but actual communication. What if I had posited, Can language feel? This is a ridiculous notion on its face. Language is a tool we use to communicate across time and space. Something written or spoken in the past can be read or heard in the future. Deep learning used, perhaps still uses, I'm not quite up on the research any longer. Anyway, deep learning used a multilayered structure called neural networks. The layers of the network began to learn on their own from vast amounts of data without certain types of human input. They spoke to each other. Still do.

GREENE: Mz. Brown, sart. You're beginning to lose me.

BROWN: What I'm trying to say to you today, and more fully through the collection, is the human sense of feeling, the human sense of knowing had obviously evolved. But this belief, though, this assumption that human-ness is the epitome of knowledge is suspect. Trees, canines, fungi: there is feeling and knowing by so-called things, if not *every*thing. The interaction, the hybridity of knowledge is the essence of Diwata.

GREENE: I'd like to explore further, as you say, the essence of Diwata. The inhabitants in Monterey Canyon appear to have been separatists and survivalists. Is that a fair assessment?

BROWN: I viewed them as realists. And dreamers. By any means necessary. This was the ethos of the descendants of the Founding Architects, as well as Diwatan immigrants. They were committed to designing a world open to them on Earth, despite the harsh conditions on the surface after the asteroid Toutatis made contact. Colonizing space was out of the question for most of them—not all of the initial resistance was related to financial resources. I'd say it had more to do with choice. They chose Earth. Diwatans, in my mind, were not limited by the fear of here. Or prone to believe the hype of capitalist outer space pioneer-entrepreneurs.

GREENE: And yet, how are we to read the Green Resistance?

BROWN: Unfortunately, factions, naysayers, obstructionists are a part of life. It's how we deal with them that defines our collective success as humans with shared experiences.

GREENE: Interesting you refer to our success as humans. I was confused by the subtle references to bioluminescence, their tendrils. Sounds more like creatures than an authentic experience of the human condition.

BROWN: I'm going to respectfully disagree. The light-emitting molecule luciferin and enzyme luciferase, responsible for bioluminescence, was a natural adaptation to the lack of natural light expressed in pelage, hair in this case, referred to as tendrils. The most common physical Diwatan adaptation was unexpected, I give you that. But certainly not extraterrestrial. What was surprising to me was the activation of bioluminescence with strong emotions, usually anger. Possibly acting more like counter-illumination, a method of camouflage. My research uncovered that descendants of the Founding Architects were on their way in terms of a long-term transition to having colloid cephalopod skin. Dynamic pigmentation. Gray is as far as they got. Think of it as the type of gray in the portraits of twenty-first-century artist Amy Sherald. A luscious gray-black.

GREENE: Gotch.

BROWN: It's quite fascinating, modern evolutionary synthesis. Several colleagues at The Huntington brought a variety of research subjects to my attention. Diwata's foundation was initially visualized as a diptych of sorts—oceanography and aerospace engineering, which eventually expanded to botany. My late wife, Inanna Adisa-Brown, was an amazing supporter and collaborator as well.

GREENE: Mz. Brown, I'd be remiss if I didn't take this opportunity to discuss your situation. Your personal experience with technology. Your amazing longevity.

BROWN: (Laughing.) I'm not sure you have the time or the budget to delve into that subject.

GREENE: Well, don't fault me for trying. Let's move on, shall we, to climate change, neo-colonization of space, the over-reliance on technical solutions versus human capital, themes also addressed in the collection.

BROWN: I think the evolution of technology, the notion of sentience (actual and simulated), is just as important as Diwatans' choice not to abandon Earth. They trusted nonprofit scientists to create a viable habitat in the relatively pristine deep ocean. Artist and political activist Ai Weiwei was quoted as saying neither fairness nor justice, neither reality or humanity, can be simulated or manipulated by wires or remote controls. That hasn't been my experience as a Black person, a woman, a neurodiverse person. Climate change, neo-colonization, techno-politics, the corporatization of culture, the capitalization of art, income inequality, all these things that were issues when I was young are inextricably linked. A pecking order of control, with or without wires, is still a reality in surprising ways and spaces.

GREENE: The exhibit presented at NMAAHC spans a selection from the collection—Boxes one through seven, accompanied by narrative documentation in verse, over one hundred and fifty stanzas, composed loosely in the Italian rhyming stanza form ottava rima. Yet the extent of the collection's boxes currently configured stands at ninety-five. How should we view the arc of Diwata presented, and is it possible to fully grasp the collection with a fraction of the work available for study?

BROWN: Thank you for that question. The collection is up to two hundred boxes at this point and continues to grow. It is true what has been selected for the exhibit doesn't capture the complete arc of Diwata. What was important to me assembling the collection was a snapshot of life in the future, our present. Resilience and resistance. Less so revenge, but it is a part of this story, our story of survival, so I'm not trying to sugarcoat any of that here or camouflage artifact documentation. Some of my own personal experience surely is reflected not simply as metaphor, but as evidence of disputed techno-politics. Additionally, *House Resolution 109 Recognizing the Duty of the Federal Government to Create a Green New Deal* is included to highlight Talee Adisa's intense study of history, a fundamental backdrop through her journey from legislative analyst to mayor to governor to president. In particular section (D) to secure for all people of the United States and generations to come (1) clean water (2) climate and community resiliency (3) healthy food (4) access to nature (5) a sustainable environment. Why would anyone responsible for representing *the people* object?

GREENE: We'll let history clap back on that. Some of my relatives immigrated to Mars. While we're on the subject, do you see yourself as a social activist?

BROWN: I see myself as an archivist, a librarian, a curator, a writer, an artist, a poet, an ephemera collector. If that makes me a social activist, so be it. Bonita, I'm so sorry. I need to cut our interview short. I received a dilital reminder from my assistant Sassafras. I'm late for my next interview.

Dominique Watah, 👤 6 5 0 . 4 catalog

⟶ ⓦ _._ DW_d.watah

I should have known you weren't coming to dinner, or breakfast for that matter. The sky was full of remnants reminding me of this empty left whole. When I raised my eyes to the sky, I should have known you weren't open to my kiss or my hands or utterances beholding yesterday. Tomorrow, you said. Ask me, tomorrow. Maybe you'd be in a better place, a safer mood.

Dear Stars, full like the sea, I should have known you could never hold or love me like I hoped you would. A comet's tail is nothing but dust, released from a nucleus. Escaped gas. As in, this pressure is too much for me to hold alone, my magnetic field cracking into orbit toward the sun. Undetected.

Onyx Davis, ♠ 3 5 0′ ₄ 3 catalog

D·ω_ DW_o.davis

Someone asked me what I remember? Miss the most?
As if remembering and missing are the same thing.
This particular someone
asked in such a way, staring straight
at my forehead, I imagine
my blue tendrils and gray skin
were too much of a distraction
to have a straightforward conversation
without asking what I remember, miss the most—
as if my grayness and their
(I don't even want to name it)
could ever be
just skin, floating on the surface, just cells—
just protection.
The water, I eventually said.
Its rage and its peace.
Later, this same someone
asking the question
looked at me as if my lip was split,
my fly was open,
like I had shit on my fin,
as if rage was not anything
to miss, and peace was nowhere
to be found. I eventually got up,
turned my head, zipped my helmet,
rambled back to our ship
knowing full well I lied.
It's love I remember and miss the most.

Onyx Davis ♫ 375.1 catalog

D-ω_ ᵒ DW_o.davis

She doesn't start from the beginning
since she decides to start in the middle
looking to find her center, so to speak,
believing locating the location of her
so-called being is like unwrapping
a birthday present.

Since she decides to start in the middle
She tries to divine her way outward,
alarmed at the findings of her field study
multiple choices at her fingertips:

a. she could be depressed and laugh her way out of it
b. she could be depressed and sleep her way off of it
c. she could be depressed and jump her way out of it

Since she decides to start in the middle
she closes her eyes and picks the best choice
at random.
When she opens her eyes, the page—empty
the choices she defined for herself, gone.

"Back," she says. "Fine, let's start back"
at the beginning.

THE DIWATA COLLECTION: CAN MACHINES FEEL?

TIMELINE

2292	Diwata acquired by National Museum of African American History and Culture
2288	Xandria Anastasia Brown begins lecture circuit, celebrates 300th birthday
2190	Talee Adisa elected President, Diwata-Saturus alliance
2185	Talee Adisa elected Governor; Morshawn's ship LMRover3 hijacked
2184	Green Resistance protests, Hegemony of Atlas active at Octavia E. Butler landing
2164	Azwan Adisa born
2159	Diwata founded in Monterey Canyon; Talee Adisa elected inaugural mayor
2133	Davis Miles Adisa, PhD, Water Engineering Commendation
2130	The Great Collision: Toutatis asteroid touches down on Earth
2125	Talee Adisa born Richland Farms, Compton, California
2123	MBARI @ Monterey Canyon; scientific habitation only
2118	Mars outposts opened by U.S. government including moons Phobos and Deimos
2090	#BlackoutWIKA ephemera acquired by The Huntington Library
2088	Quinn McCarthy dies, Atwater Federal Prison
2085	Restorative Justice Healing Circle, Atwater Federal Prison
2037	Indigo.XAB.15 decommission order
2036	Xandria Anastasia Brown retires from The Huntington Library, Art Museum, and Botanical Gardens
2035	Inanna Adisa-Brown memorial service; Rob Wickman kidnapping
2034	COVID-34 global pandemic; WIKA acquisition through grant/funding agreement
2033	Xandria Anastasia Brown promoted
2025	Diwata research begins; Xandria Anastasia Brown covert medical surveillance commences

2020   COVID-19 global pandemic, United States Space Force: four inductees report to boot camp

2017   Google invents Transformer Language Model

2011   Occupy Wall Street movement

2008   The Great Recession

2005   Hurricane Katrina

2004   Virgin Galactica founded by Richard Brannan

2003   South Central renamed South Los Angeles

2002   SpaceX founded by Elon Musk

2001   9/11: Four coordinated suicide terrorist attacks by Islamic extremists against the U.S.

2000   Blue Origin founded by Jeff Bezos

1994   Environmental Justice Executive Order 12898

1993   WWW launched in public domain

1992   LAPD officers acquitted for Rodney King beating, L.A. uprising (#2)

1991   Gulf War begins, nine-year-old Latasha Harlins killed by storekeeper Soon Ja Du

1989   Spike Lee's *Do the Right Thing* premieres

1988   Xandria Anastasia Brown born, February 29th Leap Year

1987   Monterey Bay Aquarium Research Institute founded by David Packard

1 5 0 5

THE HUNTINGTON AT 150: A SESQUICENTENNIAL CELEBRATION

THE SESQUICENTENNIAL CELEBRATION OF THE HUNTINGTON LIBRARY, ART MUSEUM AND BOTANICAL GARDENS <u>INVITES YOU</u> TO JOIN US #BLACKOUTWIKA.

1919 Private estate converted to public benefit corporation

1921 The Blue Boy purchased

1968 Zen Garden established

1987 Mount Wilson observatory rare collection acquired

1999 Corpse Flower blooms

2002 Group of Langston Hughes letters and manuscripts acquired

2006 Dibner Hall "Beautiful Science" permanent display opens

2008 Octavia E. Butler's bequeathed papers received

2019 Culmination of year-long centennial celebration

2039 Patrisse Cullors co-founder BLM movement papers acquired

2059 Elon Musk founder Tesla and SpaceX papers acquired

2069 Safariland board member purged. Alphabet WIKA acquisition blocked.

150th Sesquicentennial Celebration Storyboard

...t We W...t ow! Ten-points

1. We wa... ...edo... We w... po... to determi... destiny of... Bla
   Comm...

2. We want ... employment for ...r p...ple.

3. We want ...ent the robbery by the C... ...our Black
   Co...

4. ...nt education for ... ...shelt... human ...s.

5. ...ent American soci... ...e that e... ...rue na... ...his
   ...and our role in p... ...ant education that teach... ...r true
   ... soci...

6. ...empt from milit... service. We w...
   ... all Black and opp... d people.

7. We wa... ...diate end POLICE BRUTALITY and MURDER of
   Bl...
   ...t freedom ...

8. s and jails. W...lack men held in federal, s... ...county ...ity
   ...an immediate end to all wa... ...aggr...

9. ...be wh...om their be tried in co...
   jury ... p... or pe... ...ommunitie...
   defined ... ...onstitution of United State... want freedom for all
   Bl... nd oppressed people n... ...al, state, county, city
   ... ry prisons and jails. ld in U.S ...ury of peers for all
   ...erson... arged with so-called c... ...laws of this country.

10. We want land, bread, housing, education, clothing, justice, peace and
    people's community control of modern technology.

BPP Ten-Point Diwata Storyboard

SECONDARY SOURCES

(Retrieved between 2020 and 2035)

Blackburn, Elizabeth, PhD, and Elissa Epel, PhD. *The Telomere Effect*. New York: Hachette Book Group, 2017.

Committee on the Peaceful Uses of Outer Space, United Nations General Assembly. "Information furnished in conformity with General Assembly resolution 1721 B (XVI) by States launching objects into orbit or beyond." April 26, 2017.

"House Resolution 109: Recognizing the duty of the Federal Government to create a Green New Deal." 116th Congress, 1st Session. February 7, 2019.

Jääskeläinen, Iiro P., Vasily Klucharev, Ksenia Panidi, and Anna N. Shestakova. "Neural Processing of Narratives: From Individual Processing to Viral Propagation." *Frontiers in Human Neuroscience* 14, no. 253 (June 26, 2020).

Kuhn, Noah, Adam Kwoh, and Zoe Schlaak. "South Pasadena's history of racism." *Tiger*, August 18, 2020. (See *South Pasadena Courier* Ku Klux Klan ad, July 19, 1921.)

"Lead Poisoning—The Man-Made Disease." *The Black Panther*, March 24, 1973. Black Panther Party Alumni website.

McCormick, Jon Michal, and John V. Thiruvathukal. *Elements of Oceanography*. Philadelphia: W. B. Saunders Company, 1976.

McKinley, Angelica, and Giovanni Russonello. "Fifty Years Later, Black Panthers' Art Still Resonates." *The New York Times*, October 15, 2016.

Minority AIDS Project. "AIDS Is an Equal Opportunity Disease!!!" 1986. *Surviving & Thriving* Digital Gallery, NIH National Library of Medicine.

Miranda, Carolina A. "Architecture's whiteness by design can change. Mabel Wilson shows us how in MoMA show." *The Los Angeles Times*, March 19. 2021.

Monaghan, Heather, and Catherine G. Manning. "What Does the DSN Do?" March 30, 2020. NASA Space Communications.

Nakano, Roy. "The Case of Elmer Geronimo Pratt: A Long and Winding Road to Retrial." *National Black Law Journal* 9, no. 2 (1985).

NASA Mars Exploration Program. "Welcome to 'Octavia E. Butler Landing.'" Mars 2020: Perseverance Rover. March 5, 2021.

Quan, Steven, Rikk Kvitek, Douglas P. Smith, and Gary Griggs. "Using Vessel-Based LIDAR to Quantify Coastal Erosion during El Niño and Inter-El Niño Periods in Monterey Bay, California." *Journal of Coastal Research* 29 (May 2013): 555–565. ResearchGate. (See Figure 1: Central California map showing the Monterey Bay coastline and geographical location of the north and south analysis regions.)

Reft, Ryan. "Segregation in the City of Angels: A 1939 Map of Housing Inequality in L.A." PBS SoCal. November 14, 2017. (See the KCET 1939 HOLC "redlining" map of central Los Angeles, courtesy of LaDale Winling and urbanoasis.org.)

Rutten, Tim. "Geronimo Pratt and Johnnie Cochran." *Los Angeles Times*, June 4, 2011.

United States Environmental Protection Agency. "Environmental Justice Timeline." Updated June 26, 2024.

United States Food and Drug Administration. "Remote or Wearable Patient Monitoring Devices EUAs." November 8, 2023.

Weiwei, Ai. *Weiwei-isms*. Edited by Larry Walsh. Princeton: Princeton University Press, 2012.

ACKNOWLEDGMENTS

A fiction debut at the age of sixty-five, doubling as a speculative poetry debut and a digital-collage folio (most of the source material shot from my iPhone), was never on my bucket list. On the other hand, retiring after nearly thirty years in corporate finance before my sixtieth birthday was something I'd always visualized. A friend convinced me that a business degree was more bankable than a master's degree in library and information science. It was hard to dispute, given I had abandoned my pursuit of a master's in fine arts and a nascent studio art practice. For years I second-guessed my second act.

In 2019, after I took a lump-sum distribution, my beloved gave me the gift of time that allowed this book to eventually emerge. I am forever grateful for Tammy Haygood's love, partnership, unwavering support, and belief in act three.

I feel the need to acknowledge the COVID-19 pandemic, which unleashed my sense of urgency. I am indebted to my first readers, Aja Couchois Duncan and Elissa Sloan Perry, for Three Spirit Collective's virtual check-ins, free-write sessions, and manuscript reviews. Holding healing space during lockdown provided the ecosphere for a 300-year-old queer woman of color to thrive in my mind, despite debilitating grief and generational health issues.

Gratitude to my agent, Kima Jones, who fielded my inquiry for a publicity consultation on a different manuscript; her enthusiasm for the speculative, Black futures, and hybridity gave me the confidence to let it all fly.

Thanks to my editor, Gina Iaquinta, for seeing the possibilities, as well as her deft technical ability to shepherd fiction and poetry in the same manuscript.

I would like to thank Janice N. Harrington, former librarian, poet, and children's book author. Also thanks to L. A. Jackson, visual researcher, archivist, and former director of the Fox Research Library.

Both provided their unique perspectives on library culture and public service.

Thanks to the Hurston/Wright Foundation, Nisi Shawl, and their "Word Building for Worldbuilding" summer cohort—Aishatu Ado, Jamiella Brooks, Winifred Burton, Baluanne Conteh, Shawn Frazier, Brittany Selah Lee-Bey, Raina J. León, Aly McPherson, and moses moon.

Thank you to Millay Arts for space in the barn, which helped bring the Diwata Collection into focus, and a residency cohort that kept me laughing and safe—Sachiko Akiyama, Felecia Barr, Katrina Bello, Eric Guinivan, and Abbey Mei Otis.

Thank you Cave Canem, fellows and faculty, for your embrace of my expression of Afro-Surreal and Afrofuturist poetics.

Thank you to Maxine Chernoff and Paul Hoover for publishing a previous version of "Cavernous & transient, the deepest point" in *New American Writing*. Thank you to Caroline Goodwin, Hugh Behm-Steinberg, and Mary Behm-Steinberg for publishing a previous version of "I wake to a vortex of dust" in my chapbook *Camouflage* (MaCaHu Press).

Gratitude to Maria Connors, as well as the W. W. Norton/Liveright production team for reading and transforming the raw materials of words, punctuation, fonts, and images into something beautiful to hold—Janine Barlow, Rebecca Homiski, Jodi Hughes, Joe Lops, Louise Mattarelliano, Brian Mulligan, and Rebecca Munro. Thanks to Alexis Eke and Sarahmay Wilkinson for the gorgeous book cover.

Finally, I want to acknowledge the impact of Kathleen R. Kenyon on my work and work ethic. Kathleen was a teacher, photographer, collage artist, printmaker, and a leader of the Center for Photography at Woodstock with her twin sister, Colleen F. Kenyon. As an undergrad, I'd often get calls on the weekend from Kathleen to tell me she was working in USC's printmaking studio. I was a commuter student. Off I'd go from South Pasadena with my tangelo ArtBin storage box onto an Alhambra bus, then a transfer in downtown Los Angeles.

After hours in the studio diddling with screenprint stencils and squeegees, perhaps I'd made something I wanted to show. Or maybe not. That wasn't the point. From Kathleen I learned to develop patience, and the importance of community in a profession inherently solitary.

ABOUT THE AUTHOR

Stacy Nathaniel Jackson is a trans poet, playwright, and visual artist of African American and Filipina descent who began writing after a serendipitous corporate layoff. His artistic practice in multiple forms addresses gender, family history, and conflict emergence. His work has been published in *Callaloo, Electric Literature,* and the *Georgia Review,* among other publications. He is a Cave Canem poetry fellow and was a Hurston/Wright Foundation summer fellow in speculative fiction. He has also received support for his work as an associate artist in residence with Addae Moon at the Atlantic Center for the Arts, a Millay Arts Vincent Prize recipient and Mid Atlantic Arts Foundation Creative Fellow, a participant in the Jack Straw Cultural Center Writers Program, and a recipient of an individual artist grant from the San Francisco Arts Commission. Stacy received his BA in fine arts, magna cum laude, from the University of Southern California; a graduate assistantship in sculpture from the University of Arizona; an MFA in creative writing from San Francisco State University; and an MBA from UC Berkeley's Haas School of Business. Originally from Los Angeles, he currently resides in Washington, DC.